Shannon Stewart had been a prostitute

Much as he wanted to, Bryce Donovan couldn't deny the evidence in front of his eyes.

"Is this some kind of a game to you?" he asked Shannon.

Shannon held herself stoically before Bryce, unwilling to credit his challenge with a response.

Say something, damn it. Don't you see that your silence is only digging you in deeper?

"What is it with you, Shannon? Why don't you even *try* to explain, to defend yourself?" The question was hesitant, searching, coming from the man, not the sheriff.

"It's what you want to believe," she said with a shrug.

"How can I believe anything else?"

She could not answer his question. If she told him what had really happened twelve years ago, and he didn't believe her, then she'd have to stop caring about hi̶m̶. A̶n̶d̶ ̶s̶h̶e̶ ̶c̶o̶u̶l̶d̶n̶'̶t̶ could bear that.

Dear Reader,

The popularity of our Women Who Dare titles has convinced us that you love our stories about Superromance heroines who do not back away from challenges. So, we're delighted to offer you three more!

For October's Women Who Dare title, Lynn Leslie has created another trademark emotional drama in *Courage, My Love*. Diane Maxwell is fighting the fight of her life. To Brad Kingsley, she is a tremendously courageous woman of the nineties, and as his love for her grows, so does his commitment to her victory.

Evelyn A. Crowe's legion of fans will be delighted to learn that she has penned our Women Who Dare title for November. In *Reunited,* gutsy investigative reporter Sydney Tanner learns way more than she bargained for about rising young congressman J.D. Fowler. Generational family feuds, a long-ago murder and a touch of blackmail are only a few of the surprises in store for Sydney—and you—as the significance of the heroine's discoveries begins to shape this riveting tale.

Popular Superromance author Sharon Brondos has contributed our final Woman Who Dare title for 1993. In *Doc Wyoming,* taciturn sheriff Hal Blane wants nothing to do with a citified female doctor. But Dixie Sheldon becomes involved with Blane's infamous family in spite of herself, and her "sentence" in Wyoming is commuted to a romance of the American West.

Please enjoy our upcoming Women Who Dare titles, as well as the other fine Superromance novels we've lined up for your fall reading pleasure!

Marsha Zinberg,
Senior Editor

YESTERDAY'S Secrets

Tara Taylor Quinn

Harlequin Books

TORONTO • NEW YORK • LONDON
AMSTERDAM • PARIS • SYDNEY • HAMBURG
STOCKHOLM • ATHENS • TOKYO • MILAN
MADRID • WARSAW • BUDAPEST • AUCKLAND

If you purchased this book without a cover you should be aware
that this book is stolen property. It was reported as "unsold and
destroyed" to the publisher, and neither the author nor the
publisher has received any payment for this "stripped book."

ACKNOWLEDGMENT

I wish to thank Judi Knox for the wealth of
technical expertise and inspiration she provided
for this book

Published October 1993

ISBN 0-373-70567-0

YESTERDAY'S SECRETS

Copyright © 1993 by Tara Lee Reames. All rights reserved.
Except for use in any review, the reproduction or utilization
of this work in whole or in part in any form by any electronic,
mechanical or other means, now known or hereafter invented,
including xerography, photocopying and recording, or in any
information storage or retrieval system, is forbidden without
the permission of the publisher, Harlequin Enterprises Limited,
225 Duncan Mill Road, Don Mills, Ontario, Canada M3B 3K9.

All the characters in this book have no existence outside the
imagination of the author and have no relation whatsoever to
anyone bearing the same name or names. They are not even
distantly inspired by any individual known or unknown to the
author, and all incidents are pure invention.

® are Trademarks registered in the United States Patent and
Trademark Office and in other countries.

Printed in U.S.A.

ABOUT THE AUTHOR

Tara Taylor Quinn worked as a journalist and an English teacher before she finally realized her dream of becoming a Harlequin writer—a dream she'd nursed ever since buying her first Harlequin Romance in a supermarket at the age of fourteen. She took to writing like a fish to water. "It's not something I want to do," she explains, "but something I need to do." How lucky for Harlequin readers that Tara's enormous talent is now being used to provide us with gripping stories like *Yesterday's Dreams.*

Tara Taylor Quinn lives in Scottsdale, Arizona, with her husband and young daughter.

For Kevin—thank you

CHAPTER ONE

SHANNON FELT A FAMILIAR tightening in her stomach as she steered her six-year-old Ford Tempo around the last bend. She shifted in her seat, sweat trickling down her back beneath her thick black hair, and she was all too aware that her car's broken air conditioner was yet more evidence of her inability to provide. The twins sat silently in the back. They did not complain about the heat, but then they didn't complain about much of anything. They were good kids.

She knew they hated going back—probably as much as she hated delivering them—but she had to adhere to the rules religiously or lose any hope of having them home again. She was allowed two hours with her children every Sunday afternoon, and those two hours were up in exactly seven minutes.

Shannon stiffened as the heavy silence was broken by muffled sounds coming from the back seat of her car. Not one sniffle, but two. Glancing quickly in her rearview mirror, she pulled the car off to the side of the road and unbuckled her seat belt. She heard the click of another belt coming loose.

Mindi hurled herself over the seat and into her mother's arms. "It's okay, baby," Shannon said close to her ten-year-old daughter's ear.

"I don't wanna go back, Mommy. I don't wanna leave you all alone," she sobbed.

Shannon brushed damp, raven black bangs away from her daughter's brow. "I know, Mindi, but we have to be strong just a little while longer. Think about all the things we're going to do when we're together again.'' Those words had become a litany for Shannon over the past three months, but they didn't soothe Mindi as they had on previous Sundays.

At that moment, despite all that had gone before, Shannon had never felt so alarmed and helplessly lost. Both her children were crying, and since the day her children had been taken from her, Michael had been so strong. He was the logical child, the take-charge-and-make-it-better one. If he was crying, something was wrong...more wrong than usual.

She inhaled the scent of her daughter's hair, kissed her soft cheek, and then looked into the back seat. Her throat grew dry as she saw the tears swimming in Michael's pale violet eyes.

"What's wrong, Mike?" she asked, her voice tender and reassuring.

"It's summer," Michael said. He looked as if he had the cares of four grown men on his skinny little shoulders. His black hair was unusually mussed, as if he'd been running his fingers through it ever since they had left the mall where she had treated them to lunch.

"You're missing Little League?" Shannon asked, not quite believing that her son was that upset over a few games of baseball.

"Naw, come on, Mom, you know I can handle that. I'll play again next summer when we're together again. It's just that, well, now that we're not in school, we kinda get in Mrs. Wannamaker's way a lot—especially Mindi."

Shannon wrapped her arms more securely around her daughter's trembling little body. Mindi was a quiet, sensitive child. How could she possibly get in anyone's way a lot?

"What do you mean, *especially* Mindi?" she asked her son softly.

Mike swiped at the few stray tears that had escaped to slide down his cheeks.

"Mindi tries, Mom, she really does, but Mrs. Wanna-maker still gets real mad."

The small form in her arms trembled harder and the blood in Shannon's veins turned cold. She twisted in her seat to get a better view of her son.

"What does Mindi do to make her angry?" she asked, her voice dangerously low. She held on to her emotions just as firmly as she now held her daughter, sensing that something was desperately wrong. But she needed to think, not feel.

"She doesn't get the dishes done fast enough, and things," Mike replied, evading her eyes.

Shannon studied her son's face. His gaze darted about the car. Dread seeped into her soul. He was not telling her everything.

"What things?" she asked. Her words were soft, but her tone said that Michael had better tell all this time. The first thing she'd ever taught her children was that they were to come to her with everything; the only insurmountable problems were those that weren't approached.

"She gets mad at us when we don't do things just right, she says things and Mindi cries, and that makes her madder," Mike said in a rush, jutting out his small chin. Mindi's tears continued to wet the front of Shannon's shirt.

"What does she say to you?" Shannon asked, stroking Mindi's hair. She braced herself, dreading what she might hear.

"Bad things about you . . . about us being your kids."

Icy fingers gripped Shannon's throat as fear became reality. "And what does she do when she gets mad?" she asked, keeping a tight rein on her anger, trying to think. She needed to know the extent of the problem before she could best determine how to deal with it. She could not allow herself to be blinded by emotion, by the fury that resulted from yet another injustice. She had grown up with snide remarks and cutting words; she would not have her children exposed to the same degrading experience.

She loosened her hold on Mindi enough to run her hand along the child's shoulders, scratching her back lightly just the way she liked it.

The child cried out, flinching, just as Michael wailed from the back seat, "Don't!"

Shannon froze, her hand suspended an inch from Mindi's back, her eyes fixed on her son. "Why not?" she asked.

Michael's chin quivered, but he held her gaze. "Mrs. Wannamaker hits her with a willow switch." The words were followed by the deluge of tears he had been trying so valiantly to withhold.

Shannon's concern turned to disbelief and then to redhot rage as Mindi sobbed brokenly in her arms. She eased her forward gently, turned her small body, and lifted her T-shirt. Shannon bit her bottom lip and held back an anguished cry as she was confronted with the ugly red welts on her daughter's soft skin.

Shannon had had enough. What kind of justice thought it better for a ten-year-old girl to be a victim of child abuse than to be in a loving home with the mother who was waiting desperately for her return?

Tight-lipped, she did not say a word. She could not. She was afraid that if she allowed a single sound to escape she would not be able to contain the wounded howls rising up in her throat. Her children were already dealing with enough anguish; she could spare them hers.

She glanced at her watch. She had two minutes to get the twins back to their foster home. She thought of the caseworker who had passed judgment against her before they had ever met. She looked at her watch again, as if somehow she would find an answer within its face. The twins were expected back in a minute and thirty seconds. She took one last look at the ugly bruises on Mindi's back and nausea rose up to choke her. She couldn't do it. She just could not do it. Easing Mindi's shirt back down, she tenderly placed the child on the seat beside her and started the car.

"Buckle up, kids. We're going home." She knew she probably wasn't thinking clearly, that she could be doing more harm than good, but she was a mother. She absolutely could not deliver her children back to a home where they were being mistreated.

Her announcement met with silence as her two children stared at her in wary disbelief. Mindi's sobs quieted.

"Are you sure, Mom?" Michael asked hesitantly. Shannon met her son's gaze in the rearview mirror. His violet eyes, so much like her own, were desperately searching for some sign of hope.

She knew better than to make false promises, so she didn't reply. She put the car in drive, and turned toward the apartment complex that had been home since that final degradation that had forced her to leave the Stewart mansion two years before. "I'm taking you home," was all she said in answer to her son's query. But amazingly, it seemed to be enough.

BRYCE COULD NOT get enough air. His lungs expanded until he thought they would explode, and still he could not get enough air. He heard the first shot, and knew she had led them right into The King's chambers, the "inner sanctum."

"Donovan!" he whispered urgently into the mike wired to his chest. And then again, *"Donovan! This is Donovan, do you read me?"*

Frustrated by the silence of the tiny speaker taped behind his ear, he crawled on his belly, edging closer to the doorway through which his partner had disappeared precious seconds before. *"Answer me, Dad, damn you. She's one of them. You never should have trusted her. This whole damn thing is dirty."*

He slipped inside the doorway and squeezed himself against the cold steel wall while his eyes adjusted to the interior of the darkened warehouse. He no longer cared about the scum he had come to take down; he just wanted to find his father and get them both out of there safely.

The room was still a black blur when the next shot rang out against the steel walls surrounding him. For the first time in his life, he felt an instant of fear. Fear for his partner, his father—the man whom he'd followed, despite a strong instinct that had told him not to, straight into this booby trap. And then razor-sharp pain hit his right shoulder, knocking him backward, ripping into his flesh—

The shrill ringing of the telephone broke into Bryce's catnap, startling him upright in his chair. He must have drifted off watching the Sunday afternoon news. The sharp pain in his shoulder was from the weight of his sleeping head, rather than the bullet he had taken the previous year. After the sleepless night he had spent—another night trying to come to grips with the fact that his entire life had been blown apart by a woman—he should have known better than to sit down in the comfortable old chair.

Rotating his right shoulder slowly, he reached with his left hand for the phone on the end table.

"Donovan here," he answered automatically, shaking away the residue of the recurrent nightmare. He was no longer a Detroit vice squad detective. As of last week he was the newly appointed sheriff to the sleepy little county of Southlakes, Michigan.

"Deputy Adams here, Sheriff. Sorry to bother you at home, but we have a situation here we thought you should know about." The woman's brisk, no-nonsense tone brought him fully back to the present.

He held the receiver between his ear and his good shoulder, freeing his hand to massage the throbbing muscles in his other upper arm. "It's my job to be bothered, Adams. What's up?"

"Shannon Stewart kidnapped her ten-year-old twins from foster care, sir. Deputy Williams was on patrol when Mrs. Wannamaker, their foster mother, called in, and he traced them to Mrs. Stewart's apartment. Williams is in a car across the street now, waiting for your word on how to proceed. The Stewarts aren't going to like this at all."

Bryce leaned forward, welcoming the old familiar surge of adrenaline. "Does the woman have a history of hurting her kids?" he asked. The children were obviously in foster care for a reason.

"Not that I know of, sir. No, I'm sure not. At least not physically. I don't really know a lot about the case firsthand, only the little I've heard around town recently. The Stewarts kept the divorce real quiet. The judge could give you the facts."

Bryce nodded to himself as the young woman deputy mentioned his uncle, the judge. "Tell Williams just to hang tight and make sure the woman doesn't go anywhere. I'll be there shortly."

Bryce disconnected the call and dialed his uncle's farmhouse. If Adams was right, and Judge Oliver Donovan had the facts, he would be Bryce's most reliable source of quick information.

"The Stewart family settled this town two hundred years ago, old-money immigrants from England according to the stories, but I don't know them well, personally," Oliver began as soon as Bryce explained the reason for his call. "They're not ones to encourage friendly overtures. I do know *of* them, however. They're the epitome of respectability and generous with their money. Their holdings include at least a partial interest in just about every business in this town, but they pay better-than-average wages, ensure decent employee benefits and working conditions, and are known as fair landlords. From what I understand, Mr. Stewart runs the financial end of things from an office in the Stewart mansion. He still controls the fortune, but his son, Clinton, oversees the day-to-day running of things.

"Shannon Stewart's a looker, but she has a past to go with it. Apparently, she grew up the daughter of a hooker down in Havenville. But I remember when she showed up here in town—must have been about twelve or thirteen years ago. Even for a kid, she had this distinctive air about her, acted real ladylike, but kind of quiet just the same. She told folks that she was from some place up in the Upper Peninsula, the only child of well-to-do textile magnates. She had a real sad story about a fire that took her folks, the factory, and wiped out the family fortune, had everyone in town feeling real sorry for her. She got a job right away working the cosmetic department at Stewart's and that's where she met Clinton."

Bryce didn't interrupt his uncle with suppositions, but he couldn't help thinking that if the woman had been trying to escape a past she found abhorrent, she would hardly have shown up in town announcing that she was the daughter of a prostitute.

And yet her lies warned him that he might be dealing with a woman just like the one who had cost him his job in Detroit. Besides, as a cop, he had seen one too many women in extreme circumstances willing to do whatever was necessary to satisfy her emotional needs.

Oliver continued. "From her first day in town, Shannon turned all the boys' heads, but once Clinton Stewart saw her, he took up all her spare time. It was obvious the boy was real attracted to her. The Stewarts seemed a little worried about the match at first, I guess because the girl produced no tangible proof of her background, but Clinton was so insistent to marry her, they gave in. They gave Clinton and Shannon a nice wedding, and when the babies came, Clinton and Shannon moved into their own wing in the Stewart mansion.

"I don't know just when things went wrong. Shannon just up and filed for divorce two years ago, and Clinton quietly gave her one. Then about three months ago, Stewart lawyers started bringing up her past, claiming Shannon was an unfit mother. They were able to create enough doubt about the woman to warrant the decision to remove the children from her home until a full investigation can determine permanent custody. Clinton claims he caught his wife with one of his friends shortly before the breakup of the marriage. The charge hasn't been proven, but she hasn't denied it, either. And since the divorce she's been working as a barmaid at the Tub of Suds, that dive out by the bowling alley. Left the kids, Michael Scott and Minda Marie, with a sitter every night but Sunday. It's been rumored that she does more for her customers than just serve them drinks. Clinton has had joint custody all along, but he's decided that she's an undesirable influence on the kids and he intends to win full and permanent custody. According to the Stewarts, Shannon only wants the kids for the child support she receives."

Bryce listened to the case history intently. "What does she do with the money?" he asked, wondering why, as the ex-wife of the town's most influential family, the woman bothered to work at all, especially since her job tarnished an already smudged reputation.

Oliver sighed. "Nothing's been proven yet, but Clinton claims she has some expensive habits. He says she's never been able to handle money. He's even hinted that she may have a gambling problem. As far as the custody case goes, what she does with the money is not the issue so much as what she doesn't do. The children aren't receiving any of the benefits the Stewart name gives them, and no account has been given for how their support money is being spent."

"It matters what she does with the money if she's gambling. Then she's in water much hotter than a simple custody case," Bryce stated, his years on the streets of Detroit preparing him to suspect the deeper crime.

"I'm sure if there's any proof of illegal action, Stewart's lawyer, or his hotshot private detective, will find it," Oliver replied.

Bryce was surprised how good it felt to be discussing a case again. But even as much as he respected his uncle, he couldn't help thinking it was his father he should be talking to.

"Why did Clinton Stewart wait almost two years before trying to have the woman proven unfit?" he asked, pushing aside his thoughts.

"My guess is he had to give her time to hang herself. The Stewarts would never enter into a battle they weren't sure of winning or that they couldn't come out of looking lily-white. They want to win, but they wouldn't want to leave the town feeling sorry for the young mother losing her children. They would want to make sure everyone is as outraged as they apparently are."

Bryce found himself growing more and more curious about the legendary Stewarts. In his experience those who looked the most perfect usually had the most to hide. But then, he had never lived in a small town before. He'd never had firsthand experience with the old-fashioned social hierarchy that apparently still prevailed in Southlakes.

"Why weren't the kids with Clinton instead of in a foster home?"

"They didn't want to go." Oliver's tone suggested that he found that hard to believe. "Could be their mother threatened them somehow, but until anything's proven, until the custody hearing is settled, I feel it's in the children's best interest to be in foster care."

"So there's a caseworker involved?"

"There is one, but to be honest with you, she hasn't played a very big role in this case as far as I'm concerned. According to her report, she interviewed Shannon Stewart only briefly before determining that the children would be better off with their father. I'm not entirely convinced that she wasn't being swayed by Stewart influence. But, for the record, I'm not discounting her recommendation, either."

Bryce computed all that he had heard, drawing a mental picture of an arrogant, rich man, who apparently believed his money set him above the rest of the citizens of Southlakes, and an avaricious, immoral woman, whose beauty only went skin-deep. He felt sorry for the twins.

"For the kids' sake we need to end this as quickly and quietly as possible," Oliver finished, voicing the conclusion Bryce had already reached.

"I'll go get them myself...." Hanging up the phone, Bryce grabbed his keys off the table beside him.

SHANNON KNEW HER TIME was limited. She had just seen the police car stop across the street. Drew Williams was sitting inside watching her door. Of all the deputies in this county, she thought, it would have to be him.

"What would you like to do first, kids? Clean your rooms or eat broccoli?" she asked, leading Mindi down the hall to the bathroom. *Keep things light. Don't let them sense your fear.*

"Gross! Broccoli!" The twins squealed in unison.

"I'm going to my room," Mike said, sounding eager rather than disgruntled.

Shannon grabbed him by the shirt collar. "Wait just a minute there, big guy. You can help here, first."

She collected the first-aid kit from under the counter, and under the pretense of needing both hands to hold up Mindi's shirt, instructed Mike in applying salve to his sister's tender skin. The twins needed to be able to take care of each other.

"Wanna play Monopoly?" Mindi asked as her brother worked diligently on her back.

That's my baby, Shannon praised silently. *Get through the bad moments thinking about better ones.*

"Sure," Mike agreed uncharacteristically. He hated board games.

After offering to clean up the mess in the bathroom, Shannon sent the kids to start their game, hoping they would have enough time to finish it.

Returning to the living room a few minutes later, she was swamped by a need to cry as she watched her children playing so restrainedly. No words were spoken, other than an announcement of rent due or purchase to be made. No fears were given credence, no mention of the fact that dinnertime was nearing, no question as to where they would be sleeping that night.

"I love you, Mommy," Mindi said, looking up from her pile of recently acquired paper money.

"I love you, too, baby," Shannon said, smiling down at the two heads of night black hair. At least her children looked like her—that was some sort of twisted justice. She glanced out the window to see that the police car was still across the street, then she sat down on the floor beside her children. It was no use trying to pretend things were normal. They weren't, and all three of them knew it.

"I'm sorry, kids," she said softly. How could she explain to her children that she had been wrong, but that there was no right? How could she possibly keep them from mistrusting the system by which they would be governed their whole lives? Especially when she doubted it herself?

Michael and Mindi exchanged a long glance, passing silent messages as they had been doing all their lives. "We're not, Mom." Michael spoke for them both. His violet eyes had never been more serious, nor more sincerely trusting than they were at that moment. "No matter what, it's great to be home."

Shannon tweaked his freckled cheek, his only visible inheritance from Clinton, and watched as he rolled doubles for the third consecutive time. "Go to Jail," she said.

It had been wrong to take them, to confuse them further, but Shannon knew she had had no choice. If nothing else, her twenty-nine years of life had taught her that justice was for those born on the right side of the tracks, and that understanding was a word that had no place in the legal system. More than likely she had crucified herself this afternoon by attempting to protect her children. And yet, what else could she have done?

The cold, hard lump in Shannon's stomach jumped up into her throat a few minutes later as an authoritative knock resounded on their front door. Not moving from her spot on the floor, she just stared numbly at the door. She could feel the children's tension as the dice lay unheeded in the middle of the Monopoly board. Nothing she'd read as a child, preparing herself to be a worthy citizen, had prepared her for this.

She didn't have a plan. She had no idea what one did when one was guilty of a crime and the law came to take one away. It was useless to run. She had known that from the first, which was why they were now sitting ducks in their own home. But neither could she just calmly open the door, send her children away, and offer herself up to the authorities. They would not treat her fairly; they never had. And the children would suffer for it.

The door rattled. "Open up, Mrs. Stewart. I know you're in there," a muffled voice called. "I'd like to do this as easily as possible." The deep male voice failed in the attempt to be reassuring.

Michael grabbed the pellet gun that he had carried from his room earlier and stood up. "Come on, Mom. We're not scared," he said, pulling Mindi to her feet behind him.

"We can't fight him, Michael, he's the law," Shannon said, but still she didn't move to open the door. She stood in front of Michael, blocking his view of the door with some absurd thought of sparing him splinters if it came crashing down.

"I'm waiting, Mrs. Stewart. If you love your children at all, don't put them through any more of this. Let me take them back where they'll be safe and sound," the voice said. Little did he know.

"Safe and sound, huh!" Michael said, moving from behind his mother.

"Don't come in, mister. I'm armed," he shouted, pointing his pellet gun at the door.

Mindi was not about to be left out of the heroics. "Yeah, and we don't want to go back there, and you can't make us," she shouted from behind her mother. Shannon silently congratulated both her children for standing up for their rights, but her heart was crying for them, as well. They didn't stand a chance.

She reached behind her and took Mindi's shaking hand in her own and reached over to Michael's shoulder with her other hand, pulling him back against her. "We can't do this, kids. It's wrong to threaten an officer of the law. Besides, the man is only doing his job," she told them. There, that was the best she could do. She was not going to tell them the law was right, only that they had to live within its confines.

And still she could not open the door. *Think,* she commanded herself. There was no back entrance to their ground-floor apartment, but even if there had been, Shannon knew she would not have fled. She thought about locking herself and the twins in the bathroom, but logic told her that would only make everything that much harder for no gain.

There was a rustling outside the door, followed by the murmur of a deep voice. Shannon thought she heard the static of a hand radio. Was he bringing the National Guard? Could she go to prison for bringing her children to their own home? How could she ever prove her suitability behind bars? Shannon's heart thumped painfully as the full realization of what she'd done washed over her.

"You've got to the count of five to open that door, Mrs. Stewart, or I'm coming in." The voice no longer sounded the least bit conciliatory.

With a child hugging each of her sides, Shannon slowly moved forward.

CHAPTER TWO

BRYCE HAD NO IDEA what he had been expecting when he finally heard the click of the lock and the cheap pressboard door swung open. It certainly wasn't the sight of haunted violet eyes gazing resentfully up at him from a slender five-and-a-half-foot woman. At the moment, she didn't look like a harlot at all, nor did she look like a woman who put on airs. Like her children, she was dressed in shorts, a T-shirt and tennis shoes, and her makeup was limited to a little mascara outlining her startling violet eyes.

But Bryce had learned the hard way that some women, especially if pushed by thwarted emotions, were capable of hiding a multitude of sins behind their sweet feminine eyes. This time, he was going to listen to his brain, to take heed of his life's harsh lessons and remain immune.

The twins, however, were another story. For a split second, Bryce just stared at his captives, as if waiting for someone else to make a move. They were good-looking children, though smaller than Bryce would have expected for ten-year-olds. And they were glaring at him with frightened and accusing eyes.

"You touch my mother and I'll shoot," Michael said. He pulled far enough out of his mother's embrace to aim his gun straight in front of him.

Bryce swallowed, uncomfortably aware of the boy's height, and where the gun was pointed. He wondered if the boy knew that the groin was the only area of the male anatomy he could damage with a plastic pellet, and if he would really shoot.

"Michael, no." His mother issued the order softly, but firmly.

Bryce was shocked by the awareness that skittered through him as he heard Shannon Stewart's husky voice for the first time. He glanced up at her as the boy immediately lowered his gun. So she was a beautiful woman with a sexy voice. If the rumors were to be believed, she made a living off that combination. And Bryce had been without a woman for more than a year; it was only natural that he react to such flagrant stimuli. It meant nothing, less than nothing. He was going to listen to his brain, not his base instincts.

"I can't let you take them," she said, and again her voice taunted him.

"I'm sorry, ma'am," he apologized, and then grew angry with the automatic response. What did he have to be sorry for? Doing his job? The woman was a conniving harlot who had broken the law. Wasn't she? The judge had suggested that she only wanted her children for the money she would get from the Stewart family. A woman like that was not worth his concern. But still, there were the children to consider.

"I'm Sheriff Bryce Donovan. If you'll all come with me, we'll get these two back where they belong," he said, as if he were suggesting an outing to the park.

"We belong here," Michael stated. Bryce had to hand it to the little guy, he had gumption.

"Mrs. Wannamaker has dinner waiting for you two," he coaxed, preferring not to argue with the boy.

The woman tucked her children more securely beneath her arms. "They're not going back there."

Shannon wondered if the sheriff would believe her if she told him the truth. The system had a funny way of ignoring what it chose not to see. She searched the far reaches of her mind for any other way to win against the twisted justice that had been against her all of her life.

"I'm afraid they have no other choice." The sheriff's words were delivered amiably, but their intent was very clear.

Michael lifted his chin toward Shannon, tears glistening in his sweet eyes. She felt the pain slice clear to the root of her soul as she met her son's confused gaze.

She looked up at the sheriff, at the brown wavy hair curling over his collar, at the light brown eyes that were as cold and hard as the ground outside during the long Michigan winters. She hated him at that moment, not because of who he was, but because of what he was, what he represented. Nevertheless, she was going to beg. He had left her no other option.

"Please don't take them back there. They're not safe there. Mrs. Wannamaker beats Mindi. My daughter has welts on her back—from a willow switch." She poured every hope she had into that single plea. The tears she choked back were not for effect. They were real—and painful. Hearing herself put Mindi's abuse into words made the crime against her daughter seem so much more frightening.

Bryce's first instinct was to believe her, until he reconsiderd. The woman was a known liar. She had had well over two hours to coach the children. The scene had been staged. She was grasping at straws. So why were his instincts telling him differently? He broke away from her stare with difficulty. There was something so compelling in her eyes. Something that touched him deep inside, in a place where he was so alone, so empty.

He looked at the twins, searching for evidence of their mother's lie, expecting shifting eyes, jittery feet or any other body language giveaways. He saw instead two sets of dejected shoulders, two young faces lined with fright, two sets of eyes filled with worry. Tears welled up in the big brown eyes that seemed to take up half of Mindi's face, sending a blurry but silent plea for reassurance. The boy's gaze was filled with belligerent expectancy. Bryce was not comfortable with the brief glimpse he had of the weight young Michael was trying to balance on his ten-year-old shoulders.

"May I see the welts?" he asked, trying to ignore the haunted look in Shannon Stewart's lovely eyes.

Without speaking she turned her daughter around and lifted Mindi's shirt far enough to expose the reddened skin on her lower back. She allowed Bryce a brief glimpse, and then quickly lowered the T-shirt again.

Bryce swallowed, hard.

He hadn't expected this. He'd come to apprehend a woman, to return her children to safe custody, and then go home. Instead, he found himself facing a wounded family unit whose largest handicap appeared to be the piece that was missing—the man who should have been there, protecting them. And he found himself filled with rage, with the need to hit something. He needed someone to blame.

His insides churned as his thoughts raced over his options, his duties, the town's limited facilities, the fact that it was Sunday evening.... He wanted to help the injured trio, and yet, there was only so much he could do. His hands were tied. He had to investigate, to question Mrs. Wannamaker, to find out if there could possibly be another cause for the sickening welts marring Mindi's skin. He needed time to make other arrangements for the twins. He had to arrest their mother.

Bryce had brought down major drug dealers, he had walked beside some of the world's most dangerous scum, but never had he found himself in a position harder than the one he found himself in now. Reaching a decision of sorts, he squatted on his haunches and addressed the children. "We'll go have a talk with Mrs. Wannamaker and see what we can do to take care of this situation," he said, giving them his best effort.

"But we don't want to go back there," Michael said, looking from his tearful sister back to Bryce. The boy's glance was leery again.

"There's no place else for you to go at the moment, but we'll see that neither you nor your sister will come to any more harm. I promise." Bryce wished with all of his heart that he could do more.

"That's it?" Shannon Stewart's voice was almost shrill as she hurled the words at him. Bitterness distorted the perfection of her features. "There's no place else for them to go so you're going to take them back to that woman? Just like that? What kind of system are you running, Sheriff? What kind of man would leave two innocent children with a child abuser?"

Bryce met her gaze with a fierceness of his own. "I intend to have them out of there within the hour," he told her, his voice clipped. "I need an hour, maybe less, to find someplace else to take them. Until then, I will put the fear of God in that woman. If there is so much as a scratch on either of these two in the meantime, her life will no longer be worth living." He did not add that leaving them with the Wannamakers for an hour was preferable to taking them to the police station where they would be witness to their mother's arrest.

Because as ridiculous as it seemed to him now, he still had to arrest Shannon Stewart. She had broken a law which he had a duty to uphold. Kidnapping, or even custodial interference, if that's what the judge decided this was, was serious business.

Shannon Stewart didn't say another word, as if realizing that she would get no more concessions from him, but

Bryce could tell she wasn't satisfied. Her shoulders drooped, as if she had just lost the fight of her life in spite of giving it all she had. He met her gaze briefly, daring to see her despair, and in that one fleeting second, his spirit reached out to her, not as cop to criminal, but as one battle-scarred human being to another.

THE DRIVE TO Mrs. Wannamaker's lasted about fifteen minutes, but to Shannon it seemed like an hour. She could barely breathe through the suffocating tension. As she reassured the twins that she loved them and that they would all be together again soon, memories of another ride in the back seat of a cruiser scurried through her mind. She tried to ignore the iron grid separating the front seat from the back, hating herself for putting her children in such a painful situation. Were lies told in desperation by a heartsick seventeen-year-old girl really to be punished this way? Had being needy enough to marry someone before she'd known how to recognize love, or the lack of it, really been such a crime?

Sheriff Donovan pulled his cruiser into Mrs. Wannamaker's cracked drive, stopped the car, and got out without saying a word. Minda was crying, and Shannon suspected that Michael's stern-faced expression was maintained with difficulty. She held her children against her and waited for the sheriff's next move. Trapped as they were, she could do little else.

He opened the door closest to Michael. "Okay, son, let's get you inside for some dinner."

Minda clutched Shannon even tighter, her little nails digging painfully into her mother's arm. "I don't wanna go back in there, Mommy. Don't let them make me. Don't go, Mommy." She sobbed against Shannon's breast.

"It has to be this way for now, Minda Marie. Their rules will only have a chance to work for us as long as we live by them. Now come on, both of you, let's get out of this hot car.''

Shannon slid across the seat after Michael, pulling Minda with her. The three of them stepped out of the car, still entangled.

''I'm not giving up, ever,'' Shannon assured them. ''Never, never forget that I'm always here for you.'' She knew that they must be frightened beyond belief to be going back into that house.

''Promise?'' Michael asked, with a searching gaze.

Shannon knew her promises were the one thing her kids could count on; she never made one she couldn't keep. ''I promise,'' she said, vowing that she would find a way.

''Then let's go,'' Michael said, grabbing her hand and pulling her forward.

''Sorry, son, but your mother has to wait here. She can wave goodbye to you from the car.'' Donovan stepped forward and took Michael's free hand, then reached for Minda.

''No!'' Minda screamed, jerking her hand away and tucking it up against her body.

Shannon squatted in front of her.

''You have to go now, Minda. I'll wave from the car just like I do every Sunday. Be a good girl, honey, so people will be good to you. Do that for Mommy, 'kay?''

Minda's chin remained on her chest, but she nodded.

Shannon reached up to brush the child's hair back from her face, then with one finger under Minda's chin, she lifted her daughter's face. ''Promise?'' she asked.

Fresh tears pooled in Minda's liquid brown eyes, but she held back another sob. ''I promise,'' she answered softly.

Shannon stood, putting an arm around each of the children. ''Can I have a hug?''

They wrapped their arms around her middle, squeezing until it hurt. Shannon wished she could feel that pain for the rest of her life, but after a moment, Sheriff Donovan cleared his throat and stepped forward. She knew she should have been thankful that he had allowed her as much time as he had to soothe the twins, but she didn't have that much control left. She hated him for what he was doing, whether it was his job or not.

Her heart sank when Donovan saw to it that she was once again locked into the back of his cruiser before he finally led the kids up the drive to Mrs. Wannamaker's run-down house. For the first time since she'd opened her door to the sheriff, she felt a twinge of fear for herself. Just how much was this foolish escapade going to cost her?

The kids turned in unison to wave goodbye, almost as if they had been instructed to do so. She blew them each a kiss before they turned away again. The sheriff guided them with one large hand resting between each small set of shoulder blades. Though she supposed he was worried that the children might balk and run, she couldn't shake the notion that his touch looked almost gentle. Was she so overwrought that her subconscious was creating a scene with which she could live? No longer able to hold back her own anguished tears, Shannon wept as the front door opened and her children disappeared inside.

CHAPTER THREE

FIFTEEN LONG MINUTES later the sheriff reappeared. Shannon quickly choked back her sobs and wiped the stream of tears from her face as he slid behind the wheel of the cruiser.

"There was a tire swing in the backyard. She said Minda sat in it, spun it too tight, got tangled up. She said they're rope burns." Shannon heard the words with dread. Was that it then? Did this mean he was not going to do anything to get her children out of that house? Had her actions that afternoon been in vain after all?

She sat silently in the back of the cruiser as he drove back toward town and tried to control her mounting panic, the strangling awareness of not having the freedom to make things right for her children. She had to think.

When the sheriff passed both turns that would have taken them back to her apartment, she blurted, "Where are we going?" But she already knew.

"To the police station. You're being arrested for custodial interference, Mrs. Stewart. You have the right to remain silent..."

Shannon's heart went numb with dread as the sheriff continued with his recitation of her rights. She had heard them all once before, twelve years ago, and her tired brain could hardly comprehend that it was happening again. After all these years, the efforts and disappointments, the pain and the humiliation, was she right back where she had started? After all these years, wasn't there anyone who

Shannon couldn't stop the instant flood of tears that met his words. She did not understand this man's compassion, and she trusted it even less. Like the rest of his kind, like the rest of this town, he believed the worst of her. She had seen it in his eyes when she had opened her door to him that afternoon.

She almost wished he weren't pretending to care. At least with the others she had known where she stood.

Wrapping herself in the protective numbness that had seen her through much of her life, she walked silently beside him, only vaguely aware that his touch on her arm felt almost as gentle as it had looked on her children.

Shannon was afraid she was going to be ill when they entered the cool interior of the police station. Much smaller than the one she remembered, it still somehow gave the appearance of housing records of all of life's undesirable deeds. Papers on the couple of desks she could see were in disjointed piles, covered with messy black ink scrawls and surrounded by dirty coffee cups.

The short-haired woman who approached, dressed in a deputy's uniform, looked as if she was never going to smile again. "Would you like me to take her, Sheriff?" she asked.

"Do your stuff, Adams. But I think I'll hang around for a few," he replied.

Shannon glanced up only far enough to read the badge of the woman in front of her. Adams. She already knew about the woman's "stuff."

She stood frozen while the woman ran her hands up and down Shannon's body. She didn't flinch when hands brushed against the sides of her breasts. She spread her legs when she was told to do so. And all the while she could feel the brown-eyed gaze of Sheriff Donovan on her. She felt dirty, exposed, as though he was touching her body just as intimately as Adams was.

"She's clean, sir," Adams announced after what seemed an eternity.

Shannon glanced up to see the sheriff nod. "Get a booking slip," he said.

Adams went behind one of the desks and came back with a clipboard filled with papers. She led Shannon over to a row of folding chairs along one wall of the station.

"Name?" she asked as soon as Shannon was seated.

"Shannon Stewart," Shannon replied in a monotone, all too aware that the sheriff stood close by, broodingly. She kept her gaze glued to a dirt spot on the gray tile floor.

Shannon answered the predictable questions in a monotone, until the woman asked, "Next of kin?"

"Minda and Michael Stewart."

The sheriff stepped forward. "Adult next of kin, Mrs. Stewart. Someone we can notify if we need to."

With her gaze fixed on the floor, Shannon watched the shiny black shoes move into her field of vision.

"None," she replied. Once she would have proudly named Clinton Stewart, but those few short months of respectability didn't seem real to her anymore.

Adams slapped a square plastic container onto Shannon's lap. "Empty your pockets, please, and take off all your jewelry."

Shannon removed the gold-plated ball stud earrings and matching gold-plated chain that the twins had given her for Mother's Day, dropped them into the container and handed it back.

"Sign here," Adams instructed next, thrusting the clipboard at her. Shannon signed, took her receipt, and returned her gaze to the dirt spot on the floor.

Sheriff Donovan stepped forward. Once again, Shannon concentrated on his shiny black shoes. "Would you care to explain the events of this afternoon, Mrs. Stewart?"

Shannon remained silent. Had she believed that she would be fairly heard, she would have pleaded her case with everything she had, but she knew better. The first time she had trusted the law she had been convicted of prostitution, and the second time she had been labeled an unfit mother. No one was interested in her side of things; they never were and they never would be. They were only looking for grounds upon which to convict her. The Stewarts had interests in most of the businesses in town, law enforcement included. At least if she said nothing she would not be in danger of hanging herself. There was a tiny smudge on the right toe of the shiny black shoes.

"You're only making this harder on yourself, Mrs. Stewart," Donovan said persuasively.

Shannon remained still and silent. The black laces were not tied evenly. You would think a man who wore shiny shoes and creased pants would tie his laces evenly.

The shoes moved a little closer. "You're going to end up spending the night in jail if you won't cooperate."

Shannon was already going to spend the night in jail. She had already been booked. Did he think she didn't know that? She could not be released until a judge was there to pass sentence on her. And unless you were someone with an inordinate amount of pull, a judge was not going to hold court on Sunday evening.

"You have the right to an attorney. If you don't have one, the court will appoint one for you."

If he had done his homework more thoroughly he would have known that Shannon could not afford an attorney, that one had already been appointed, which was precisely why she was in this mess to begin with. Clinton and his highly paid hotshot lawyers were wiping the streets of Southlakes with her. Of course, it helped that Ron Dinsmore, the attorney the court had appointed to her for the custody hearing, had graduated from the same fancy boarding school as Clinton. Shannon did not believe for a minute that it was merely coincidence. She kept her mouth firmly closed.

Leather squeaked. The tops of the shiny black shoes were pushing upward, and she could tell he was bunching up his toes.

"You also have the right to a phone call. Is there anyone you want to contact?"

Shannon closed her eyes briefly in reaction to the words. She desperately needed to speak to her children for a moment, to assure herself that they were okay.... But she knew the answer to that request before she made it. There was no one else. Again, she said nothing.

The big black shoes backed off. "Adams, get her finger-printed. I'm going to put in for previous record."

Fear rolled down Shannon's back. She had one. She had a previous record. But Clinton and his family had never found out about it. It was the one thing she had managed to keep hidden all these years. If they ever found out about her conviction, her custody hearing was going to be finished before it had begun. Shannon held no hope that Sheriff Donovan would keep the information to himself. Her only hope was that he wouldn't find it. Her name was different now, and the small police station in the town where she had grown up had never advanced to the computer age. It was possible he wouldn't find it.

She submitted to fingerprinting and then stood in front of a black square of cloth to have her booking picture taken. Wondering about the system that treated human beings as guilty until proven innocent, she followed Adams to a little cell that was empty except for the skinny, regulation cot. She had a feeling she was in for a long night.

NIGHT, DARKNESS AND HEAT were Bryce Donovan's three worst enemies. He turned in his king-size bed, looking for

She hugged her arms across her chest as Sheriff Donovan's van pulled up in front of the little police station. The gesture was as protective, as instinctive as it had been twelve years before, and the feeling of sickening dread that seeped through her was the same, as well. Was this it? Had she really come full circle?

Sheriff Donovan pulled the car up to a wall in front of big black letters spelling Reserved. He turned in his seat.

"Doesn't seem much point in cuffing you, Mrs. Stewart," he said, half in question, as if giving her a choice. It almost sounded as though he was trying to make things a little easier for her, but Shannon rejected that idea. After all, in his eyes she was already a convicted criminal.

"I'm not going to leave my children, Sheriff," she assured him, trying to keep the distress out of her voice. "I made a promise that I intend to keep."

Donovan got out of the car and moved quickly to release the back door, reaching in a hand to help her out.

His gallantry surprised her. A gentleman cop? Things had changed in twelve years. "No, thank you," she said, dismissing the hand he offered.

"It's either that or the cuffs," he said.

Shannon felt the heat of embarrassment creep into her face. He wasn't being gentlemanly; he was keeping her in custody. She put out her hand.

"Do you believe in your system, Sheriff?" she asked, sliding from the car.

"Most of it, most of the time."

Shannon walked beside him, careful to stick close enough so he wouldn't need to assert pressure on the arm he now held. "And do you believe in your ability to determine if it's working?" she asked as casually as she could. Coming suddenly, almost painfully, like a blood-pressure cuff, and she was ready to protest when, just as suddenly, his touch became impersonal once again. "I'm a good cop," he finally said.

Shannon heard the tension in his voice, but she was not about to back down. She had made a promise.

"And do you believe that your system is correct in taking children from the mother who loves them and giving them to a woman who mistreats them?" she asked, thinking only of her determination to help Mindi and Mike. Those marks on Mindi's back had not been left there by the rope of a tire swing.

"I'm already planning to move on those allegations, Mrs. Stewart. It will only be a matter of a couple of phone calls to have your children moved to different foster care."

Shannon was so surprised she stopped walking and stared straight up into his solid brown eyes. "Then you believe Mrs. Wannamaker has mistreated them? You believe the children?"

He returned her gaze for a long, heart-stopping moment, seeming to look straight into her soul, to see the tortured misadventures of her past, to understand. Shannon wondered if maybe she had finally found an ally on the right side of the tracks. And then he looked away.

"Yes, I believe them," he said softly.

"Where will they go?" she asked, needing to know, knowing she would get through whatever lay ahead by picturing her children safely in their new place, waiting until they could all be together again.

"Until the judge passes a ruling on you, you cannot be allowed to know where they are." The words came cautiously, laced with unmistakable apology.

CHAPTER FOUR

SHANNON SLEPT LIKE a frightened child, curled up in a fetal position as if warding off any evils that might befall her during unconsciousness. And Bryce, after several hours of tossing and turning in his own comfortably soft bed, had showered, dressed in a clean uniform, shined his shoes, and driven to the station with one purpose in mind: he had to see Shannon Stewart again. He stared at the round lump she made under the blanket, unsure why he was even there.

The cot she lay on consisted only of a thin sheet of metal mounted on four legs. Bryce had been surprised and bothered when he had first toured the jail weeks ago, to see the outdated accommodations. And, for some reason, the sight of this woman huddled there made the sorry excuse for a bed seem inhumane, indecent.

In the eery predawn light the empty cells surrounding him seemed to echo the loneliness of life at an end. He did not like the picture his mind was drawing of Shannon Stewart huddled all alone among those cells.

She was facing the wall, with her chin tucked down and the old, too-small blanket pulled up, but he recognized the long black tresses that lay forlornly around her head and shoulders. He was also familiar with the tiny patch of faded blue jean that was showing beneath the small blanket. Bryce had a sudden urge to cover up that exposed piece of material and the nicely rounded hip that it clothed.

He turned impatiently from the bars separating him from the woman who had occupied so many of his thoughts during the long night and headed back to the lighted and livelier part of the police station. Stopping in the tiny storeroom that served as a kitchen, he pulled an opened, half-gallon carton of chocolate milk from the shelf of the miniature refrigerator and took several long swigs. It was time to go to work.

MUCH LATER THAT MORNING, Bryce was not at all certain that the sunshine outside had brought any improvement to his state of mind. He opened the courtroom door with more force than necessary, prepared to do his job to the best of his ability. He was the arresting officer; he would testify to what had transpired, relating the incidents exactly as he had perceived them. It was up to Oliver to determine the extent of the crime and the resulting punishment.

Shannon was already inside the brightly lighted room, standing to the right of the judge's bench. Ron Dinsmore, the lawyer who had been appointed to Shannon several months before, stood beside her. Williams had told him the night before that Dinsmore was one of the best. Bryce looked him over and had to admit that the man wasn't some loser off the streets. Dinsmore's impeccably tailored designer clothes screamed success.

"Officer Donovan, describe for us please the events of yesterday afternoon as you remember them." Oliver's voice rang out in the near-empty courtroom just moments after Bryce had taken his place at the left side of the bench.

"I approached Mrs. Stewart's door at approximately five o'clock yesterday afternoon, acting on a report that she was holding her missing children inside her home. No force was necessary to remove Mrs. Stewart from the apartment, and she aided in the return of her children to their foster home." He glanced only briefly at her, but he heard her sharp intake of breath and wondered at its cause. As far as he was concerned, he was only reporting the truth.

"The children did not wish to return to the Wanna-makers'?" Oliver asked, though Bryce knew his uncle was fully aware that that was the case. Oliver had backed him up last night so he could make arrangements to remove the Stewart children from the Wannamaker home.

"No, sir, they did not," Bryce replied.

"Do you know why that was?" Oliver asked, drawing the facts from Bryce as if Bryce were a stranger to him. Bryce respected his professionalism, his fairness. Oliver would judge the woman, and punish her accordingly. Bryce didn't have to make any decisions, or rely on his own judgment where Shannon Stewart was concerned. All he had to do was report the facts.

"Yes, sir. There was evidence of physical abuse, several welts on the girl's back. The children also expressed a strong desire to be with their mother." Bryce knew that was conjecture and wouldn't sway his uncle, but he wanted the children's obvious affection for their mother to be part of the official record, anyway.

Oliver nodded once, slowly, as if digesting what he had heard, and then turned toward Shannon. "Counsel?" he stated, giving Dinsmore a chance to speak on her behalf.

"My client wishes to plead guilty, sir," Dinsmore said. He glanced down at the papers in his manicured fingers as if conscientiously checking his facts, preparing his argument. But he said nothing more.

Following Oliver's piercing brown gaze as it settled on Shannon, Bryce frowned as he saw her almost imperceptible nod, her blank expression. He looked quickly back at Dinsmore, waiting for the man's next move.

Dinsmore remained silent. "Do you have anything more to add in behalf of your client?" Oliver finally asked.

"Just that she found the marks on her daughter's back as reported by Sheriff Donovan, something that could excuse a mother for an irrational act. However, my client admits to knowingly, illegally removing her kids from foster care,'' Dinsmore replied.

Bryce shot a sharp glance at Shannon. She did not seem the least bit surprised by her lawyer's double-edged defense. Her world-weary eyes were focused someplace beyond Oliver's left shoulder. Her expressionless features appeared to have been set in a mold, showing neither surprise, nor noticeable distress. It was almost as if she saw no point in fighting, as if she had known that Dinsmore was going to let her down. And yet, when he looked closer, Bryce saw that her fists were clenched in desperation.

Once again he found himself struggling to figure her out. Who was this woman? And why in the hell did he care?

"Due to the circumstances brought forth by Sheriff Donovan in this courtroom, and backed up by your own counsel, I am going to lessen the charge to a misdemeanor, Mrs. Stewart. You may have had justifiable reason to remove your children from their temporary place of residence, but there is no justification for not taking them immediately to the proper authorities. Therefore, I am sentencing you to thirty hours of community service and am hereby suspending all visitation privileges previously granted in connection with Michael Scott and Minda Marie Stewart until the July 18th custody hearing that has already been scheduled on their behalf."

Oliver's last words hit the room, shattering the brief moment of relief Bryce had felt upon hearing of the lessened charge. His first thought was of Minda Marie, the frightened little girl who had sobbed so brokenly in the back seat of his car the day before. Was keeping their mother away for close to six weeks a move in the children's best interest? And yet, Bryce had to admit that he wouldn't trust Shannon Stewart.

Bryce stood silently by, an onlooker as Oliver finished with Shannon and told her she was free to go. There was nothing in her expression to indicate that she cared one way or the other that she had just lost the right to see her children, but Bryce had a feeling, somehow, that she was crying inside.

He waited for her by the door of the courtroom, holding it open for her, then followed her out into the hall.

"You got lucky, Mrs. Stewart," he said in an effort to test the ground, to determine if she was feeling the anguish he suspected, or if he should just believe the facts as he had them and accept that she was the kind of woman this entire town believed her to be.

She looked at him then with eyes that reflected years of hard living, and Bryce felt their impact like a physical blow to his stomach. "Lucky?" she asked, confused. Her tone was not belligerent, sarcastic, or friendly, either. It was mostly dead, and it reached into Bryce more effectively than any tears or tirades would have done. It spoke of a pain that ran too deep for expression, a suffering too intense to acknowledge. It was the same kind of agony Bryce had been battling for more months than he cared to remember.

In the second it took Bryce to recognize that kinship, it became suddenly important to him that he do something to ease Shannon's loss. She might have loose morals. She might be guilty of the sins her ex-husband's family believed she had committed. But she was also a human being, so full of unbearable feeling that she was about to overflow.

"Yeah, lucky," Bryce finally answered as he walked beside her down the hall. "You could have been sentenced to prison."

"You don't think it's a hell worse than prison to be told I am no longer permitted to see my own children?" she asked, and her even tone didn't fool him this time.

Bryce had no answer to her question. He had no idea how it felt. "They've been moved," he told her, though technically she had lost the right to know.

She did not ask where they were; she knew he couldn't tell her. His respect for her grew.

They reached the end of the hall that led back into the police station, and Bryce saw Deputy Adams standing by the door holding Shannon's belongings. Apparently Shannon saw her, too, because she stopped walking and turned to face Bryce, her eyes meeting his for the first time that day. "Will they be told?" she asked, her voice trembling a little.

Bryce couldn't look into those eyes and lie to her, yet his throat felt too dry to form words. He didn't want to cause her more pain; he wanted to reach out to her, to smooth the tension from her face, to offer her the comfort of a warm touch. Holding his hands firmly in his pockets, he welcomed the pain in his shoulder as it rebelled against his tensed muscles, and he nodded.

She walked away then, without another word, without a backward glance, but Bryce couldn't do that. He went back to his office, he went to lunch, he went out on a couple of calls, but no matter where he was, he could not get away from the sight of the beautiful, downtrodden, violet-eyed woman who had opened her door to him the day before, knowing that he was going to take her children right out of her arms.

AS MUCH AS SHE WANTED a shower to wash the night's grime from her skin, Shannon went straight to the phone in her bedroom when she got home. She had spent the long, dark hours of the night wrestling with what she knew she had to do, but sitting with her children in the back of the squad car, she'd realized that dignity and pride were worth very little in the face of losing them.

She had to call directory assistance for Darla's number, but she'd never doubted it would be listed. If there had been a legitimate way for her to get it in the yellow pages, Darla would have had a listing there, too.

The phone only rang twice. "Darla's place." After ten years the voice was still the same.

"Darla, this is Shannon. I need your help." The words almost stuck in her throat.

"Shannon? Where are you? Is something wrong?"

"I'm fine," Shannon lied, knowing that Darla really did care, as much as she was capable of caring.

"Are you still married?"

Shannon had to remind herself that Darla loved her more than anyone, besides Darla. It was just that Darla's love for herself had ruined Shannon's life. "No."

A tense silence fell over the line. "Oh." More silence. "Has it been long?"

Shannon knew what Darla was asking. Was it Darla's fault that Shannon was no longer living the life of luxury with Clinton Stewart? Of course, it was Darla's fault, she thought, at least partially, but she wasn't going to say so. It would serve her purpose better for Darla to be in a willing mood, rather than a defensive one. Shannon didn't think she could stomach more of Darla's guilt-ridden apologies. And no matter what, Shannon could not forget the fact that Darla was her mother. Of course, Shannon hadn't been allowed to call her Mom since she was four years old and had inadvertently cost Darla a client.

"Two years," she answered.

"And your baby. You had your baby?"

Shannon knew how much it was costing Darla to ask that one. She was under no illusions about Darla Howard. The woman had stayed out of Shannon's life at Shannon's request, but she had not tried, even once, to change Shannon's mind. And Shannon knew why. Darla's only asset in life was her looks. She was obsessed with maintaining a "young" image, and having a grown daughter—let alone a grandchild—was the kiss of death in her business.

"I had two, Darla, and that's why I'm calling. I need some money." Shannon just wanted to get this over with, then see if she could take a long enough shower to wash off some of the shame she felt crawling along her skin.

"You have *two* children, Shannon? When did you have the second?"

Shannon gritted her teeth. Darla sounded more distraught than pleased.

"I had twins. Minda Marie and Michael Scott. Clinton has had them taken away from me, and he's trying to prove I'm an unfit mother. I need money to hire a good lawyer or I may lose them to him for good." She could not wait any longer to get to the point.

"Maybe you should consider letting him have them, Shannon. They couldn't help but be better off with Stewart money. Especially if you don't have enough of your own to hire a lawyer."

Shannon stood ramrod straight, staring at her bedroom wall. She understood that Darla actually meant well by her statement. Darla Howard had never had anything given to her in her life, so to her, taking was second nature. She didn't understand about unconditional love. Still, knowing that didn't take away the rage; it was only the thought of Mindi and Mike that kept her from slamming down the phone.

"Can you give me some money?" Never had she dreamed it would be this hard to ask.

"You know how sorry I am about things, don't you, Shannon?"

"Yes, Mother, I know." Shannon did know, but she did not want to hear any more. She did not even want to think about it any more. Some things just came too late.

"You were underage, Shannon. The most you could get was a slap on the wrist, a little counseling, maybe. I would have been sent to jail. And then what? Who would have come back to me then? Havenville is just too small, and it had taken me years to build up my clientele to the point where I could support us comfortably. It was too much of a risk."

Shannon walked to the door of her room, stretching the phone as far as the cord would allow. She looked across the hall to Mindi's room, to the rainbow-colored comforter stretched neatly across her daughter's bed. She fought the images her mother's words invoked, the degradation she had lived with for years as a child, going to school in clothes purchased by the other kids' daddies. And the final humiliation...

"Will you send the money?" Shannon simply could not respond to her mother's plea for understanding.

"I'll see what I can do, Shan." Shannon heard the resignation in Darla's voice. "Give me your number and I'll call you later in the week."

Shannon rattled off the numbers, too numb to feel relieved, too full of the past to feel good about what she was doing. But she thanked her mother before she hung up.

And then she dialed the phone again, before self-disgust had a chance to eat her up. She had to keep moving forward.

"Ory, I need a favor." Shannon sat on the side of her bed, clutching the phone to her ear. She could hear the cacophony of the lunch crowd at the Tub in the background.

"You need the night off?" he asked. Shannon heard the harsh intake of breath as he drew deeply on the ever-present cigarette. She smiled as she pictured the huge, dangerous-looking, beer-gutted teddy bear who was her boss.

"No. I need a lawyer." Ory practically lived in his reputably seedy bar on the outskirts of town, but he knew the identities of every upstanding citizen in Southlakes, and some surrounding cities as well.

"You in mo. trouble?" Ory demanded, and then hollered for somebody named Jake to have a seat and he'd send someone over.

"Clinton's puppet, Dinsmore, is going to lose me my kids," she told him when he came back on the line.

"You got money?" A spasm of Ory's chronic coughing followed his words and Shannon winced.

"Probably," she said when she knew he could hear her again.

There was a long pause. Shannon heard Ory bark an order to his daytime bartender, telling him to see what Jake wanted and then bring up another keg.

"Brad Channing." Ory's voice finally came back over the line. "He grew up here, one of eight or nine kids with a father who couldn't hold a job. He lost a girl to Clinton once, took it pretty hard. Smart kid, though. I heard he got a scholarship to one of them fancy schools. He's with some big-to-do place over in St. Joe but he'd pro'bly take you on, for a price. Dunno how much he charges."

Shannon wrote down the name, knowing that whoever helped her would have to be someone willing to go up against the Stewarts. It sounded like this Brad Channing had a reason to welcome a chance to beat Clinton Stewart at something. "Thanks, Ory, see ya tonight."

"I sure dunno why you don' just leave this town, kid," Ory said.

Shannon felt his caring even though he always tried so hard to hide it behind criticism. "Yeah, you do, Ory. And you think they're worth it, too."

"Yeah? Well, you just don' be late tonight, missy, 'cause I ain't coverin' for ya."

Shannon smiled as a heavy click resounded in her ear. Ory had not denied her charge that he had feelings. Though he wasn't the kind of friend you took to court as a character reference, he was the best friend she'd ever had. He was always there for her, unconditionally.

She put in a call to Brad Channing's office and was told that he was on vacation and that her call would be returned.

SHANNON MADE IT through the next week simply because she had no other choice. Sometimes she felt nothing, as if every bit of emotion had been sucked from her body; other times she felt a soul-destroying hatred as she thought of the people and the system—neither had been on her side even once in her life. But mostly, she just felt a loneliness so deep, so abiding, that it scared her. For the first time in her life she was tempted to give up.

She spent several hours a day planting flowers up and down Main Street that first week, fulfilling her community service, but what started out as just another lesson in humility turned out to be the grace that saved her. The delicate brightly-colored little petals she buried beneath the dirt gave testimony to the resilience of life. They not only withstood the elements that threatened them—the rain and harsh winds—but they also took their sustenance from those very elements. Shannon found in their example a reinforcement of her will to stand up in the face of her own adversity. Their beauty renewed her strength. She began to have hope.

The first letter arrived five days after the twins had been taken. Her hands trembled as she carried the little white envelope back inside, holding it as if it were glass, fragile and breakable. She could not wait to open it, and still she held back. Like a child at Christmas she wanted to savor the moment of sweet anticipation, and yet she was half-afraid the message inside might contain bad news. With her

stomach churning excitedly and her heart pounding with
dread, she carefully slit open the envelope.

Dear Mom,

Minda's childish cursive script brought a rush of tears to
her eyes, momentarily blinding her to the words her
daughter had written.

Bryce said I can write to you but I have to let him
check the letters for spelling and stuff. He must think
that's what you do with kids even in the summertime.

Bryce? Who was Bryce? The only Bryce that Shannon
had ever heard of was the sheriff who had ripped her life
apart the previous weekend. Of course, Shannon grudg-
ingly remembered, he had also been responsible for the
lessening of her charges.

Michael and I are in a much nicer place now. We have
chores to do but nothing more than we did at home. I
have to clean the kitchen after meals and Michael has
to take out the trash and mow the lawn but we get to
play a lot. There's a pool but we can only swim when
someone is outside watching us. Michael says we're
being treated like babies that way and he's right but I
like to swim anyway. Bryce has come twice since we
moved. Once to tell us that you were busy working for
the judge to make up for taking us away from the
Wannamakers without permission and the second time
I don't know why he came but he's nice to us. I hated
him at first but he got us away from Mrs. Wannamaker so now I'm glad.
    Michael says to tell you hi and he'll write next time
but I don't know. You know how much he hates to

write anything. I miss you, Mama, and hope you're done working soon. I love you, Mindi.

Shannon smiled through teary eyes as she saw the penciled-in *X*'s and *O*'s along the bottom of the page. She would give anything to be able to collect on those kisses and hugs.

On Saturday there was a letter from Michael. Shannon did not hesitate this time before she tore into the envelope, anxious to hear more about her children. She had already read Mindi's letter so many times that she knew every word by heart.

Mom, Mindi says I won't write but I will you know. Bryce gave us paper and stuff and he's mailing them for us. He said we should write to you every day but when will you write back? I figured out that you got into trouble for taking us home and I just hope you aren't in jail. Bryce said you were working for the judge but I don't believe him cause no judge hires someone because they were bad and I know if you could you would be here so since you aren't that means you can't. And we aren't allowed to call you, either. I don't really believe you're even getting these letters but just in case you are I'm going to keep writing them. Other than the fact that he lies Bryce is an O.K. guy. He told us to call him Bryce except I don't know why but we do. He's been here to see us a couple of times and the lady we live with told us that she knows his uncle and that its because of him that we're here so I'm glad about that. We have to be babysat to swim but other than that everything's O.K. here. Mindi is treated real good and I am too. I miss you and all that. Your son, Mike.

Despite the letters, Shannon woke up the next morning with her spirits in the gutter. It was Sunday, her day to see the twins, and she felt their absence so severely that she wanted to bury her head beneath her pillow and cry the day away. Strangely, it was thoughts of the twins that finally got her out of bed. Maybe she couldn't see them, but they were still out there somewhere, thinking about her as surely as she was thinking about them. And they would be missing her, drawing on her strength.

After forcing herself to concentrate long enough to complete a couple of pages in the new accounting textbook she'd received in the mail the day before, she collected her keys, unearthed a couple of dollars, and drove down to a nearby market to buy some flower seeds. She knew what she wanted as soon as she read the name on the package—Peace Lilies. She could not afford pretty pots, but she had enough money for a bag of potting soil. She headed home with her purchases, feeling better than she had all day. As long as there was life, there was hope.

She kept busy that afternoon planting the tiny seeds carefully, following the package directions implicitly. She poked holes in foam containers for drainage and used them for pots, placing them on saucers from her cupboard.

All the while she worked, the letters from her children played over and over in her mind, sometimes comforting, sometimes not, but at least, in some way, she had her children with her. She thought often of the new sheriff of Southlakes, too; it was hard not to, with his name popping up so often in the letters she had committed to memory.

She was honestly baffled by the man's actions, starting with the testimony he had given to the judge last Monday morning. She had never had a cop do anything that even slightly resembled helping her before. And according to the kids, he was continuing to do so. Donovan could not have known that Michael wouldn't buy his story of a job keeping her away, but she was warmed by the fact that he had at least tried. She was also more grateful than she could ever say that he had found a good home for the twins. The fact that he was also providing them with writing materials was outside her realm of understanding.

She still didn't trust him, but she was grateful to him. She found herself wondering if he gave Mindi a hug or two when he visited. Her little girl was a hugger. As she remembered the sheriff's big, warm hands guiding Mindi gently up the walk the previous week, those same hands that had been almost comforting when they had touched Shannon that afternoon, she had a feeling that one way or another her children's needs were being met.

She carried that feeling of well-being with her through Monday and Mindi's second letter, into work Monday night, and all the way until the mail came on Tuesday. Michael's second letter upset the precarious balance she had managed to find.

Dad came to see us last night, her son had written. Shannon's heart began thudding hard beneath her breast as soon as she read that first line. Clinton had started visiting the kids after they'd been put in foster care. He had ignored them their whole lives, unable to see beyond the fact that they were her children, that they were conceived under false pretenses, and now, suddenly, he was visiting them. She wished she knew what he was after. She wished that whatever it was, he would find it someplace else and leave the twins alone. He was a virtual stranger to the children and his visits upset them, especially Mindi.

Dad says that you're home and that you're just not coming to see us anymore that you got into too much trouble last week and that you don't love us that much. He wants us to come live with him, and Grandma and Grandpa Stewart too, instead of here. Mindi and me talked and we don't mind it here so much as we would

there but if you aren't ever coming to see us again then
why are we here? Don't worry Mom, we know that
Dad just doesn't understand about love and stuff but
it kinda seems like you could try harder to see us or
something. Are you still looking forward to the day
when we can all three be together again or not? Dad
says he's coming back in a couple of days. Mike.

Shannon's whole body was trembling by the time she
finished Michael's letter. She jumped up from the faded
beige couch upon which she had been sitting and paced her
small living room, trying to control her panic long enough
to figure out what to do. But what could she do? What options did she have? She didn't even know where her children were.

Should she go see Clinton? Try to reason with him, to
convince him how badly their children needed to be loved?
But what good would it do? A Stewart always did what was
"right," but in matters of the heart, Clinton's education
was sadly lacking. He had been raised to command respect, not affection. How could he be expected to understand that his children needed something he had never had?

He would not listen to her. He had no respect for her.
And she had no way to make him listen. If only she knew
why he was doing this to them. Why after two years, after
the agreement they'd made, was he suddenly so interested
in the children? It was not, as everyone believed, because
the twins were Stewarts; Shannon knew better than that.
Clinton had denounced them while they were still in her
womb, at the same time that he had denounced her. They
were a constant reminder of what he saw as Shannon's attempt to make a fool of him. He had never gotten beyond
the fact that Shannon had trapped him into unknowingly
siring a bastard's brood.

Only the elder Stewarts had ever recognized the twins'
Stewart ancestry, but then they had not known the true

circumstances behind their maternal parentage until two years ago. They had already been laying claim to them for years. It would not have looked good had they suddenly turned their backs on two innocent children. Shannon believed that in their own way, the elder Stewarts were fond of the twins. Clinton's parents had lived by the old adage that "children should be seen and not heard," which had provided for some uncomfortable hours for the twins on their weekly visits to their grandparents' wing of the mansion, but the elder Stewarts had never once canceled.

Clinton, on the other hand, had been avoiding Mike and Mindi for as many years as his parents had been accepting them. He, after all, was the one who had been made a fool of. He was the one who had been stained by their mother's lies. Shannon cursed herself for the millionth time for being naive enough twelve years ago to mistake Clinton's desire for affection. Clinton's attentions, though coupled with his respect for her, had brought warm feelings into her life for the first time. She had been unable to resist Clinton's offer to give her a lifetime of the same, and had gladly married him, determined to be the best wife he could ever want. She had been so certain that if the passionate kind of love she had read about truly did exist, it would just a take a while to grow....

Going to see Clinton, she knew, would be a mistake, but neither could she simply do nothing. Minda and Mike's entire futures were at stake, their security, their beliefs in their own worth. There had to be something she could do, someone who could help.

She dismissed the idea as crazy when it first came to her, but after staring helplessly out her living-room window for several moments, wondering where in the county her children were residing, she began to consider it again. Ordinarily she wouldn't dare ask the law for help. But after Mike's last letter, she knew her son was hurting and frightened. And that Sheriff Donovan was her only chance. He knew where her children were. Since he had gone so far as to provide them with letter-writing materials, he had to care about them at least a little bit. Surely, under these extreme circumstances, he would be willing to deliver just one letter from her. She would insist on letting him read it first to set his mind at ease....

She cringed at the thought of asking for anything from someone who represented the "system," but compared to calling Darla, she thought, this would be a walk in the park.

Her hands were unsteady as she thumbed through the front of the phone book, looking for the number to the sheriff's office. She picked up the phone to dial and then set it down again, stopping to water the foam containers of fresh dirt that lined her windowsills, and talking herself into making the call. The worst that could happen would be that he would say no, which would leave her no worse off than she was already. And there was always the slim chance that he would say yes....

BRYCE LEANED BACK in his desk chair and tipped up his pint-size carton of chocolate milk, swallowing lustily as the last of the cold liquid trickled down his throat. He could very well become addicted to the stuff, he thought. His deputies were threatening to give a carton or two to the prisoners so that there would be room for something besides milk in the station refrigerator, but so far Bryce had been lucky. There had been no prisoners.

There hadn't been a prisoner in their small jail since the night Shannon Stewart had been there over a week ago. Bryce lifted the empty carton one more time, hoping to catch a last drop or two, trying once again to banish thoughts of the beautiful woman he had met so briefly, but who seemed to have gotten under his skin, anyway.

He'd been wrestling with himself for two days over a simple decision to call her. He had been to see her children again, though, and despite his warnings to himself not to get involved, he was a little worried about them. After their father's visit they had become withdrawn and bewildered about their mother's absence. Mindi had tearfully asked about Shannon almost as soon as he had arrived on Monday.

And Mike. The boy had been such a tiger when Bryce had first met him, sure of himself and his place in the world. But the day before, Mike had been listless, and self-conscious. If something wasn't done soon, he figured, those two well-adjusted kids might suffer damage that could take years, a lifetime even, to fix.

The damnable part was, Bryce knew he could help. That is, if he could convince Shannon to cooperate with him. But how could he convince her if he couldn't bring himself to call her? And how could he call her when he knew that for his own mental health he needed to stay as far away from her as the county lines would allow?

Bryce rubbed his sore shoulder. Maybe if he just saw her again and got it over with, he would discover that he was making a problem where there was none. He'd tended to blow things out of proportion more easily since his release from the hospital, he reminded himself. He would probably take one look at the woman and wonder what all his fuss was about. He'd been tired last week, worked up over things and maybe he'd only imagined the pull Shannon had on him. Besides, this was not about Shannon; it was about two children who were suffering as a result of a system that they were supposed to be able to depend upon.

With a decision of sorts finally made, Bryce headed for the locker room to change into his jeans and polo shirt. This would be an off-duty, unofficial call. He didn't need to go armed.

CHAPTER FIVE

SHANNON DIDN'T LEAVE a message for Donovan. She needed his help, but she didn't have to trust his deputies. She would call back.

In the meantime, she decided she would bake some of the kids' favorite cookies. She swept through her cupboards like a woman possessed, collecting peanut butter and flour, cream of tartar and vanilla. Mindi loved peanut butter cookies, and Mike's favorite were snickerdoodles. If she had enough margarine, she could make a double batch of each. Then, when she finally reached the sheriff, he could deliver the cookies to the twins. Michael would not doubt her love with a plate of her snickerdoodles on his lap. She refused to contemplate the very real possibility that the sheriff would refuse to help her.

She yanked open the refrigerator door, relieved to see the unopened pound of margarine sticks nestled along the back of the top shelf. She pulled it out to place it alongside the rest of the baking supplies on her one small counter. She preheated the oven and set to work with a vengeance. The cold, hard margarine was no challenge to Shannon as she whipped it by hand, creaming in the sugar and eggs to begin the dough. She was not going to allow the stiffness of a dairy product, or the strength of the entire judicial system, to stop her from mothering her children.

An hour later, there were two full cookie sheets in the oven, another two on the table cooling, and two more were sitting on top of the stove holding raw dough, when the doorbell rang.

Pushing the hair away from her face with the back of a sugarcoated hand, Shannon left the small ball of dough she had been rolling in the bowl of cinnamon sugar and went to answer the summons. She only had a couple of hours before she had to get ready for work, and she was going to need every second of that time to finish her baking.

If not for the mouth-watering smell permeating her small apartment, she would have forgotten the cookies altogether when she pulled open her door. The last person she had expected to see on her front step was Sheriff Donovan. The sight of him in tight-fitting blue jeans and a snug white polo shirt, unbuttoned at the neck, was something she could never even have imagined. Her first reaction was relief, thinking that he'd come because he was willing to help her. But in the next instant, her heart was pounding with something more akin to dread. She had left no message. He didn't know she'd even been trying to reach him.

"I'm sorry if I'm interrupting something important—" he indicated the hand full of cinnamon sugar that she was holding out in front of her "—but I'd like to speak with you for a moment."

Shannon thought she detected a hint of a grin behind his words. The sheriff? A grin? Her stomach was fluttering from nerves, she knew, but she stepped back and motioned him into her tiny living room. "My kids. Are they all right?" she asked fearfully.

"They're in perfect health," he assured her. It occurred to her then that dressed as he was, he was hardly on an official call. But that thought worried her, too. Bryce Donovan out of uniform was having a rather disturbing effect on her nervous system.

He was smiling at her and Shannon suddenly realized how ridiculous she must look with her hair around her shoulders, no makeup, and wearing Michael's oversize Teenage Mutant Ninja Turtle T-shirt over a pair of old shorts. Not to mention her sticky hands hanging out in front of her. She supposed, were she in the sheriff's place, she would smile, too. And since she knew her children were all right, and since she very badly needed a favor from this man, she smiled back.

"I'm, uh, baking cookies," she said, smiling at him over her shoulder as she headed back through the archway into the kitchen. "If you don't mind watching, we can talk in here." She would keep busy, let him say his piece first, maybe let him eat a cookie or two, and then she would ask him to help her.

"Good Lord, woman, do you always bake like this?" Bryce exclaimed as he followed her into the sweet-smelling kitchen.

Shannon turned to see him surveying her bowls of dough, trays of cookies in the making and piles of finished confections with something akin to awe. "Not always," she replied, but she didn't elaborate on her reason for doing so today.

"Help yourself," she said instead. "I can get you a glass of milk if you'll wait while I rinse my hands."

"Milk would be great." Bryce watched as Shannon leaned over to rinse her hands at the kitchen sink. His mother had left him and his father almost immediately after Bryce's birth so he'd missed out on many of the feminine touches most kids took for granted. The closest he'd ever come to a woman baking homemade cookies was his TV set.

He didn't know what he had been expecting when he had knocked on Shannon's door unannounced. An artfully made-up woman in a miniskirt maybe, but not this homespun beauty making enough batches of cookies to feed an entire Boy Scout troop. At the moment, surrounded by all those cookies, she looked the furthest thing from the self-ish and cold person the Stewarts were painting her.

Bryce sat down hard, reminding himself that he was not here to get involved with Shannon Stewart in any way. He was here strictly and solely for the sake of two ten-year-old children who deserved better than they were getting. Nevertheless, he couldn't control the hammering of his heart in his chest when Shannon leaned over the table with his glass of milk.

Swallowing thickly, he reminded himself once again of the reason for his visit. "Thanks," he said as she placed the glass in front of him.

"No problem." She shrugged away his gratitude. Taking the seat opposite him at the Formica table, she started to roll little balls of dough in a bowl of brownish sugar.

Bryce had never before seen Shannon in any kind of natural situation and he was amazed by her ease with herself, her lack of brittleness, the absence of any obvious resentments. She looked over at him expectantly, as if waiting for him to speak.

"I've come about your kids," he stated baldly. Her beautiful violet eyes widened in alarm.

"You said they were okay." Her hand hung suspended above the bowl of sugar. The dough she held fell into the bowl with a plop.

"They're fine," Bryce assured her, meeting her gaze directly.

"Then why are you here?" she asked, pinning him with her steady gaze.

"They're fine, but they're confused. I read Mike's letter before it went out," he admitted apologetically and then hastened to explain. "I couldn't let them write to you otherwise, in case they told you where they were." Having delivered his justification, Bryce didn't feel much better.

Shannon's gaze never wavered from his as she nodded softly, accepting his explanation. Again, Bryce felt a growing respect for her. Lord knew, he had plenty of reason not to trust her, but he continued to be pleasantly surprised by Shannon Stewart. And therein lay the danger of what he was about to do.

"The thing is, if you're willing to cooperate, I can probably help you." He heard himself make the offer just as he was about to change his mind and return to the safety of the police station. He told himself that his instinct had made him do this, and the last time he had ignored his instincts, it had cost him more than he could afford to lose again.

"How?" she asked steadily. The ball of dough continued to lie unattended on top of the mound of sugar.

"I have a couple of questions for you, first," he said, looking for this last bit of reassurance.

She lowered her lids enough to mask her expression, but she did not return to her cookie making. "What?" she asked. She sounded as though she wasn't going to like whatever he was planning to ask.

"You expected Dinsmore to let you down in there last week." Shannon did not attempt to contradict him. "Why?" he asked.

She looked up with weariness clouding her eyes. Her slender shoulders slumped forward. "He went to boarding school with Clinton," she said and her shrug filled in the rest.

Bryce didn't like the implication behind her words, but he couldn't refute them, either. He had seen Dinsmore's behavior at Shannon's court appearance. Of course, if she talked to her court-appointed attorney as little as she had talked to Bryce at the station a week ago Sunday, Bryce's sympathies lay with the attorney. It was possible that Shannon, knowing Dinsmore's association with her ex-husband, had just assumed no help would be forthcoming and had refused to cooperate.

She broke into his thoughts. "You said two questions."

The second was not quite so easy to ask, and twice as important. "Why do your children hate their father so much?"

"They don't know him well enough to hate him." She was looking him straight in the eye as she spoke. "You have to understand, Sheriff. Clinton was nurtured with respectability and the importance of the Stewart image, not love. He was taught to temper his emotions in the cradle because rampant emotions cause scandal. Control is all the Stewarts know—it's all they are comfortable with. To them it's security, contentment. But to Mindi and Mike it's a sign of being unloved. Add to that the fact that Clinton resents the twins because they are a constant reminder that he made a mistake, that he was fooled, and you have little grounds to form a relationship. The children don't hate their father, they just sense that he doesn't love them."

Bryce wondered how, if what Shannon said was true, the children had grown up to be as affectionate as they were. They'd spent the first eight years of their lives in a Stewart household. Was it Shannon's influence on them, or had she just fed him a line concocted to raise his sympathies?

"So how can you help?" she asked, interrupting his thoughts for a second time.

"Let's just say that your case was not pleaded to your best advantage last week. It has also become obvious that the children's needs should be reevaluated. I believe there is a chance that with proper supervision you may be granted provisional visiting rights. Your kids miss their mother," Bryce finished softly as Shannon sat, unmoving, across from him.

Bryce could have been fooled into thinking that his words meant nothing to Shannon, were he to judge by the lack of expression on her face. But he was beginning to realize that it was when she was feeling the most, that Shannon's face revealed the least.

"Why are you doing this?" she finally whispered. Bryce didn't miss the telltale tremble of her chin as she asked the million-dollar question.

Why *was* he doing this? "I like your kids," he answered simply, accompanying the words with a shrug of his good shoulder.

"You really think there's a chance?" Her words were obviously measured carefully, but Bryce saw a glimmer of hope shining from within her too-wise eyes.

That small glimpse of hope was his undoing. "With the county sheriff as a chaperon, I don't see why not." The words came out before he could even consider the wisdom of his offer, but he had a feeling he would have uttered them anyway. He was beginning to believe that possibly all Shannon Stewart needed was a friend. From what he had seen so far, she had very few of them in this town.

Shannon smiled then, a bright, big beautiful smile, a real smile. It made her eyes glisten like moonlight over the ocean. Bryce had never seen anything so lovely in his life. The voice of reason that was whispering annoyingly behind his ears was just going to have to understand that he was only trying to help.

"Thank you," Shannon whispered, but the happy tears shimmering in her eyes were all the thanks he needed. He had a feeling that he was seeing a Shannon Stewart that very few people saw.

SHANNON PRACTICALLY floated around the kitchen after the sheriff left, packaging up cookies, imagining what the kids' faces would look like if she was actually able to deliver them herself. She played different scenarios in her head, until she was almost giddy with delight. She could not remember a time when she had felt so good inside.

Being honest with herself, and Shannon always made a point of doing so, she had to admit that though the good majority of her bliss resulted from the prospect of seeing the twins again soon, some of it was also due to the sheriff of Southlakes. She was too smart to believe that Bryce Donovan was quite the good Samaritan that he seemed, but she was human enough to cherish the hope that she finally had a little bit of justice on her side.

The fact that the man was sinfully handsome, with his broad, burly shoulders and lean waist, his shaggy dark brown hair, and warm brown eyes, really was of no significance at all. So she had noticed his good looks; she was alive, wasn't she?

Shannon finished in the kitchen with fifteen minutes to spare before she had to squeeze into the tight black skirt and tank top that made up her uniform at the Tub. Even her distaste for the less-than-wholesome clothes, the less-than-wholesome job, could not mar the delight singing through her veins.

She was actually chanting one of Mike's irritating rap songs on the way to her bedroom when the phone rang. Fearful as always when the kids were away that the summons indicated bad news, Shannon hurried into her bedroom and grabbed up the receiver. "Hello?" she said breathlessly.

"Okay. Here's what I've got. I hope it will make up for the way I acted twelve years ago..." Shannon barely had time to recognize Darla's voice before she slumped down onto the bed, stunned. She'd been hoping for hundreds, not thousands. With that amount of money she could afford to hire Brad Channing and pay him in cash.

"Shannon? Are you there?" Darla's voice rang louder over the line.

"I'm here, Darla. But are you sure? I never expected so much. I don't want to take all your savings, or anything." Shannon knew Darla would always take care of herself first, but no one could give away that amount of money without sacrifice.

There was a pause on Darla's end of the line. "Business has been good," she finally said, and Shannon stopped questioning her mother's generosity. Darla's occupation had caused Shannon nothing but grief since the day she was born and Shannon did not want to think about any of it.

But neither did she want to be responsible for wiping out the savings of a fifty-year-old woman. "I just don't want to rob you of your retirement," she said, knowing how badly she needed the money and how hard it would be to take it.

"You're not, Shannon. I can afford it. I'll have a money order to you in a couple of weeks. Now I gotta run. I have an appointment in fifteen minutes."

Shannon was still holding the phone, a mixture of relief and revulsion coursing through her, when the dial tone came on the line in place of Darla's voice. She did not want to take the money; it was as tainted as the first seventeen years of Shannon's life. But deep down, there was still a small part of the little girl Shannon had been who rejoiced because, for once in her life, her mother had come through for her.

"RON...DINSMORE, isn't it?" Bryce asked later that same evening. He had finally tracked the lawyer down at South-lakes's one and only country club, catching him alone outside the locker room. It would seem he had pegged the man at least partly right.

For a brief second, Dinsmore looked irritated at the interruption until he recognized Bryce. "Right!" he replied, holding out a slim-fingered, hairless hand. "Sheriff Donovan! Good to see you again."

Bryce shook the man's hand, but he dropped the contact as soon as was politely acceptable. "I'd like to speak with you about Shannon Stewart." Bryce came right to the point.

"Why?" Dinsmore asked, scratching his head as if he was faced with a perplexing problem. He dropped his gym bag at his feet.

Bryce was quick to note that Dinsmore did not offer him a drink at the bar, which is where he presumed the man had been headed before Bryce had stopped him.

"To have her visitation rights reinstated," he said.

"What?" Dinsmore looked at him as though he had lost his mind, and then seemed to remember to whom he was speaking. His voice took on a convincing tone. "I'm sorry, Sheriff. I know you're new to town, and I really respect that uncle of yours, so maybe you just don't know enough about Shannon Stewart yet. The Stewarts are just sick about this whole thing. The lies that woman told just to get her hands on Clinton's money," Dinsmore said, shaking his head. "Of course, that's all water under the proverbial bridge now, but take my word for it, Sheriff, those kids are better off without that woman around." Dinsmore nodded his preppy head as if giving emphasis to his credibility.

But rather than swaying him from his quest, as Bryce had halfway hoped the lawyer would be able to do, Dinsmore's practiced delivery convinced Bryce more than ever that Shannon had received the short end of the judicial stick the previous week, and that her children did not deserve to suffer any more because of a fight between adults. "Have you seen those kids recently, Counselor?" Bryce asked.

His only satisfaction in the whole conversation came when Dinsmore opened his mouth to speak and no words came out. Bryce had his answer. He turned at once and walked away, leaving an openmouthed Dinsmore in the hallway behind him.

FIFTEEN MINUTES LATER, Judge Oliver Donovan opened the door of his big rambling farmhouse to his nephew. "Bryce! What brings you out here so late?"

"Shannon Stewart," Bryce answered honestly, coming right to the point.

Oliver stepped aside for Bryce to enter the beautiful old house, calling out to his wife to bring some coffee and a glass of chocolate milk to his den.

Babsy, Aunt Martha's spoiled toy poodle, jumped at Bryce's heels as he followed his uncle to the den. She jumped into his lap as soon as he'd settled himself in one of Oliver's huge leather chairs. Bryce rubbed the dog's ears absentmindedly as he waited in silence for his aunt to appear with the refreshments. Oliver cleared some papers off the top of his desk.

"Bryce! I didn't know you were coming out!" Aunt Martha said, smiling warmly as she entered the room and handed her nephew a tall glass of the chocolate milk she had been buying since Bryce had moved to town.

"Thanks, Aunt Martha, neither did I." He returned the old woman's smile, adding a wink for good measure. "You're sure looking nice tonight," he said. He loved to see his aunt blush, loved the fact that someone her age still could.

"Bryce is here on business, darling. I didn't know he was coming myself," Oliver explained, patting his wife's hand as she placed a cup of coffee on the desk in front of him.

Martha turned back toward the door, smacking her lips together for Babsy to follow her. "Then I'll leave you two boys alone, shall I?" she asked, smiling over her shoulder at both men.

"Thanks for the coffee, my dear," Oliver called to her retreating back.

Bryce shared the grin his aunt had left on Oliver's face, amazed as always that two people could still share such obvious affection after almost forty years of marriage. He wondered if there were any women left like his aunt.

"Now, what about Shannon Stewart?" Oliver asked, looking at Bryce over steepled fingers. His lined face was completely serious once again.

"I believe it would be in the best interests of her children that her visitation restriction be lightened somewhat," Bryce stated evenly.

Oliver stared silently, taking in Bryce's steady demeanor before replying. "Why?" he asked.

Bryce's answer was critical. Oliver knew him. If there was any validity behind Bryce's doubts, behind the possibility that Bryce might be making a big mistake, Oliver would have a better chance of seeing it than most. "I've seen them," he admitted. There was no getting around the fact. "They deserved to be told not to expect their mother, and they deserved to hear the news from someone they knew."

Oliver nodded. "Go on."

"In just one week's time I've noticed changes that concern me. They're bewildered, frightened, blaming themselves. The boy is suddenly unsure of his mother's love."

Oliver leaned his forearms on his desk. "This could all be a matter of adjustment. Kids are resilient. By next week it could have all blown over."

Bryce met his uncle's shrewd gaze head on. "It could," he conceded, biding his time. He was not about to appear overeager.

"So?" Oliver questioned, shrugging his shoulders.

"Their father has been to see them. He told them that their mother did not love them enough to put up with all of the trouble. He's trying to convince them to agree to move in with his parents,'' Bryce reported.

Oliver picked up a paper clip, turning it end from end on the desk in front of him. ''Maybe that would be for the best.''

Bryce had been afraid his uncle would see it that way. Apparently the whole town saw it that way. Bryce had even entertained the idea himself. ''But not under these circumstances,'' he said, expressing his concern. ''Those children seem to adore their mother and allowing them to believe she does not love them back, when in reality she has been banned from seeing them, is neither healthy nor fair.''

Oliver was silent for several minutes after that, watching Bryce. And though Bryce was not completely sure that he was doing the right thing, he was confident that his uncle was considering everything Bryce had said, was weighing it fairly, in the best interests of all concerned.

''This is highly unusual, Bryce,'' he finally said. His words cracked the tense silence in the room.

''But it can be done. It's legal,'' Bryce returned, recognizing his edge.

''A chaperon would be required at all times,'' Oliver stated, in a let's-just-say-if tone of voice.

''That could be arranged.''

''This county cannot afford to pay a chaperon, Bryce. Especially since the Stewarts are not only our most lucrative taxpayers, but our largest donation source, as well.'' Oliver had a point there, but Bryce had a solution.

''I'll do it myself, free of charge.'' He did not even blink as Oliver studied him intently. Bryce's doubts were his own.

''Is that wise?'' Oliver asked, but he was no longer looking at Bryce. He seemed to have found something interesting along the rim of his coffee cup and was running his finger back and forth across it. The air hung heavy with the knowledge that Oliver had just stepped over the thin line

between personal and professional ethics. Had Bryce revealed more of himself than he had intended, after all?

"Are you doubting me?" Bryce asked.

"Not for a second," Oliver returned, raising his gaze
once more to meet Bryce's unwavering stare.

"Can she see them tomorrow?" Bryce pressed his advantage.

"Give me until the day after and make sure you stop by
my office in the morning, Sheriff, to put this request in
writing."

Bryce stood. "Thank you, sir. I will." He felt a twinge of
uneasiness at the relief that was flooding through him. This
was a professional matter and should not be affecting him
emotionally one way or the other. He told himself he was
just overtired, and bade his aunt and uncle good-night.

He called Shannon as soon as he got home, and then
again every half hour for the next three hours, but she never
picked up the phone. Finally, he realized she must be
working. When he pictured the Tub—the honky-tonk,
jukebox-blaring-hole-in-the-wall where he had been told
she worked—he hung up the phone in disgust and went to
bed. Instead of sleeping, he lay on his back staring at the
shadows on the ceiling, angry with himself, and angry with
Shannon Stewart, too. It galled him to think of her ped-
dling drinks to the questionable characters he knew fre-
quented the Tub, and the fact that it galled him bothered
him even more. Maybe he was not impartial enough to
carry through with his plan to help her kids. Maybe he
should quit trying to be a good Samaritan and just do the
job he was being paid to do. Bryce stared at the darkened
ceiling and wondered if he shouldn't just listen to his head
and stay away from Shannon Stewart.

CHAPTER SIX

MICHAEL STEWART DID NOT like the way things were going at all. He had really thought that his mother would show up to see them on Sunday, no matter what Bryce had told them. Bryce just didn't know his mom. She had never let them down before. Yet he and Mindi had waited all day and she had never come; he still couldn't believe it. He didn't know what to tell Mindi, either. She needed Mom even more than Mike did. And now, here they were, walking down Main Street with their father for the second time in a week.

He looked over at Mindi and felt kind of scared at the lost look on her face. He wished their father would talk to them. Maybe then Mindi wouldn't feel so funny with him.

"Do you children need any clothes or anything?"

Mindi looked at Mike. "No, sir," Mike told his father, who had asked them the same thing during the last visit. He wondered if their father thought they ripped clothes a lot, or if he just forgot he had already asked.

Mike couldn't figure out why their father even bothered with these visits. They never went anywhere, except to check on his father's stores and watch while he smiled at everybody but him and Mindi. They only ever talked about dumb stuff that didn't mean anything, not like when they were with Mom. With her, they had so much to say that the time flew by so fast it made them sad. The time with their father went way too slow, but at least they were glad when it was over.

"I need to stop here at the bank for a moment, children. We will go quietly inside, and sit still in the chairs by the door until we are finished, understand?"

Mike looked at Mindi and they both nodded. They grinned a little, too, but not so their father could see. Sometimes he and Mindi made fun of the way their father said "we" when he didn't mean we at all.

When their father finished his business, he and Mindi stood up to leave right away. Their father held the door open and Mike went first, so he would be on the sidewalk when Mindi came out. It was probably dumb, but he felt kind of like he was protecting her that way.

His eyes were still adjusting to the bright sun so he didn't see just what happened, but their father must have come out between him and Mindi because Mike heard her cry out and then he saw her fingers caught in the door of the bank. Their father quickly released them, and even looked at them, like maybe he really cared if Mindi were hurt.

Mike could see that she wasn't bleeding or anything, but it must have hurt bad, because she was crying hard. She even leaned against their father, like she wanted him to hug her.

"Minda!" their father said, holding Mindi away from him. "You mustn't smudge Father's shirt with your tears, child. You're a big girl now."

And that's when Mike knew he would rather die than live with his father. He would've cried himself then, except he knew his father would hate him for sure if he started bawling. He blinked back his tears and grabbed Mindi's other hand, pulling her to his side.

SHANNON DIDN'T HEAR from the sheriff on Wednesday. She stayed close to the phone just in case, going outside only long enough to check her empty mailbox, but he neither called nor stopped by. Telling herself not to be disappointed, not to automatically conclude that he was letting her down, assuring herself that these things took time, she tried to concentrate on the next lesson of the correspondence courses she had begun the year before. It helped to remind herself how proud the twins were going to be, how much better their lives together would be when she finally completed the course and obtained her degree. Worrying served no purpose; it would not reunite her with her children.

In spite of her resolve, by the time she went to work Shannon's stomach was a mass of tight little knots. An entire day had passed and she had accomplished nothing more than miles of senseless pacing. Her spirits were sagging down around her ankles.

A dejected cocktail waitress did not make good tips, Shannon discovered when she filled out the disclaimer on her time card at two o'clock that morning. The bar was closed, though her cleanup work had not yet begun, and she had only half of her usual earnings weighing down her money belt. Her black pumps clicked on the now-vacant wooden floor as she made her way through the sticky tables, wiping up beer spills and peanut shells.

Ory hollered from the back room, "Hey, Shan, I got a hot one. You okay to lock up?"

"I got it, Ory, see you tomorrow." She was glad for once to be left alone with the stench of male sweat and stale alcohol. She had no reason to hurry home, no one waiting for her return. The dank interior of the Tub fit her mood admirably.

When the twins were home, Shannon worked the early shift so she'd be back by midnight. Not being as familiar with the closing procedure of the bar as she could have been, it took her twice as long to straighten, wipe and sweep as it should have. And with Ory gone, she was also responsible for restocking the inventory behind the bar.

It was close to four o'clock in the morning when Shannon finally opened the door to her apartment. She stumbled into the shower, too exhausted to care about anything besides getting rid of the grime coating her body. On the way into her bedroom, she towelled herself dry, then fell naked into bed. The coolness of her soft, clean sheets was like heaven. Her last conscious thought as she drifted off was that this day had brought her something good after all—for once she wasn't going to have trouble falling asleep.

IT SEEMED LIKE ONLY a few moments later when Shannon was rudely awakened by pounding on her front door, followed by the pealing of her doorbell. She flew out of bed and was halfway through her living room before she remembered she wasn't wearing any clothes. The pounding on her door continued as she turned and fled back to her room, grabbed her printed cotton robe from the closet and hurried back through the apartment to the front door.

"Just a minute," she called irritably when the bell rang again. She was buttoning as fast as she could. The pounding stopped.

Shannon glanced quickly at the clock over her living-room couch as she fastened the last button and was shocked to see that it was almost noon. She hadn't intended to sleep so late. She slid back the dead bolt.

Bryce Donovan, in full uniform clear down to his shiny black shoes, stood in the open doorway staring at her sleepy dishabille. Feeling self-conscious, she blurted out the first thing that came to her mind. "You didn't call yesterday."

"I'm here now," he answered, somewhat defensively, as if maybe he was having second thoughts about being there at all.

Shannon's looked him over, until her gaze settled on the holster resting across his hip. She had to remind herself that this uniformed police officer was the same man who had sat in her kitchen dressed in tight blue jeans and offered to make one of her dreams come true. Brushing her uncombed hair out of her eyes, she took what little control she could of the situation.

"So what did they say?" she asked, afraid to hear the answer. When she was faced with the badge in front of her, her hopes suddenly seemed so foolish.

"Your kids are waiting for you to take them out to lunch," he replied. And then, as if he had been holding back until then, he smiled, the same smile that had made him so approachable the other day in her kitchen.

It was his smile, more than his words, that got through to Shannon. "I can see them?" she repeated slowly, keeping a tight rein on her joy until she made sure she had heard him correctly.

The sheriff stood out on the step with his hands in his pockets. "I have to chaperon, but you can see them. I couldn't take time off yesterday," he added, almost as an afterthought.

Tears of relief flooded Shannon's eyes, and without thinking, she flew forward to wrap her arms around his neck.

"Thank you," she whispered hoarsely, choking back happy sobs.

Bryce Donovan's arms came around her back, holding her steady, pressing her near-naked body against the firmness of his own for the instant it took her to realize what she had done. Mortified, she pulled back abruptly.

"I'm sorry," she said quickly, stepping back into the apartment. "If you'll just give me five minutes, I'll be ready to go."

Without waiting for a reply, or giving him a chance to reassess the situation, Shannon turned and hurried through the living room to her bedroom, leaving Bryce standing in the open doorway.

After visiting the bathroom, Shannon slipped into a cotton sundress, ran a brush through her hair, applied what little makeup her trembling fingers would allow, but still she was not at all ready to face Bryce Donovan again.

She thought she'd long ago lost all interest in sex, if she'd had any to begin with. In her experience, there was nothing particularly interesting about it. So why now, after her marriage, followed by years of peaceful celibacy, would she suddenly be feeling things she had never felt before in her life? She wanted to think it was gratitude, an outpouring of appreciation for the sheriff for helping her when no one else would, but she could not lie to herself. She was attracted to Bryce Donovan.

Shannon supposed she ought to be celebrating the fact that she was a normal woman after all, that life's early lessons had not completely obliterated her chances to feel the yearning a woman feels for a man, to experience the tug of sexual desire. But she didn't feel like celebrating; she felt nothing but frightened.

Sheriff Donovan was a member of the system Shannon had reason to mistrust. He was also a man who had the power, through his judge uncle, to take her children away from her. He was the man waiting for a report of a possible police record—her police record. She would just have to see that her awakening hormones went right back into hibernation, she decided. As long as he was willing to help her, to provide the means for her to see her children, she needed Bryce Donovan.

SHANNON WAS SILENT on the short drive to the home of Bessie Thompson, a widow who was now the twins' foster caregiver, but Bryce wasn't even curious about the thoughts she was hiding. He was too busy battling his response to her soft, clean scent and an overload of forbidden stimuli. He had been so sure of his control. He'd planned to take her to the kids, keep a safe distance during the visit and then leave, not seeing her again until the next visit, which would progress in exactly the same manner. He had been certain of his ability to remain impartial, right up to the moment she had launched herself into his arms.

There had been nothing the least bit sexual about her advance, but Bryce was having a hard time convincing his body of that. Of course, it hadn't helped that he'd reached out to steady her, and discovered that she had nothing at all on beneath her thin cotton robe. The curves her loose clothes had hidden up to that point had been so obvious that Bryce had immediately hardened in response. So much for remaining impartial.

"So what were you planning to do with all of those cookies the other day?" he asked, indicating the foil-lined shoe boxes she now held on her lap.

Shannon had wondered when he would get around to figuring out the fact that she had been making the cookies *before* he had arrived with his offer to help her see the children.

"Prove to Michael that I still loved him," she replied.

"And just how were you going to do that?" he asked, smiling over at her as he waited at a red light.

Shannon felt the warmth of his smile pool inside her, mixing with the excitement she could hardly contain as she counted down the seconds until she could see Mindi and Mike again. "Through you," she replied. The light turned green, and he turned his attention to the road. He was driving his own sedan, rather than the cruiser with handle-less back doors. Shannon peered out the window, anxious to see where they were going, to know the moment they got there.

"Me?" he asked, clearly surprised.

Shannon saw no harm at this late date in letting him know that she'd been counting on him even before he had offered his help. "When Mike's letter came, I knew I had to do something, and as far as I could see, you were my best chance. I was hoping to convince you to take a letter to the twins for me along with the cook— Oh look! There they are! Hurry, Sheriff, let me out!" Shannon said, reaching for the door handle before he had even slowed beside the curb where Mindi and Mike were waiting.

Bryce turned off the engine, but he remained seated in the car, trying not to watch, to intrude, as the kids hurled themselves into Shannon's open, welcoming arms. But he need not have worried. The small family hugged together in a circle that looked impermeable, seemingly unaware of the world around them, or of Bryce waiting silently in the car. He didn't even try to hold back the grin spreading across his face.

There was no mistaking the children's need to feel their mother's arms around them, or the joy that embrace brought to them. Whatever else Shannon Stewart was or had been in her life, her children obviously adored her.

They went to Aunt Hattie's, Southlakes's one fast-food hamburger joint, and the only awkward moment during the whole afternoon came when Shannon pulled a leather pouch out of her purse to pay for their meals and came up short fifty-nine cents. Bryce was uneasy, remembering what Oliver had said about her suspected gambling, but he was not going to put a pall on the day by asking her about it. He pulled out his money clip and paid the whole bill, telling her to put her money back in her purse.

The kids continued to talk all through lunch, filling their mother in on everything that had happened to them during the past week and a half, inconsequential or not. Bryce was glad to see that his presence on their outing did not seem to faze either one of them in the least. If he were a vain man, he might even be offended by the ease with which the other three occupants of his booth carried on as if he was not even there.

They chattered so much that Bryce could barely follow who was saying what, but Shannon didn't seem to miss a single word. It was as if simply having two ears automatically allowed her to hear two completely different conversations at once.

"He came to see us again," Mike said as he chewed his last couple of French fries.

"'He' has a name, son," Shannon chastised softly, seeming to know immediately who they were talking about.

"He doesn't deserve it," Michael said, mumbling over a French fry.

"Whether he meets with your approval or not, the man is still your father. To put him down is to put yourself down as well," she said.

Bryce felt his respect for Shannon Stewart rise another notch; at the same time his cynical inner voice murmured praise for her consummate acting skills.

"He did come, Mama. And I don't want to go live with him. Are you gonna make us?" Mindi entreated.

Bryce sat awkwardly next to Mike, trying to be as inconspicuous as possible, listening while the twins voiced their private fears.

"You will be staying right where you are for now, Mindi," Shannon stated. Bryce suspected that her calm certainty, as she looked from one child to the other, did more to reassure them than any words. She was good, he would give her that.

He noticed that she did not make any promises for the future. Mindi nodded and reached for the saltshaker, sprinkling more of the white crystals into her bag of fries.

"And that's enough salt, young lady," Shannon said, reaching over to remove the shaker from her daughter's hand.

"I don't get why he's showing up now," Mike said. He sucked on his milk shake, looking at Shannon over the top of the straw. "He never had time to do stuff with us before, and now when he does take us out he keeps looking at his watch like he has to be somewhere or something."

Bryce sensed, more than saw, Shannon stiffen. "Your father's a busy man, Mike," she said.

Mindi pushed the rest of her French fries away. "He doesn't love me, Mommy," she said, sounding more grown-up than Bryce had ever heard her. And suddenly he wasn't the least bit hungry anymore, either.

Shannon pulled the little girl up against her side. "You don't know that for sure, Min. We can't know for sure what's inside somebody else unless they tell us. But you do know that I love you enough for ten families, and that's more than a lot of children have. And you've got a pretty terrific brother, too. Now, who wants dessert?"

The straw dropped out of Mike's mouth. "Me," he answered promptly.

Shannon smiled across the booth at her son. "You've got it," she said, reaching over to poke him playfully in the chest. "How did I ever end up with a human garbage disposal?"

Bryce liked the teasing glint he saw in her eyes.

"I guess you just got lucky," Mike answered his mother with an impish grin. He looked just like any one of a million other boys who were secure in a parent's love.

"How'd you get to be so smart?" Shannon asked her son while riffling through her purse for the money Bryce had told her earlier to put away. She passed it across to her son and squeezed Mindi back up against her side. "How do you live with him?" she asked her daughter, nodding toward the preening boy in the seat opposite her.

"It's tough, but someone's got to do it," Mindi said sending a "so there" grin across to her brother.

Despite his attempts to remain unaffected, the familiar bantering filled Bryce with a curious sense of well-being. For a moment, he wondered if he was witnessing the results of years of nurturing. It certainly seemed like it. It struck him suddenly that to an impartial onlooker, the four of them would appear as happy-go-lucky as any other family out for a quick lunch on the way to someplace else. No one could have guessed that he was a sheriff guarding a restricted mother while she spent her two hours a week with her children, or that the only place the four of them would be going was back to Bessie Thompson's foster home.

The jovial mood continued up until the moment Bryce pulled up at Bessie's home an hour later. He had been planning to suggest taking the kids to the park, but they had seemed content to spend the entire visit sitting at Aunt Hattie's, soaking up their mother's undivided attention.

Bryce put the car in park, but didn't turn off the engine. The sound of the back seat belts opening was like a shotgun blast in the suddenly silent interior. Shannon's belt clicked next, and she turned around in her seat.

"Show Mama your back, Mindi," she demanded. Her soft tones held a wealth of love, but they left no room for refusal.

Without a word, Mindi turned, lifting up her shirt to reveal the faint welt marks still visible there.

Bryce felt his gut clench at the sight, and could only imagine the rage that Shannon must be feeling. He watched her reach out to trace the tips of her fingers lightly along her daughter's healing back.

"Does it still hurt?" she asked. There was no evidence of distress in her voice, but Bryce knew it was there just the same. He saw the telltale tremble of her chin.

"Not anymore," Mindi mumbled.

"Are you getting lotion on it every night?" Shannon persisted.

"I'm putting it on for her every night, Mom, just like you said," Mike quickly assured her.

"Then we've made it through an ugly time, and put it behind us, haven't we, guys?" Shannon asked, lowering Mindi's shirt back down over the top of her shorts.

Bryce did not turn around, but he watched in the rearview mirror as Mindi sat back down and both children trustingly held the gaze that Shannon passed back and forth between them. Together, almost as if the move had been choreographed, they nodded, not with smiles, but not with tears, either. As matter-of-factly as possible, the problem of Mindi's abuse was being dealt with and put to rest.

Bryce had to hand it to Shannon; she certainly seemed to have a grasp on motherhood. In one afternoon he had seen her discipline and tease, love, laugh, and handle sensitive issues. And she had done it all so naturally. She had waited until the end of the afternoon to mention the aftereffects of Mrs. Wannamaker's brutality, a subject that needed to be brought out, but could very well have put a damper on their short time together. And yet Shannon had still managed to send her kids off happy. Bryce thought their grins might split their faces in two when she pulled out all those cookies. They had trudged up the walk to Bessie's front door, proud as a couple of peacocks, with their arms full of their mother's love.

The drive back to her apartment was as silent as the ride over had been, but Bryce sensed a peace in Shannon that had been absent on that earlier trip. It was almost as if she had regained some measure of control just by knowing where her children were. He found it hard to imagine anyone suspecting her of wanting custody of those two children for the money that came with them. It just didn't fit.

All the same, he walked her up to her front door with his emotions held firmly in check. There were still some pretty stiff accusations floating around against her that had nothing to do with stealing her children, or losing her visitation rights. She was supposedly receiving quite a lot of money in child support, yet she worked long into the night, way past the time most respectable people were in bed asleep, at a job that was considered by many to be unsavory, and still she didn't have enough money in her purse to buy her kids hamburgers. He was a long way from trusting Shannon Stewart.

He had some doubts about the other party in this battle, too. Why was Clinton Stewart squiring his children around town all of a sudden if he had never done so in the past? So he'd look like a dedicated father? Or because he really cared?

"How's next Thursday for you?" he asked as Shannon searched in her purse for her house key. He moved back a step or two when her fresh womanly scent drifted around him.

"Thursday?" she asked, looking up at him from the jumbled mess in her hands.

"I'm on duty most Sundays. Your visiting hours have been moved to Thursdays," he explained, reaching for the key that she had finally unearthed.

"Then Thursday will be fine," she stated in a tone of voice that suggested that she would make it fine if it were not.

Bryce unlocked her door, telling himself to hand her the key and walk away, but he reached toward her instead, putting a hand against her back and ushering her through the opened door. He barely had time to be aware of how good she felt to him before she was gone—not just casually, "we're in the door now," gone, but really gone. She shrugged off his touch almost as quickly as he had given it and scurried into the apartment.

The man in Bryce was not at all pleased with her reaction.

"I'll pick you up at noon on Thursday then," he said, still holding on to the door.

Shannon turned to face him. She looked as if she was going to say something, but finally she just nodded.

Disappointed, Bryce released his hold on the door, letting it close. He started back to his car.

"Sheriff?"

He turned around. She'd opened the door again. "Yeah?" he called.

"Thanks."

The satisfaction he felt hearing that one word worried him more than anything else had all day. If her simple expression of gratitude was going to have that kind of effect on him, then Bryce was failing drastically at keeping Shannon Stewart in the distant niche he had allotted for her in his life.

THE PHONE RANG just as Shannon shut her door behind Bryce.

"Shannon Stewart, please," asked a pleasant male voice after Shannon's breathless hello.

"This is Shannon," she offered, wondering who on earth he could be.

"My name is Brad Channing, ma'am. I just returned from vacation and have a message here to call you."

Shannon's heart started a nervous tattoo. The lawyer Ory had recommended. The next couple of minutes could very well affect the rest of her life. "Mr. Channing! Yes, I called. Thank you for being so prompt," she said, trying to gather her scattered wits, to plan her words carefully.

"My assistant said something about a custody case."

"Yes, sir," Shannon agreed and then filled him in on the basic facts of her divorce, and told him about the past two years, when Clinton had only come for the children on command from his parents. She mentioned the home-study course she was taking in the hopes of eventually obtaining an accounting degree, the child-support money she wasn't receiving, as well as the rest of the allegations currently against her. She spoke factually, tonelessly, asking for legal assistance, not sympathy. She even told him about Clinton's claim that he had caught her with Deputy Drew Williams shortly before the divorce.

"Did Stewart catch you with his friend?" Channing asked.

Shannon's face and neck warmed with embarrassment, but she appreciated the fact that it was necessary for the man to know all of the facts. Dinsmore had never even asked.

"No. Clinton and Drew got drunk one night. Clinton had been doing that a lot toward the end of our marriage, though as far as I know, he never drank where anyone might recognize him. That particular night, Clinton had had more than usual and he offered his friend my hospitality. He insisted that I be a good wife and make Drew feel welcome. It was obvious there had been some pretty heavy promises between the two men, a trade of some sort agreed upon."

"And?"

"I took the children, left, and never returned," Shannon replied.

"But you stayed in town?"

"I had to. Clinton had joint custody of our twins. I couldn't leave with them, and I won't leave without them."

As Channing continued to question her about some of the other facts she had related, Shannon's faith in the man grew. He appeared to be listening carefully to her, taking her seriously, giving her a chance.

"How *do* you justify leaving the kids six nights a week?" he asked a few minutes later. He did not sound accusatory, just interested.

Shannon was eager to reply. She believed she had a good explanation, and she was finally going to be able to give it, even if only to this one man. "I am home to get my children ready for school in the morning, to drive them if it's raining, to come pick them up if they get sick during the day. I am waiting for them when they get home from school, to help with homework, or projects or problems, to carpool to Scouts or softball or Little League. I fix their dinner every night, and I eat it with them. I supervise their baths. Then, when they're ready to go to bed, to go to sleep, I go to work. What could be more ideal?" She had had no idea how good it would feel to finally get that off her chest.

"Tell me more about the money."

"It's been his word against mine, but I don't see how he can prove he gave it to me when he didn't. There would have to be canceled checks or something, wouldn't there?" she asked. Shannon had thought long and hard about that, and had decided that even in spite of Clinton's sterling reputation, the town's inclination to believe Clinton over her, he still could not prove something that had never happened.

"Anything's possible, Mrs. Stewart, but you have a good case here."

"What about Dinsmore? The court appointed him to represent me, but he's more interested in seeing me lose."

"It's just a matter of your signature and a couple of phone calls to have him removed from the case. I can take care of it. We should be free of him long before your next court appearance."

Shannon held her breath. "We?" she asked, latching on to that single word. "Does that mean you're interested in taking it on?" She strove to keep the hope from her voice.

"I think I can help, yes. To be perfectly honest, I would welcome the chance to see Clinton Stewart get his due for once."

Shannon's eyes flooded with happy tears. She was finally going to have her chance to be heard.

CHAPTER SEVEN

"HEY, BABY, HOW 'bout hightailin' a cold one this way!" The suggestive voice was loud enough to be heard over the din of the country crooning that blared from the juke box.

"Gotcha, Jack!" Shannon called over her shoulder, threading her way quickly between tables. She stopped and smiled down at the group of jean-clad men whose whiskey-filled shot glasses and beer chasers weighted down the tray she was balancing on her open palm.

She ignored the leers a couple of the men shot toward her cleavage when she bent to place the drinks on the table. She made sure to smile at all of them, though, thinking how much better Mindi's back had looked that afternoon. The ugly redness was gone, and even more to the point, Mindi seemed okay emotionally.

"That'll be eighteen dollars, guys," she said and slapped down another cocktail napkin, then placed the last bottle of beer, dripping with condensation, on top of it.

The biggest of the four men sent her a lewd grin, displaying a mouthful of crooked teeth. He held up a twenty-dollar bill just out of her reach. "Give us another one of them pretty smiles and you can keep the change," he drawled. The three men sitting with him waited expectantly.

She thought of Channing's offer to "take care of" Dinsmore for her. Life was treating her well; she could afford to be generous. In her mind's eye, she pictured Clinton's face when he heard that Dinsmore was no longer going to be around to guarantee him a sure win. She flashed a saucy smile at the four men in front of her, grabbed the twenty-dollar bill and pocketed her tip.

She made her way back to the bar for Jack's beer, her thoughts once again on her afternoon with the twins. *The cookies were a good idea. The twins practically floated up the walk to Bessie Thompson's front door.*

"Shannon, love, we're all out of peanuts," a voice called.

"Be right there!" she shouted back. *Mike better not have eaten all those cookies at once or he was going to be sick tonight. I should have thought of that, and given them to him in separately wrapped packages,* she decided.

Shannon delivered Jack's beer, along with several others', and made her way along the edge of the room toward the pool table.

"Anyone need anything over here?" she asked.

"I could sure use a taste of your sweet-lookin' lips," Derek Miller answered.

"Ory'd fire me for loafing on the job." Shannon sidestepped the man with practiced ease. "How about a refill on that drink, instead?"

"Sure, if you'll bring it over here to me," the brash young man challenged.

"You see anyone else working in my station?" Shannon asked over her shoulder as she left to collect more drinks. *Michael's lips were so sweet, already covered in cookie crumbs, when I kissed him goodbye....*

A slightly unsteady hand reached out to brush the soft black leather molding her hips, and Shannon slapped it away, making a note to pass on the other side of table number nine for the rest of the evening. *Mindi's arms felt so good around me, so needy, so loving....*

Shannon continued to keep her customers' glasses full and their arms empty, pocketing more tips during that first hour Thursday night than she had during her entire shift the night before. She only wished it were enough to pay for Brad Channing's services. As thrilled as she was to have him behind her, it still made her sick when she thought of Darla's money paying his bill. She tried to find comfort in the fact that, for the first time ever, her mother had come through for her. As she continued to weave through the crowded tables, she fought the knot in her stomach. If her mother's guilt could be wiped away with the thousands she was sending, then that alone would make it worthwhile. Shannon didn't want retribution for the past; she just wanted it over.

BRYCE WAS RUNNING as fast as he could, adrenaline pumping so hard through his veins the sensation was almost painful. The thickest fog he had ever seen swirled around him, muffling sounds, confusing his sense of direction. His shoulder was aching, but he had to go on. She needed him, and God help him, he needed her, too. Visions of her flawless skin, her soulful eyes spurred him on, hardening his body as he ran, impeding his progress.

He was running through a maze—the streets of downtown Detroit. His breath came in gasps, not filling his lungs. He was losing air, running out of breath, and his chest was going to explode from his effort to keep going. He found the end of the maze, but she was not there. She was outside somewhere, calling to him from a bed of tall grasses in a huge country field.

Bryce ran on, determined to find her, promising to save her. He stumbled through the grass, needing to hurry but slowing down to search for her among the waist-high growth. The grass caught at his feet and ankles, holding him back, dragging against him. He stumbled, falling against the hard ground, onto his bad shoulder. Pain shot down his arm, but before he could cry out, she was there, taking it away, whispering soothing words of love and need.

Bryce worshiped her body, kissing away her clothes. He lifted his suddenly naked body between her legs, supporting his greater weight with his arms and shoulders, two perfectly healthy shoulders. He thrust once, but she flinched. The air was filled with sounds of exploding gunfire. Children were crying. An acrid stench filled the air. Her nails bit into his shoulder, and the searing pain returned. He wanted to drown it all out, to lose himself in her, but she was gone. . . .

Bryce sat up with a start, automatically reaching for his aching shoulder, which he must have rolled over on in his sleep. He flung away the single sheet covering his naked body and slid off the bed. The bedroom still lay in the total darkness of night, but Bryce didn't need a light to see where he was going. He had taken more cold showers than warm ones since the last time he'd seen Shannon four days ago.

It was obvious to Bryce, as he toweled icy rivulets from his cold body, that he was going to have to do something about Shannon Stewart, other than trying to pretend she affected him no more than Deputy Adams. That plan was not working.

He glanced at the clock when he entered his bedroom and was surprised, as well as a little irritated, to see that it was only a little before midnight. He had been asleep less than an hour. He would bet Shannon was still at work—for hours yet.

Bryce had driven by the Tub of Suds several times lately, dismayed by the run-down appearance of the local dive, the raucous laughter that drifted out to the gravel parking lot outside. But never once had he stepped inside the darkened interior of the bar. Perhaps it was time he did so. Perhaps it was time he saw the real Shannon Stewart.

BRYCE STEPPED INTO the smoke-filled bar fifteen minutes later with hair still damp from his shower. His blue jeans and "boaters do it on the lake" T-shirt would have fit right in with the Monday-night crowd if he had worked in them all day, or at least worn them more than once without washing them. As it was, he felt like a shiny new penny in a collection of old coins.

His arrival went unnoticed, and he picked a vacant table in the darkest corner of the room, grateful for the anonymity. At the table next to him, a man with more hair on his face than on his head, was overtly fondling the curves of the voluptuous woman draped across his lap. Neither of them was aware of his presence and Bryce could not help thinking that it was time they moved their party to a more private place, like maybe the back seat of their car, for instance, or the seedy motel out on County Road E.

And then he noticed Shannon. She had just come into the room through the swinging door beside the bar. One look at the skintight, black leather miniskirt she was wearing and the too-brief black leather top and Bryce's insides were churning. Never before had he known what it felt like to go wild over something and hate it at the very same time, but that pretty well summed up the way he felt about Shannon Stewart.

Bryce was used to seeing Shannon dressed in loose-fitting, figure-concealing clothes. And now, in one fell swoop, he was seeing every curve she had been hiding behind those formless garments. Her shapely bottom was everything a man could wish for, and . . .

She leaned over to serve the three men seated a couple of tables in front of Bryce, revealing a cleavage that would have made a lesser man drool. Bryce glanced away before he became a lesser man and noticed the hungry looks on the faces of the men she was serving. He could cheerfully have broken a nose or two.

How could she do that? Those men were eating her up and she was smiling at them as if she enjoyed their attention. He felt his temper begin to boil. Too late he realized that what he should be feeling was disgust, not this, which felt an awful lot like jealousy. Placing a firm grip on his emotions he sat back, concentrating on remaining impartial.

He knew the exact moment when Shannon saw him. She had been making her way efficiently around the tables, collecting empties, taking orders, chatting with her customers, but her steps faltered, slowing almost to a stop as she finally approached his table and recognized who was sitting there.

She was fidgeting with the stack of napkins on her tray as her high-heeled pumps clip-clapped hesitantly up beside him.

"Sheriff. I've never seen you in here before," she said.

The first thing Bryce noticed was that she seemed to be inordinately interested in the slogan on his T-shirt. The second thing he noticed was that the face that had been smiling easily only seconds before was now wiped completely clean of expression.

"That's probably because I've never been here before," he replied, watching her closely. Her long black hair was tied back loosely, baring her slender neck to his gaze.

"Uh, did you want a drink or something?" she stammered.

Bryce had never heard her stammer before. His being there was making her uncomfortable. Or was she just feeling guilty? Maybe, he thought, it was a little bit of both.

"That's usually why someone comes into a bar, isn't it?" he asked, doing absolutely nothing to put her at ease.

She placed a little white napkin on the table in front of him. "What can I get for you?" she asked. Her fingers had returned to shuffling through the remaining pile of napkins on her tray, betraying her nervousness.

Bryce looked around the room. No chocolate milk here. "A beer would be fine," he said, wondering how long he was going to have to stay in the place before he figured out what he'd come here for.

"Coming right up," she replied before hurrying away toward the bar.

She was stopped twice on her way to collect his beer, but she was no longer smiling at her customers. She had disappeared behind her mask.

He never took his eyes off her as she moved across the room. Her long, gorgeous legs were filling his mind with possibilities, with enticing fantasies.

"That'll be a dollar fifty," she said as she leaned forward to place his beer in front of him. Bryce stared at the tempting cleavage that was once again revealed to him. And then he raised his gaze to meet the knowing look in her large eyes. The lighting was dim, shading her skin, but Bryce thought he detected a hint of a blush. Shannon Stewart, blushing? Did women like her blush? But then, what kind of woman was she, exactly?

"Would you like me to run a tab?" she asked uneasily when he failed to reach for his wallet.

He leaned back to reach into his pocket. "No, here, take this." He pulled the top bill from his money clip, catching a brief glimpse of a number five in the corner of it. "Keep the change," he offered.

He frowned as anger tightened her face. "That won't be necessary, Sheriff," she said through clenched teeth, digging in the pouch strapped around her waist. She withdrew several bills and slapped them on the table beside his untouched beer.

Bryce took one look at the amount of change she was laying down and felt sick to his stomach. He had forgotten he had stopped by the bank on his way home that evening. Tight-lipped, she turned to leave.

"Shannon," Bryce said, grabbing her wrist. He couldn't let her think what he knew she was thinking.

She flinched at his touch, reminding Bryce of the ending of the dream he had had such a short time before. "Let go of me," she said, keeping her voice low. Bryce barely heard her above the noise in the bar, the people getting louder with every beer, the music, the clacking of pool balls. He barely heard her, but he felt the fury behind her words as surely as if she had screamed them.

He could not let her go because she would walk away, but he lessened the strength of his grip, keeping her captive as gently as he could. "Shannon, I'm sorry. I thought I had given you a five."

She stood stoically within his grasp, staring at the wall behind his left shoulder. Her face looked like molded porcelain.

"Shannon, look at me, please," Bryce said, uncertain why it was so important that she understand he hadn't meant to be insulting. She continued to stare straight ahead.

"Come on, man! Share a little!" someone called out from a few tables away. "Yeah, we need some beer over here," another voice rang out.

Bryce was not going to be badgered from his purpose by a couple of drunk cowboys. "In a minute," he called, raising his voice above the din.

"I'm not letting you go until you look at me, Shannon," he continued, lowering his voice for her ears alone.

Her fiery gaze pinned him to his chair. "I'm sorry," Bryce repeated, meeting her gaze, accepting her anger. "If I'd wanted to proposition you, Shannon, I would have done it the other day, when I had you in my arms."

He got the response he'd wanted, sort of. Her face flushed for the second time that evening, and Bryce knew he had made his point. He could feel the muscles beneath his fingers begin to relax.

He knew he should let go of her wrist, let her get back to work before he got her fired, but her skin felt so good, so soft, against his callused palm. He rubbed his thumb along the inside of her wrist, thankful that the darkness in the room hid his body's reaction from her. The memory of the dream was still too vivid.

"You handle this whole place by yourself?" he asked, nodding toward the roomful of round cocktail tables.

Shannon nodded. "Just since midnight," she said. "There's me, and Ory behind the bar." Her chin was trembling. Now what had he done to upset her?

"Then I guess I better let you go get 'em, huh?" he asked, reluctantly releasing her wrist.

"Guess so," Shannon said, glancing over her shoulder at the tables full of patrons awaiting her attention.

"Shannon," Bryce said, as she turned to go.

"Yeah?" she asked, still looking nervous.

"Your kids call me Bryce. Do you think you could manage it, too?" he asked, giving her a little grin.

She hesitated, as if about to argue the wisdom of his request, or maybe the point of it, but another raised voice broke into their conversation, demanding a drink or else. Shannon nodded quickly at Bryce and hurried away. He didn't bother to deny the revulsion he felt toward the crude men who thought she owed them something, or toward her for giving it to them.

He stayed until closing, nursing his one beer and watching Shannon work the roomful of men, and the odd woman or two, with a skill that he could not help but admire. His burgeoning respect for her returned as the half hours passed. She walked like a lady, even in the tight, suggestive clothes, refused advances with a smile and artfully dodged wandering hands. He also noted, with his sober, detective's eye, that the pouch slapping against her hip when she walked was beginning to hang mighty low beneath the weight of the money she had been slipping inside, and it was only a Monday night. She probably made even more on weekends.

When Bryce was the only customer left in the bar, he finished his beer, waved across the room at Shannon who was busy clearing dirty glassware off tables, and stepped outside. He filled his lungs quickly with the warm, smokeless air, thinking he'd just spent two hours in a place he would never frequent ordinarily, and all he'd accomplished was to decide that he still didn't like how Shannon made a living. He was no closer to discovering what secrets lay behind her too-old eyes. Was she for real, or was she just a very good actress? Had her irreproachable behavior been an act she put on for his benefit?

Whatever, it was a fact that she wanted her children back. It was also a fact that Bryce was in a position to influence the outcome of her custody hearing. He decided he couldn't leave just yet.

He had to wait almost an hour before Shannon followed him outside. As soon as he saw her shoes hit the parking lot, he called, "Shannon..."

She whirled around, with no sign of fatigue in her body as she swung into a stance that looked something like a karate move. Then she recognized him.

"B-Bryce! You scared me to death. What on earth are you still doing here?" she asked, relief obviously weakening the tight rein she usually held on her tongue.

Bryce liked the way his name sounded on her lips, soft and familiar. He smiled, and shrugged. "Seeing you home," he said. He wasn't about to tell her that he had been waiting to see if she was going to go home by herself.

She was. But now that he knew that, he figured he might as well follow her home in case she had someone waiting there for her—a customer, perhaps, with whom she had made arrangements for a late-night rendezvous.

She looked pleased. "That's really not necessary, you know. I've been seeing myself home for years." Bryce concentrated on her smile rather than her words.

"I'll follow you just the same," he said, telling himself that as soon as he was convinced she had made no other plans, he would leave her alone.

"I'm too tired to argue with you about it," Shannon replied, heading toward her car.

Bryce climbed back into his own car and waited for her to pull out, then followed her to her apartment complex, parking in the slot next to hers and pocketing his keys. He would see that she made it safely to her door.

"You like muggy air?" he asked as he approached her car, and watched her roll up the open window.

"It's better than no air at all," she replied, sliding out to join him in the parking lot. "My air conditioner went out over a month ago."

Bryce walked beside her as she led the way to her porch. "So why not get it fixed?"

"I've got two children to support."

He recalled her sagging money pouch hanging low against her hip. He thought of all the Stewart money she was receiving, and he thought of how little money she carried in her purse.

"You've had support checks to cover the twins' needs," he reminded her.

The conversation was beginning to leave a worse taste in his mouth than the cigarette smoke he'd been inhaling all evening, but it was important.

Shannon turned her head, sweeping him with her jaded gaze. "Have I, Sheriff?"

The answer to her question should have been an obvious yes, and yet Bryce hesitated to push the issue. Her look, her tone, was bitter. He had never felt such negative emotion from her before. He motioned her toward her apartment without another word.

Shannon remained silent until they reached her door and then, before putting her key in the lock, she turned toward him.

"Why did you come tonight?" she asked, watching him by the light over her front door, holding his gaze with her own. It was hard to lie to her when those tired eyes looked at him with such confusion.

Bryce pushed his hands into the pockets of his jeans, stretching the material taut across his fly. "I guess I'm trying to figure out just who Shannon Stewart really is." He was being as honest with her as he could. Bryce considered himself a decent man, and so far, he had seen nothing in Shannon's actions that told him she did not deserve that decency.

"Why?"

Bryce was beginning to feel more uncomfortable by the minute, thinking it would probably be best if he turned and walked away.

He reached out to brush a stray strand of hair back behind her ear. "Isn't it obvious?" he asked, not at all sure what he meant by the remark. Was he getting personal with her, or was he still just concerned about her rights, her kids?

Shannon swallowed. Her face was impassive again. "Not to me, it isn't," she said. Bryce knew by her blank expression that she was bothered by their conversation, but she was not letting it drop.

He could not give her what she was asking, even if he had wanted to. He did not know the answers to her questions himself. "Then I guess that makes two of us," he heard himself admit.

She opened her mouth as if to say something, but bit her lip instead. Bryce couldn't take his eyes away. He wondered how she tasted. He wished his teeth were biting gently into the full, tender flesh.

Shannon turned away, pushing her key into the lock with shaking fingers. "I need to go in."

Bryce almost reached for her, tempted to see how hard it would be to convince her to let him join her, but then he remembered who he was, who she was, and knew that he could not take things any further. Despite what he had seen thus far to the contrary, there were still too many rumors stacked against her, and too many memories crowding his heart.

With a quick "See ya Thursday," he turned and walked away.

"HELLO. THIS IS THE Friend of the Court. Financial information is unavailable by phone. You need to have your case number to obtain information. Please hold if you wish further information. Thank you." Bryce twirled his pen between his fingers as he listened to the elevator music that followed the recorded message. He had been put on hold, and he did not have a case number. The call was his first step in finding out the truth behind Shannon Stewart, to help himself and, maybe, to help her, too. After seeing her in that bar last night, he wanted to believe that there was some reason she had to be there, some moral reason, that is—like necessity. His mind kept replaying her bitter "Do I?" in reply to his comment about her child support.

The phone clicked right in the middle of a catchy violin solo. "Hello, this is Pam, may I help you?"

"Yes, Pam, I hope so. My name is Bryce Donovan. I'm the sheriff over here in Southlakes and I need some information." The woman sounded friendly enough; maybe this would be as easy as he had first thought.

"I'll do what I can, Sheriff. What kind of information did you need?"

"Financial and, no, I don't have a case number," he offered before she could ask.

There had to be a way for him to find out if Clinton Stewart had indeed been paying Shannon child support for two years.

"Do you have a subpoena?" she asked. She still sounded eager to help, even while she was laying roadblocks in his path.

"I wasn't aware that I needed one," he admitted. Hell, he was a sheriff, not a lawyer. And he had never paid child support.

"There are a couple of other ways for you to obtain the information," she offered.

Bryce poised his pen above the legal pad in front of him, ready to write. "Such as?"

"You can have one of the parties involved give you a written release for the information, or obtain written permission from either attorney of the parties involved."

Bryce threw down his pen. That was just swell. He was not sure he could trust either of the lawyers involved, and he sure as hell did not want either of the parties involved to know what he was doing. Not now. Not yet. Not until he knew just why he was doing it, why it was so important. Was he an officer of the law, investigating a possible gambling charge, or was he a man investigating a woman he...what? A woman he *what?*

"Thank you for your time, Pam. You've been very helpful." He spoke into the phone, but his mind was already racing ahead.

He did not want to go to Stewart or Shannon. He could not go to either of their lawyers. That left him one option—Oliver. Bryce picked up the phone and dialed.

The young law student who was working for Oliver during her summer break from school answered his call.

"Hello, Betty. This is Sheriff Donovan. Is the judge available?"

"One moment, sir. I'll check." Bryce was put on hold again. An easy-listening rendition of "Lady in Red" filtered through the line.

"Donovan here." Oliver's voice interrupted the song almost as soon as it had begun.

"It's Bryce, Judge." Bryce used the formal address to tell his uncle that he neither expected, nor wanted, any personal favors. He wouldn't even have called on Oliver again, except that after Dinsmore's performance Bryce wasn't sure which members of the Southlakes County judicial system would be impartial to his plea.

"What's on your mind, Sheriff?" Oliver returned.

"I need to subpoena the Friend of the Court for some financial records."

"Are you planning to file formal charges?" his uncle asked.

Bryce picked up his pen again, twirling it back and forth. "It's too soon to tell. At this time, the investigation is informal, merely following up a lead. Substantial child-support payments are reportedly being paid, and yet there is no evidence that those payments have been made."

"Whose records are you petitioning?"

Bryce's heart was hammering. Had he convinced Oliver that the investigation was a professional one? If his uncle believed it, couldn't Bryce believe it, too? "Shannon Stewart's," he answered.

"Then you don't need a petition because there aren't any," Oliver stated as if he knew exactly what he was talking about.

"There aren't any?" Bryce repeated, surprised. Everyone was so sure that Shannon was receiving that money, and yet the judge residing over the case was calmly stating that there were no records of child-support payments.

"It happens that way sometimes," Oliver explained. Bryce could picture the older man's shrug. "A petition was put forth to forego the court, allowing the defendant to pay the plaintiff directly. The Stewarts have more money than they know what to do with, and a sterling reputation in the community besides. I saw no reason not to approve the order."

"And has Stewart been paying her?" Bryce asked.

"He says he has, and there's no reason not to believe him. The man has enough money to pay support for fifteen kids, so why would he get himself into trouble over two? The Stewarts never take chances with their good name."

Bryce thanked his uncle and rang off, leaning back in his desk chair. Oliver's news had raised more questions than given him answers. When he'd assumed that Clinton's payments were being run through the Friend of the Court, he had been certain that Shannon was receiving the money. But Clinton's freedom to pay her personally, once a month, left a lot more room for delinquency. It was possible that Shannon was not receiving any money from her ex-husband.

Of course, as Oliver had said, there was no reason for Clinton Stewart not to make the payments. He could afford them, so why would he risk trouble with the law by not paying them? What could he possibly gain? Could he have a motive of which everyone was unaware, or did Shannon simply mismanage money? Did she have some hidden, expensive habits as everyone seemed to believe, or was there something else entirely going on?

Once again, Bryce was left with many questions, but no answers.

CHAPTER EIGHT

SHANNON SAT ON A BLANKET on the hot beach Thursday afternoon with her knees pulled up to her chest, and her arms wrapped around her legs. Her hair fell around her shoulders, protecting her bare arms from the burning sun. Her terry-cloth short set was sticking to her in places, but she didn't care. She was too busy smiling at the twins as they frolicked like a couple of dolphins in the icy waters of Lake Michigan.

"I got thirty for the kids, and fifteen for you and me." Bryce's voice came from behind her. She turned and saw him walking toward her down the beach, carrying a couple of bottles of sunblock lotion.

There was no denying it. The man was gorgeous. He was wearing white shorts and a black muscle shirt today, displaying his assets rather blatantly, in Shannon's opinion. She looked at the dark hairs curling along the contoured muscles of his legs, and trickles of awareness slithered down her belly.

"Thirty's good," she said, forcing the words past her constricted vocal cords.

Bryce dropped the lotion on the blanket beside her, and reached down to grab the bottom of his shirt with both hands. Shannon watched as he slowly revealed, inch by inch, his smooth, taut stomach. Shannon's gaze followed the thin dark shadow of hair from the waistband of his shorts up to where it swirled around his navel and then farther until it burst into a full mass of tight black curls over bulging pectorals. Her eyes settled briefly on the scarred flesh of his right arm at the juncture of his shoulder, the one flaw that made the rest of him so perfect—so very perfect. She quickly looked away.

He dropped his shirt and slid down beside her on the blanket, looking over at her. Shannon felt his glance as surely as if he had swept his fingers from her toes to her head.

"You're starting to burn," he announced.

She was burning all right, but it wasn't from the sunshine beating down upon her. She was absorbing Bryce's body heat through her pores and it was turning the blood flowing through her veins into lava.

"I always get red the first time out, but it'll turn brown by tomorrow," she replied, hoping she sounded calm, unperturbed, normal.

"You still ought to put some of this on." He held up the sunscreen. "It would be a shame to mar that beautiful skin in any way." His last words were softer, not quite as impersonal as Shannon needed them to be.

She was embarrassed by her growing and very inappropriate desire for Sheriff Bryce Donovan. Her body was reacting to the man in ways it never had before, with anyone. And she was reading in his words, in his eyes, that he felt the same. But was it really there or had she just conjured it up out of her own need?

Bryce opened the bottle of sunblock lotion and squeezed some cream into his palm before setting the plastic bottle down on the blanket between them.

"Why aren't you wearing a suit?"

It took a moment for his question to register. "I don't have one," she said, hoping she didn't sound as distracted as she felt. She counted the sailboats out on the water.

"You don't have a swimsuit?" he asked, smoothing the lotion over his arms. Shannon gave up counting boats and tried to concentrate on the kids splashing in the shallow water several feet in front of her, but the coconut aroma of the lotion floating between her and Bryce was filling her mind with forbidden visions of slick hot skin covered with coarse dark hair.

She had to think for a second before she remembered the question he had just asked her. "Uh . . . not this year," she finally said. She leaned back, digging her hands into the sand behind her. "I . . . um . . . need the money for other things."

Get ahold of yourself, Shannon, she admonished harshly. She was behaving like an adolescent. She watched as a wave blew in, sweeping over Mindi's head, leaving the little girl drenched and shrieking with delight.

Bryce reached for the bottle once more. How much of that stuff was he going to use? Was he deliberately dragging out the process, or did it just seem that way? She was still watching the children, but from the corner of her eye she saw Bryce's hand leave the bottle, full of lotion. By the time she realized where he was going with it, it was too late.

"Stop!" Shannon pulled her leg away from Bryce and the warm lotion before he could discover the goose bumps he was raising. "I can do that," she added in what she hoped was a more normal tone of voice. It was bad enough that she was suddenly besieged by this startling awareness of him; she didn't want him to know about it.

Bryce's hand lingered above her thigh for a long, silent minute before he pulled it away, wiping it on one of the towels. "Fine with me," he said shortly. "I'll go get the kids so you can rub them down, too."

Shannon glanced up as she heard the strange tightness in his voice, expecting from his tone to see anger stamped across his features. But there was no sign of ire, or even frustration, as she met his troubled gaze. He looked just plain sad as he turned from her and headed down the beach. She stared after him as he walked away, her lotion-smeared hands suspended above her leg. She was more moved by that last brief glimpse she'd had of him than by anything else that had transpired all day. What could possibly have brought that pained look to Sheriff Donovan's earthy brown eyes? Did he, too, regret that their circumstances prevented them from exploring what might have been something special? Or had he been thinking of something else entirely...?

The kids ran up from the lake, squawking about the hot sand under their feet, spraying water on everything in their path. But they came up alone.

"Come here, rats, so I can get some of this stuff on you before you melt away right before my eyes," she ordered as her giggling children tickled her with drops from the icy lake.

"Aw, Mom, do I gotta?" Mike moaned, clearly offended by this blow to his budding masculinity.

Shannon opened the lotion Bryce had purchased for the twins, with money that had not come from her.

"Yes, you gotta," she mocked playfully. "You know as well as I do, Michael Scott, that your shoulders will be redder than ripe apples tonight if we don't plaster you now."

As Mike plopped down between her legs, shocking her heated skin with his icy-cold suit, Shannon was not thinking about sunburns and shoulders. At least, she wasn't thinking about Michael's shoulders. She was watching the lake, watching the back of Bryce's broad shoulders as he swam surely through the waves. Was he propelled by a need to cool off as desperate as her own?

Bryce stayed in the lake for almost half an hour, swimming several laps between the buoys and the shore, until Mindi and Mike returned to the water, clamoring for his attention. Shannon watched as he tossed each of the twins out into the waves over and over again. Though he was primarily using one arm, he looked strong and wonderful out there playing with her children. Warm waves of gratitude swept over her. Male companionship was something the twins had never received from their father. A good name, yes, but never time. Clinton hadn't been mean to his children; he'd just avoided them. Shannon smiled as Mindi's squeal rang out over the beach. She was content with life for the moment, feeling good about the future for the first time in many months.

Her smile turned into a frown of concern, however, when she noticed Bryce walking slowly back toward the blanket, rubbing his scarred shoulder. There was a grimace of pain on his face.

"What's wrong?" she asked as soon as he was within hearing distance.

He followed her glance to his upper arm and immediately dropped his hand. "Nothing," he said. His tone warned her that the conversation was going to end right there.

And Shannon would have let it, if he hadn't winced again when he sat down and rested his weight against his hands.

"What happened?" she asked.

He reached for his shirt and pulled it on. She wasn't sure he was going to answer her, aware as she was that she might be crossing into private territory, uninvited. But things were becoming different between them, slowly changing. She wanted to know more about him. Especially since they were going to be spending several hours in each other's company over the next few weeks, hours that were the only high point in Shannon's life at the moment. She decided that she could lower her guard just a little.

Bryce continued to sit silently beside her, giving no indication he had even heard her softly spoken question. She glanced at his profile, liking the character lines around his eyes; they gave evidence that he'd lived life, experiencing its trials and its joys. His nose was straight, his lips firm and full. He was staring out at the horizon, but Shannon had a feeling his attention was directed inward.

"I was injured in the line of duty." The words dropped into the silence just when Shannon had decided he wasn't going to answer her.

"It's a bullet wound?" She knew she should be no more than casually empathetic, but she felt frightened by the realization that he was not as invincible as he seemed. And that his job entailed a lot more than escorting divorced women and their estranged children through a sleepy little town.

Bryce just nodded, still staring out toward the lake. Sailboats bobbed along the choppy waters, disturbed now and then by the wake of a passing speedboat, the occasional skier. The peacefulness of the scene did nothing to calm the jumbled feelings raging through Shannon. She couldn't help it. She had to know more.

"What happened?" she asked again, hoping that he was going to say somebody's gun had misfired, hoping that his reticence was due only to a too-healthy male ego.

Her eyes bore into him. Whether it made sense or not, was right or not, was even wise or not, she needed to know what had happened, to know that the danger had passed. But she had a feeling that what she was really searching for was the assurance that it was never going to happen again— an assurance that he surely couldn't give her, one she had no reason, no right, to even need.

Bryce turned to look at her then, and Shannon met his gaze fully, hiding neither her concern nor her sympathy. The desire for him that had been burning so close to the surface all day was there, too, but at the moment she didn't care. The stark pain in his expression cut her to the quick.

"As I told Michael on the way here, I was a detective on the Detroit vice squad before coming to Southlakes. My... partner... and I had spent months on the tail of the king of crime in downtown Detroit. The man was into drugs, major car theft, prostitution, you name it. But every time we got close to him, things seemed to crumble like dirt in our fingers. Then one day a year ago last spring, we got the break we'd been waiting for, or so we thought. We went in, things went sour, and all hell broke loose." Bryce gave the account tonelessly, as if reading from a report, but his words were thick with pain.

Shannon had long since stopped reaching out, unless she was reaching for her children, but she lifted her hand, anyway, linked her fingers with his, and squeezed.

"I'm sorry," she said.

Bryce clutched her fingers so hard that, for a moment, Shannon feared they might break. He brought them up between both of his hands, holding them captive. And then he released them. He reached for his tennis shoes and stood up. "We need to head back. I'll go tell the kids." And then he was gone.

Shannon gathered up towels and lotion, shook the sand out of the blanket, folded it and shoved it back into the carryall she had packed so cheerfully when Bryce had suggested this trip to the beach. She could not shake the feeling that he hadn't told her everything, that the anguish he was suffering went deeper than a shoulder injury earned in the line of duty. She admonished herself for being ridiculous, replaying the past several moments over and over again in her mind, trying to convince herself that she was an oversensitive idiot. And then she remembered the halting way he had mentioned his partner. What had happened to Bryce's partner that day? Had he been the reason the deal went sour? Had he been a crooked cop?

Shannon had no answers to her questions, but as she stood alone on their little section of beach, she felt Bryce's pain as if it were her own, bringing home the fact that he had somehow become more to her than just a means to see her children. She was not happy about it, but she wasn't going to waste energy trying to convince herself that it wasn't so. She'd need every bit of energy she had just to get through the weeks ahead.

Slipping into her sandals, she watched as the twins lingered, pleading for the chance to dive into one last wave. She saw Bryce nod. He had told her all he was going to tell her, but Shannon was almost certain that there was more to be said. She didn't know what exactly. There was nothing specific, just an inflection in his voice, his rigid posture, his drawing away from her after already having confided painful facts. But then, she could hardly blame him for keeping some things to himself; she had her secrets, too.

THE TWINS' CHATTER filled up the car on the half hour drive back to Southlakes. As he had on the ride over, Mike threw question after question at Bryce, the big-city detective. Though he would have chosen another subject, Bryce was happy, at least, to have something to fill up the quiet between him and Shannon. All the while he was replying to Mike's interrogations on bank robberies and high-speed chases he was kicking himself for the need that had prompted him to share such an intimate part of himself with Shannon that afternoon.

When it had just been a matter of his being attracted to a woman he, as an officer of the law, was trying to help, his problem had been simpler; he'd merely had to control his baser instincts. And then she had looked at him with that mixture of caring and desire, an incredible display of feeling that he had never seen before on her face, and he'd gone and made things so much more complicated. He'd opened himself up to her, talking to her of an episode he had heretofore refused to discuss with anyone, not even the district psychologist. Bryce did not like this turn of events, not one little bit.

"Have you ever done a stakeout?" Mike asked as Bryce entered Southlakes city limits.

More than willing to be distracted from his thoughts, Bryce quickly thought through the hundred or more stakeouts he had participated in, looking for one that ended well. "Once or twice," he replied, glancing in the rearview mirror at the boy.

"Yeah?" Mike asked, awe glowing through eyes that were a younger, more innocent version of Shannon's. "What happened?"

"One of our wealthier citizens was convinced his daughter had been kidnapped and was being held in a vacant apartment building downtown," Bryce said, pausing for effect.

"Yeah, so?" Mike prompted.

Without thinking, Bryce glanced over at Shannon, meeting her twinkling gaze, sharing a smile with her over her son's eager anticipation. The car started to close in on him and he pulled his eyes quickly back to the road.

"We sat outside that building for two days, with no one coming or going except the father, who drove by every few hours to check on our progress. Of course, we hadn't really expected anyone to come or go—we'd known they weren't in there from the beginning."

"You did?" Mike asked, clearly surprised at this turn of events.

"Sure we did," Bryce said, enjoying himself.

"Why'd ya sit there for two days then?" Mike asked, not quite hiding his disgust.

"'Cause we found out that the woman had run away to be married, but it wasn't our place to tell her father. We did try to tell him that we had reason to believe his daughter was safe, but since we couldn't produce her, he insisted we continue the stakeout."

"Was the girl too young or something?" Mike demanded with a mixture of confusion and disappointment.

"She was forty-two years old!" Bryce finished, savoring his moment of surprise.

"You're kidding!" Shannon said, giggling.

He had never heard Shannon laugh before. The husky sound was as sexy as the rest of her, and Bryce was sidetracked from his story, wanting to hear that burst of delight again...and again....

"Nope, it really happened," he said a second or two later than he should have.

"How'd you figure out she hadn't been kidnapped?" Mike asked, his interest piqued again. His voice suggested that he cared little about the marriage, but if Bryce had done some real sleuthing to find out the truth, that would be worth hearing.

"The ransom note for one," Bryce said, turning on to Bessie Thompson's street. "The woman sent it herself, and the amount she asked for was so little, it was obvious that it wasn't a real kidnapping. Anyone who's going to break the law and risk getting caught is going to make it a lot more worth their while than the five thousand dollars she asked for, especially from a millionaire. She should have asked for a hundred thou' at least."

"What else?" The voice came from the back seat, but it was not Michael's. Bryce glanced back, startled to see that Mindi was just as enthralled with the story as her brother was.

"The note also specified the meeting place—the apartment complex—but didn't give a time. A real kidnapper would never do that because it gives the police a chance to stake the place out."

"Did they call with a time then?" Shannon asked, her amusement obvious.

"No, but that was another clue, really, because nine times out of ten a kidnapper is real nervous. He gets to a phone or a mailbox to make his demands as quickly as possible."

"But how'd you know she was getting married?" Mindi piped up again.

"Well—" Bryce pulled to a stop in front of the twins' foster home and turned off the engine "—when we checked at the library where she volunteered, we discovered that the head librarian, a man, was missing, as well. We did some discreet checking and found that the two had taken out a marriage license."

"Now," he continued, gripping the wheel with both hands, "give your mom a kiss, kids, before we're all in trouble for making you late for dinner."

Shannon kissed each child, hugging them to her breast with a fervency matched only by theirs. Bryce hated watching these goodbyes; he could only imagine how torn Shannon was. No one would have known to look at her. As she watched her kids run up the walk to their temporary home, she smiled, waving cheerfully as they turned before going inside. She was a great actress, Bryce determined, when he noticed how her fingernails were digging into her hand.

He pulled away from the curb.

"Has Clinton been paying you child support since the divorce?" Bryce asked bluntly. There was no easy way to build up to the things he needed to know. He was getting in way too deep to be able to continue without some answers. Somewhere along the way he had begun to invest a part of himself in Shannon Stewart, and he needed to get things back in a professional perspective. He needed to know why she couldn't afford something as basic as a new swimsuit.

"Is this an official question, Sheriff?" she asked. The sudden change in her was almost frightening. It was hard to believe that she was the same woman who had touched him so tenderly that afternoon.

Bryce turned the corner, dismayed by her stiff tone. He wasn't only doing this for himself, he thought. Whether she knew it or not, she needed someone on her side, but he couldn't be that someone if she wasn't willing to help him help her.

"I would rather not think so," he replied.

"Then I don't have to answer you?"

Bryce glanced away from the road just long enough to see the expressionless mask firmly back on her face. Instead of putting him off, her withdrawal made getting answers that much more important, because he now knew what lay behind the mask, and he wanted to see it again.

"You don't have to, no, but I'll be disappointed if you won't," he admitted. "I'm doing what I can to help you, Shannon, but I need your help, too."

She was silent for so long Bryce thought she was reenacting the scene at the police station weeks before when she had given a pretty fair imitation of a deaf woman.

"I haven't received one cent from him since I walked out of the Stewart mansion two years ago."

He almost didn't hear the words when they finally came. She was turned toward the window, speaking hardly above a whisper.

"But he was required by law to pay you on the fifth of each month," he said, sounding like a cop even to his own ears.

"And he says he has done so," she finished for him, saying the words he had left hanging between them.

"If you haven't received the money, why haven't you done something about it? Called someone?" Bryce continued, needs stronger than compassion driving him on. He knew he was pushing her.

"I did call. Several times. But it's his word against mine and who do you think will be believed?" There was no intonation in her voice, no plea for understanding, no defensiveness.

Bryce knew who would have been believed. He knew he should have been believing Clinton himself. It was more logical. It made the most sense. "You could have taken him to court," he told her.

"It would have cost me more money than I had, and it just wasn't worth it to me," she said in the same dead voice. "I didn't really want his money, and he knew it. As long as he was going to leave me and the kids alone, that was all that really mattered."

"And he was willing to do that, turn his back on his own children?"

"If Clinton had known who I was before he sired the twins, they would never have been conceived. He said that I tricked him, that the twins were mine and he was only too willing to let us be."

Bryce wanted to believe her. Her explanation made sense, up to a point. But why would Clinton not pay a debt he could easily afford, and then lie about having done so? This from a man who had supposedly been waiting two years to collect enough evidence to win back his children?

"And now?" Bryce asked softly.

"Now he's going to have a mighty hard time proving that he gave me money when there is no evidence whatsoever to show that he did." Her conviction rang through the car like a ship's horn blasting entry into the harbor.

Shannon's words were strong enough to plant some heavy doubts in his mind, strong enough to ease his doubts about *her* considerably. But there were still too many pieces missing for him to trust her completely. He had a hard time believing that appearance-conscious Clinton Stewart would take a chance on exposure if he *couldn't* prove that he had been paying child support for the past two years.

CHAPTER NINE

SHANNON WAS IN TROUBLE. Two days after their trip to the beach, her mind was still crowded with thoughts of Bryce. She dreamed about him at night and woke up filled with nervous energy which she channeled into cleaning. Her apartment was beginning to reek of pine-scented disinfectant.

She talked to her seedlings incessantly, despite the fact that they were still covered by mounds of dirt. She knew they were in there, and that was all that mattered.

"I don't think he trusts me," she confided early Saturday morning as she moved from one foam container to the next, administering plant food and cool water, "which means I can't trust him. Deep down, he may be no different from all the rest. But I've known that all along, so why does it matter this much?"

She reached out a finger, running it tenderly over the top of a mound of dirt, feeling for nubbins of growth much as she had searched for evidence of teeth on the gums of her twins when they had been babies. She thought about the scar on Bryce's shoulder and about the agony she had seen so briefly on his features, telling her that there was more to the story than she had been told. She thought about how much she cared, and about how much his inquisition later in the car had hurt.

"He doesn't believe me about the money. And he's surely not going to believe me once he finds my police record," she told an embryonic Peace Lily. She recognized the truth of her words, and knew that she was not going to be able to prevent the pain that would follow. Whether she liked it or not, Bryce's opinion mattered. She only hoped that if the record did show up it would be after the custody hearing, after she had her children back home with her. She could bear anything if they were with her.

"It's only been two days and I miss them so...."

Shannon's one-sided conversation was interrupted by the ping of her mailbox lid. She hurried through the remainder of her gardening chores, went straight to the box mounted outside her front door, and grabbed up the stack of envelopes inside. She was as anxious as a kid waiting for a letter from Santa, thinking there might be another letter from the twins.

She leafed through the envelopes, swallowed her disappointment that none sported childish scrawl, and then went through them more slowly. She recognized her mother's handwriting on one letter. Darla wrote as she dressed, carefully feminine, and like a schoolgirl—no lazy letters or undotted i's—her script was small, neat and written with lavender ink.

Shannon stared at the envelope for more than a minute, as if its contents couldn't touch her if she didn't open it. Mixed emotions swirled within her—relief that she could now count on Brad Channing's services, disbelief that Darla had really come through for her this time, shame for how low she had stooped, and a small piece of a little girl's love for the mother she had always wanted to be able to count on.

She tore open the envelope slowly and, like a person drawn to the sight of a gory accident, pulled out the folded sheet inside. It was blank. Not a word was written on it— no message for the daughter Darla had not seen in more than ten years. But it was wrapped securely around a money order for the thousands of dollars Darla had said she would send.

Guilt money. Shannon knew she was looking at another of Darla's attempts to rid herself of twelve-year-old guilt. Darla had shown up ten years ago not because she was worried about the daughter who had disappeared, but to seek atonement. She had said she could not get the trial off her mind. It weighed on a heart that had always been light, free of entanglements. It had been driving Darla crazy. Apparently it still was.

Shannon did not want her mother's apologies—some things just went too deep to forgive—but neither could she hate her. The woman had given birth to her when she could have chosen not to; she had kept her and had provided for her. Shannon detested what Darla did with her life. She was sickened by her own association with her, but she did not hate her mother. And she was going to keep Darla's money if for no other reason than because Darla's guilt told Shannon that, in her own convoluted way, Darla cared.

BRYCE HEATED A TV DINNER Saturday night and sat in front of the television while he ate it. He chewed, he swallowed, he chewed some more, all without tasting a bite. The television rambled, but after fifteen minutes, Bryce still wasn't sure what he was watching. He had been preoccupied all day. No matter what diversion he sought, his brain refused to be swayed, and continued instead to juggle the pieces of the puzzle that was Shannon Stewart. None fit snugly enough for his peace of mind.

He reached over to push a button on his remote control, silencing the television, then carried the remains of his dinner into the kitchen, poured a second glass of chocolate milk, gulped it down, rinsed the glass and put it in the dishwasher. Maybe he needed to see her with a rowdy weekend crowd. He reasoned that if she had any customers who were used to receiving more than drinks from her, chances were they'd be at the Tub on a Saturday night.

His mind made up, Bryce strode back to his bedroom to shower and change. The irony of that action, considering his destination, was not lost on him.

Twenty minutes later Bryce was driving through town on his way to the Tub. He inhaled the potent scents of after-shave and car leather, liking the combination, trying to convince himself as he sped along at five miles over the speed limit that he was not looking forward to seeing Shannon again.

He pulled to a stop at a red light in front of Stewart's hardware, thumping the steering wheel with his fingers while he looked around, checking to see if the streets were quiet. After so many years in law enforcement the reaction was second nature.

A vintage white Jag pulled up to the light on the other side of the intersection, stopping directly under the glare of a street lamp. *Nice car,* Bryce thought. There were two men sitting in the front seat, one in back. Bryce could see them well enough to make out that there was a blond, pretty boy driving. An older, darker man sat in the passenger seat. And the man in the back, leaning forward between the headrests was... Deputy Williams.

The light turned green and the cars passed in the inter-section, leaving Bryce to wonder about his deputy's impressive connections.

"WE NEED SOME BEER over here!" The summons came from over by the juke box where six or eight obnoxious men sat around a cocktail table. Shannon nodded her aching head, increasing her pace as much as her sore feet would allow. The only good thing about the night so far, other than booming business bringing in good tips, was the fact that it was her night to leave early, if midnight could be considered early.

"Keepin' you hoppin' tonight, ain't they?" Ory grinned as she stopped at the bar long enough to drop off more orders and fill her tray with drinks.

"That they are," Shannon agreed, returning his grin. Her boss had been good to her over the past two years, understanding when she had to miss work because of the kids, not holding it against her. Besides, it wasn't his fault that Shannon hated everything about the place. She turned toward the bar, hiking up her black leather top, which tended to slip when she got sweaty. Etiquette books had not taught her how a lady should wear black leather.

"Looks like that sheriff friend of yours just came in again," Ory half shouted just as Shannon was spearing an orange slice with a toothpick. She poked her finger.

"Where?" she demanded, sucking on her finger. She hated her sudden breathlessness, the way her stomach jumped in anticipation.

"Same table, way in the back," Ory hollered, trying to be heard over the roar of the blender he had just switched on.

Shannon looked back to the table she remembered from the last time. Sure enough, there he was. He looked good, too. His ankle was crossed over his jean-clothed knee, while one arm rested on the table beside him. The top couple of buttons on his cream-colored shirt were unbuttoned, revealing just a few of the mass of dark curls she knew was hidden beneath it. His hair hung over his collar as always, and she could not tell, from this distance, if he was freshly shaven or not. She sucked in her stomach encased in the black leather skirt, hoping the action would lower the hem a little.

The blender stopped. "I'm always glad to have new customers, but I'm not real crazy about the sheriff bein' one of 'em. Might hurt business," Ory said, following Shannon's gaze. He shook his head and pushed two more glasses along the bar toward Shannon's already loaded tray. "Best git these out."

She found room for the extra drinks and, bending slightly at the knees, slid the tray off the bar. She had no business being glad to see Bryce Donovan again, especially not after Thursday. She should be angry with him for turning cop on her again and ruining the end of what had been a nearly perfect day. Or, more to the point, she shouldn't feel anything at all. She had work to do, money to make. The twins were going to need school clothes soon.

She approached his table a few minutes later, unable to stall any longer. Her tray was empty except for the pile of napkins. "Checking up on me, Sheriff?"

She hated the defensiveness in her voice, hated that he must have heard it, too. She hated even more the shame she felt, standing before him, dressed as she was. It had not seemed to matter so much the last time he had been in.

"Are you this nice to all your customers?" he replied, and then continued without giving her a chance to answer his question. "We're long past the stage of Sheriff and Mrs. Stewart, don't you think?"

Shannon stared at him, teeth clenched to hide the trembling of her chin. She had thought they were, too; he was the one who had switched back to "sheriff" on her. Did he think she hadn't seen the doubt in his eyes?

"Okay, Bryce, what'll it be?" she asked, telling herself that capitulation was smarter than caring enough to defy him. Her emotions, all of them, were under control again.

"You're still upset about the questions I asked the other day," he said, ignoring her attempt to take his order. "Damn it, Shannon. How can I find out the truth if I don't ask?" he charged, taking the wind out of her puffed-up sails. His brown-eyed gaze bored into her, while the tenderness in his voice flowed smoothly over her skin. He didn't smile at her, or attempt to charm her. He simply tried to help her understand actions that he was under no obligation to explain—something no one had ever bothered to do before.

Shannon softened, knowing then that there was something vitally wrong with her defenses. He did have a point, but it should not have been enough. She had heard the disbelief in his voice when he had informed her that Clinton *had* to be paying her. She didn't want him to believe her because he'd found proof; she wanted him to believe her because he trusted her.

"And did you find out the truth?" she asked, ignoring the clamor around them. She was not sure why she bothered to ask; she was only opening herself up to more disappointment, but her need to know was stronger than her protective instincts.

He held her gaze for several silent seconds and Shannon wanted more than ever to know what he was thinking. Was there a chance that he was trying? That he wanted to believe her?

"Let's just say that I haven't yet found the untruth." His words were accompanied by a hesitant grin.

It wasn't trust, but it was the closest thing to it Shannon had ever had. "I guess that'll do, for now," she said, smiling back at him. She told herself she had made the decision logically, consciously, but for the first time in as long as she could remember, she wondered if she was lying to herself.

Music blared, booming laughter filled the smoky air, raised voices clamored for attention, but for one moment, lost in Bryce's smile, Shannon was taken away from it all to a place that was warm and good and wholesome.

"Hey, baby, you gonna have any left for the rest of us?"

Shannon jumped, scattering the pile of napkins on her tray, as the slurred demand brought her back to an awareness of where she was and what she should be doing. Her heart was beating rapidly, her stomach was trembling, but she was back.

"Beer, wasn't it?" she asked Bryce with an apologetic grimace. She knew it was. She knew what brand it was, too.

"Beer's fine."

She had to give him credit, Shannon thought, as she turned back toward the roomful of people impatiently awaiting her attention. He had hidden his disapproval of the catcall rather well. His frown had hardly been apparent at all.

Bryce stayed until she was finished for the night, nursing the same beer all evening. Other than to check his drink, she didn't return to his table for the rest of the night, not wanting to take the chance of angering her tipping customers by showing a preference for one man over another. Her refusal to do that was what kept them all coming back. But she knew Bryce was there, every second of the next three hours. In a bar full of brawny men, she felt his presence as if he had been the only male left alive on the continent.

He waited for her outside while she tipped out and signed her voucher, and then watched her walk to her car just as he had done that other time. She saw his headlights in her rearview mirror all the way to the apartment, and she grew more nervous with every mile they traveled. It was late at night, they were two adults, alone, with no children to buffer them. There was no denying the attraction between them anymore. And she was dressed like a woman ready for anything. Bryce had no way of knowing that that impression could not have been further from the truth.

Bryce was frowning as he pulled into the driveway, parking in what he now thought of as his usual slot next to

Shannon's. He climbed slowly out of his car, aware that she was probably wondering why he was there. He wasn't even sure.

"Why do you do it?" he asked as he walked beside her up the walk to her door. After spending the last three hours watching her run around a roomful of ogling men, his frustration was near to boiling point.

"Do what?" Her bare arm brushed against his.

"All of it. The Tub. That getup." Immediately, he regretted sounding so judgmental. His arm burned where she'd brushed against him. He, like dozens of other men in the bar, had been fantasizing about touching her all night long. And then he'd come across holier-than-thou.

Shannon shrugged her gloriously bare shoulders. "It's all I know," she replied, seemingly without taking offense. "I have no training. The only other positions I was offered were entry-level, minimum-wage jobs. Respectability has a price, Sheriff." She finished just as unemotionally as she had begun. She *was* offended.

And there it was again, her lack of money. He was going to have to find some evidence that Clinton Stewart had paid his obligations to her, or find out why he hadn't. It was becoming crucial that he find some answers somewhere, but the last three hours had done nothing but confuse him further.

"I'm sorry, Shannon. It seems I can't be with you for five minutes without making you defensive," he admitted, frustrated with his desire for her, and his inability to trust her completely.

She shrugged again. Bryce couldn't see her face, but he would bet a year's salary that it was as expressionless as stone. "I guess that comes from walking on opposite sides of the street," she said, almost as if she understood.

Bryce touched her hand. "Seems like we're walking pretty good together right now," he said into the sultry night air. He had to touch her, to push her a little, to see if she was as affected as he by their strange relationship.

"But it's such a short distance to the door." Shannon gave him her answer before he had even asked the question. She was not ready to explore any possibilities.

He waited while she searched for her key, standing behind her while she slid it into her dead bolt and pushed open the front door. He told himself not to touch her again, that so much bare flesh was more temptation than he could handle, but the strip of skin that was visible between the two pieces of leather covering her had been taunting him all night. He just had to see if it was as soft as it looked, to see if she was really as cool as she looked.

She turned back once the door was open, as if to say good night, but Bryce reached out, cupping her hip, before she had a chance to dismiss him. He pulled her a little bit closer to him, but left her far enough away that their only point of contact was his hand on her hip. He stood still for a brief second, waiting to see what she would do, flooding with pleasure when she did not pull away as she had before. She did not move forward, either.

The night was hot and sticky, she smelled like smoke, and it was too dark to see the expression in her eyes, but never had Bryce felt so much like he was poised on the brink of a wonderful discovery. Forgotten was his job, her children, her ex-husband's money. He moved his thumb slowly upward, seeking the smooth flesh above her waistline, needing to touch her body, skin to skin. The contact, when it came, nearly scorched him.

He heard her suck in her breath as his thumb caressed her tender inch of flesh, back and forth, back and forth, between her waistline and her top. She was hot, he was hot, and the two of them together created a combustion within Bryce that he was not sure he could stop. It was not enough, and it was far too much.

He knew the moment that she started to pull away from him, though her withdrawal was not physical. He could feel her tension just as surely as he felt her heat, and it was enough to cool his ardor for the moment. His slid his hand from her hip, trailing it down to her thigh before letting her go. The next move was up to her.

"G'night, Bryce. Thanks for seeing me home," she said, remaining motionless in front of him. The huskiness in her voice almost had him reaching for her again.

He did not pull her into his arms, but he couldn't just leave her like that, either, with so many questions hanging between them. She was right to refuse to confront the attraction between them. But even while he knew that it was imperative that they keep distance between them, that he stay far enough away from her life to remain impartial, he needed it understood between them that he was more to her than just a sheriff and a chaperon.

Slowly, hesitantly, he leaned forward and touched his mouth to hers. His lips were closed. His hands were clenched behind his back. He was keeping his distance. But, even then, he was not prepared for the response her soft, sweet lips ignited within him. He needed to taste her and it took everything he had not to deepen the kiss.

Shannon's lips did not welcome his, but she did not pull back immediately, either. Bryce was excited even by that small bit of encouragement; for now that had to be enough. He pulled back long before he was ready.

Releasing his hands from their death grip, he reached up to brush her hair back from her face. "Sleep well," he said, and turned to walk back down the walk. It was Saturday night and again there had been no strange cars waiting for her to get home, and none suspiciously cruising by, either. Despite the liquid heat uncomfortably filling him, Bryce was feeling better than he had all day.

SHANNON STOOD in the shadows with trembling limbs and watched Bryce go. "Sleep well," she whispered as he climbed into his car and drove away.

An hour later she lay in bed wondering if she was going to sleep at all. She had showered and changed into a thin cotton gown, her apartment was sufficiently cool without being cold, but as tired as she was, her body still would not rest. None of her usual positions was comfortable to her, nor were any of the new ones she tried. She punched her pillows; she pushed off her covers; she yanked on the sheet; she hugged a pillow. Nothing worked.

She got up and visited her plants; she even drank some warm milk, but nothing could calm the buzzing in her veins. She tried to read, but could not concentrate. Nothing on television held her interest. Finally, out of desperation, she filled her bath with water as hot as she could stand it, stripped off her summer cotton gown, and stepped into the tub, hoping the heat would relax her. The water caressed her body, seeping up her thighs, touching her femininity, flowing over her belly as she slowly lowered herself into its warmth. She leaned back, laying her head along the back of the tub, and the water lapped at her breasts, touching them like tender fingers. Her nipples hardened instantly. And suddenly Shannon understood what was wrong with her. For the first time in her life, she was suffering from sexual frustration. She didn't need a hot bath; she needed a cold shower.

Her heel hit the drain plug, her fingers stretched to turn the knob marked C, and her toe pulled out the lever above the faucet.

SHE AWOKE SEVERAL HOURS later to the ringing of her telephone. Reaching over to pick up the receiver, she didn't even bother to open her eyes. She'd been dreaming about that kiss—Bryce's kiss—the most chaste caress she had ever received, and yet....

"Shannon? This is Bryce. What you need is another lawyer." The words barely registered in her sleep-glazed mind, but the identity of her caller did.

She sat up, shaking the fogginess away, trying to forget the dream she had been enjoying just seconds before. She clutched the sheet against her breast.

"I, uh, have a lawyer," she said, trying to calm her pounding heart and make sense of his words at the same time.

"Forget Dinsmore. He's not much help to you," Bryce said. He sounded frustrated about something, but Shannon was too shocked by his words to care. The sheriff had just admitted that his precious system, or a small part of it anyway, was not working. Was she finally getting through to him?

"I've already forgotten Dinsmore," she told him, glad he could not see the giddy grin spreading across her face. "My lawyer's name is Brad Channing. His office is in St. Joe," she said.

"Channing? In St. Joe?" Shannon could not miss the pleased surprise in Bryce's voice.

"Yeah, do you know him?" she asked.

"No, but it's probably best for you that he's out of town. I was going to suggest that it might be best if you find someone outside Southlakes," he said, surprising her again. She did not believe that Bryce was fully convinced of her innocence just yet, but at least he was giving consideration to the things she had told him. It was not enough, but it was a good start.

"Brad Channing grew up with Clinton, but he wasn't part of that crowd," she told him, wanting him to know that Brad was not going to be swayed by the Stewarts' sterling reputation.

"You need to call him, Shannon. Make sure he's running a check on Clinton's bank accounts, his spending habits. He's probably already on it, but call him anyway, just in case. It should be easy enough for him to prove that you never received your payments if there are no canceled checks," he said.

A week ago Shannon would have taken offense at his order; now she felt all giddy and warm inside because it showed signs that Bryce was looking out for her. But then, a week ago she had not yet admitted that she cared about him, that it felt good to be cared for.

"Doesn't he need a warrant for that, or something?" she asked.

"He needs to subpoena the records, yes, but he won't have any trouble doing so."

Shannon let go of the sheet, and lay back against her pillows. "I'll call him," she promised.

"Shannon?" Bryce's voice sounded more hesitant than she had ever heard it before.

"Yes?" she asked, her stomach tightening with fear.

"What about his fee? I mean, I thought you didn't have your own lawyer because of the cost."

"I borrowed the money from my mother." The words stuck in her throat. Though she knew Bryce must know about Darla, Shannon never spoke of her mother to anyone, ever. And she could not afford to give Bryce anything more to be suspicious about. She braced herself for his response, his disgust, his disappointment that she would accept tainted money.

"That must have been difficult for you." His words were softly spoken, sincere. They meant more to her than an avowal of undying love.

"Yes." She blinked back silly tears. No one had ever understood before. No one had ever figured out that just because she had been exposed to Darla's way of life from birth, that didn't mean she condoned it, or even accepted it. No one ever seemed to realize that she was ashamed of her mother. "Bryce?" she asked hesitantly.

"Yeah?"

"Like I said last night, respectability does have a price, but I'm not planning to stay at the Tub forever. I've been enrolled in a home-study business course for a while now and I'm well on my way to earning an associates degree in accounting." She was more embarrassed by the words than anything else. He might not even care.

"Somehow that news doesn't surprise me, Shannon. I had a hard time believing that you'd be content to peddle beer for the rest of your life...."

SHANNON WAITED long enough to shower and dress, and then she did call Brad Channing. Her faith in her new lawyer solidified as soon as she heard that he was already working on a petition for the records in question. She rang off with a heart so light she barely recognized it as her own. A couple of weeks ago she had been all alone in the world, buckling under the weight of her burdens. And now, miraculously, she had two men of the law willing to take some of the load off her shoulders.

Shannon was not naive enough to believe that Bryce had done an about-face and decided to trust her. She had not missed the telling "if" when he had mentioned the canceled checks. But the fact that he was listening to her, giving credence to what she told him, was a huge step in the right direction. She was almost ashamed to admit to herself that it almost meant more to her to think about Bryce believing in her, man to woman, than it did to think about the advantages of having the sheriff on her side during the custody battle, even with his uncle as the presiding judge.

CHAPTER TEN

"YOU'RE HAVING a triple scoop, Bryce? Can I have one, too?" Mike asked his mentor as he stood with Shannon and Mindi in the middle of Mason's old-fashioned ice-cream parlor.

Shannon figured if she was not so taken with Bryce herself at the moment she might have been jealous that her son had just turned to someone other than herself for permission to do something. As it was, she met Bryce's pleasantly surprised expression over her son's head and nodded.

"Sure, sport, if you think you can finish it." He stepped up to place their orders.

Bryce paid for the cones and Shannon let him, wondering if her single dip of French vanilla really tasted better than ever before, or if her enjoyment came more from the fact that it had been so long since anyone had invited her out for a treat. She could almost forgive herself for imagining, just for an hour or two, that they were a normal family with nothing more pressing on their minds than an afternoon outing.

They left the ice-cream shop behind, walking down Main Street as they ate their cones, enjoying the blue sky above, watching the hustle and bustle of Southlakes's citizens as they hurried past. Shannon remembered a time when the townspeople used to go out of their way to greet her. Now they avoided her.

The foursome strolled by Stewart's department store, past a diner the Stewarts had invested in a few years earlier, and on toward Stewart's hardware. Bryce, Shannon and Mindi finished their cones, but Mike forged diligently on. Mindi teased him mercilessly, giggling so much at the faces he was making she could hardly speak.

Shannon smiled at their teasing, but at the same time she felt a little sorry for her son, for having bitten off more than he could chew, literally. She did not want him to be embarrassed in front of Bryce, knowing how much the boy had come to like the sheriff, knowing, too, that their rapport was very important to a boy her son's age. And yet there was no way she could think of to help him without embarrassing him further.

"You don't have to finish that if you're getting full," she told him, trying anyway.

Mike shook his head a little too quickly. "No, I've still got lots of room, Mom. I could probably have handled four dips."

"You know, sport, I'm still a little hungry. Would you mind terribly if I shared that with you just a little bit?" Bryce asked, finding a permanent place in Shannon's affections as he rescued her son's pride.

Mike appeared to be considering the situation, as if he really didn't want to part with a single swallow of ice cream. "I guess if you're really that hungry, you can have just a little," he finally agreed.

He handed the cone to Bryce, and nobody said a word as Bryce proceeded to finish the whole thing.

"Uh-oh," Mindi said under her breath a few minutes later. She was walking between Shannon and Bryce as they approached Southlakes's one bank.

Both adults glanced down at the child. "What's wrong, honey?" Shannon asked with concern.

"Look," Mindi said, motioning up ahead of them with a slight nod of her head.

Shannon looked. "Oh," she said, slowing her pace. *Oh God, no.*

Bryce looked ahead, too, surprised when he saw the preppy blond man who had been driving the vintage Jag the other night. Bryce also recognized the older, dark-skinned man who had been in the car with Williams and the blond man that night. Nowhere did Bryce see anything that should have caused Mindi's distress.

Mike was walking slightly ahead of them, but he obviously saw something that Bryce had not. He turned around and stopped, halting them all where they stood, and looked from Shannon's concerned eyes to Bryce's confused ones.

"It's our father," he finally said, his words directed mostly toward Bryce.

Bryce felt the words like a physical blow to his chest. He glanced over Mike's shoulder. Was it the pretty boy, or the older guy? Bryce decided he didn't want to know.

With growing frustration, he took in the three unsmiling faces surrounding him. He wanted to scoop up all three of them and whisk them away.

He stood stiffly, watching the men approach, wondering in spite of himself which one had married Shannon, and fathered her children. He was not proud of the jealousy shooting through him.

The two impeccably dressed men came to a halt a few feet away from them. Their expensive cologne wafted toward Bryce, reminding him of the one time he had lit a stick of incense in his bedroom. He had been about fourteen then, and he had been free to gag.

"Hello, children. I didn't expect to see you in town today." So, it was the pretty boy. Bryce could not determine whether the man was pleased about the unexpected meeting or not.

Mindi leaned against one side of Shannon, while Mike took up a straight stance on his mother's other side. Shannon placed a protective arm around each of her children. The three, dressed in shorts and T-shirts, could have been posing for a holiday picture, if they had been smiling. After a half-mumbled hello to their father, the twins stood silently, watching Clinton Stewart. Bryce was more convinced than ever that something was wrong with the Stewart custody case besides Shannon.

"You have some ice cream on your chin, Michael." Clinton reached into his pocket, pulled out a handkerchief, and handed it to Mike. "Please get rid of it." The words were clearly an order. Though Stewart's dress, his manners, his speech were beyond reproach, Bryce found the man lacking, somehow. Stewart seemed completely unaware of the embarrassment he had just caused his son.

Stewart did not even bother to nod in recognition of Shannon, but Bryce watched as he ran a quick, insulting glance up and down her body, blatantly undressing her with his eyes and finding her beneath his contempt. Cars drove slowly by, their bored passengers staring at the tense sidewalk meeting. Clinton turned his appraisal on Bryce.

Bryce stepped forward, throwing out a carefully unclenched hand to Clinton Stewart. "I don't believe we've met. I'm Bryce Donovan."

Stewart clasped Bryce's hand firmly, his expression easing. "Hello, Sheriff. I didn't recognize you in shorts and tennis shoes. I've been looking forward to meeting our newest law man. Drew speaks highly of you," he said. So Bryce had not been mistaken; Deputy Williams was on friendly terms with Clinton Stewart.

Stewart extolled the virtues of Southlakes, but while Bryce nodded appropriately, he grew more and more curious about Stewart's silent companion. It could be nothing more than his overactive imagination due to the tense situation at hand, but he thought that as soon as the older man had become aware of Bryce's identity, he had turned away toward the street. He had the air of a man bored with the present situation, and yet Bryce, always the cop, noticed the tightly clenched jaw, the unnaturally stiff shoulders. The man looked like a trap ready to spring.

"I've liked what I've seen so far," Bryce interjected when Stewart paused in his recitation. Stewart was being sincere in his welcome, but after Stewart's treatment of Shannon, Bryce was not in a mood to make friends.

"I'm sorry your first taste of your new duties had to involve our little family squabble," the man said, glancing at Shannon with barely concealed disgust crossing his perfect features. "But we'll have things wrapped up soon enough." Bryce sensed the tension in his three companions as Stewart's confidence rang out around them. An older couple approached, looking curiously at the six people gathered rigidly outside the bank. Stewart nodded at them as they passed.

Bryce would have loved nothing better than to take the man down a notch or two, and had to quickly remind himself that he was, after all, merely an observer, the impartial sheriff. He clamped down on his tongue and shrugged, as if chaperoning Shannon were all in the line of duty.

Apparently satisfied with Bryce, Stewart glanced from his watch to the twins.

"I've got business to attend to for the rest of today and this evening, children, and due to the holiday tomorrow, your grandparents and I have duties to see to this weekend, but I'll be there to see you next weekend. I will be able to spend at least an hour, maybe two, with you. Is there anything special you would like to do?" Clinton was clearly ill at ease as he addressed his children.

Mindi stood mute beside her mother. Mike shrugged. They didn't exactly seem afraid of their father, just uncomfortable. Despite the brightness of the sun, the day had lost much of its beauty as far as Bryce was concerned.

He felt extremely uneasy as he compared the twins' stilted, unemotional display with their normally affectionate outgoing behavior. Was their lack of response Shannon's doing as the Stewarts' were claiming? Bryce was not so sure. He had seen Shannon reprimand Mike for simply referring to his father as "he." Surely that did not depict a woman who was turning her children against their father. Or had the incident at Aunt Hattie's been enacted for Bryce's benefit?

Clinton was frowning at the children, clearly unsure what to do next. It was equally clear that he was bothered by his children's cool response to him in front of an audience. He glanced over at Bryce and then back at his daughter. Putting his hand into his pocket, he pulled out a wad of bills. "How would you like to head down to Ben Franklin and pick out a brand-new tea set, Minda?" he asked, holding a twenty-dollar bill out to the girl.

Minda's hands remained at her sides. "No, thank you," she replied. Getting more flustered, Clinton turned toward his son. "How about you, Michael? Take this and get yourself a new BB gun." He handed out the same twenty-dollar bill.

"You got me one for Christmas," Mike told him.

Clinton's nostrils flared unbecomingly as he stuffed the money back into his pocket, but there were no other outward signs of his displeasure. And he didn't give up. Bryce had to hand it to him for that.

"You realize that if there's anything either of you need, you only have to ask...."

Bryce felt Shannon tense beside him as Stewart spoke. A quick glance confirmed that her nails were once again biting into her palms.

"We'll go visit your grandparents next weekend, then," Stewart was saying. "They've made some plans for your future of which I highly approve. I'm sure that as soon as you hear them, you'll realize that it's in your best interests to be under our care. I expect the judge will see that, too, and then this ugliness will all be behind us.''

Bryce intercepted the look of pure fear that the twins exchanged and decided that it was time to go. Maybe they weren't his children, but for what was left of their visit with their mother, *he* was responsible for them.

"It was nice meeting you, Stewart." Bryce held out his hand.

The blond man took his hand again, meeting Bryce's gaze head-on. "I'm relieved that a big-city cop like you is too smart to fall for a pretty face," Clinton said.

Bryce narrowed his eyes, not sure if Stewart was merely assuring himself of the fact aloud, or if he had just issued a veiled warning to the new sheriff in town. He didn't dignify the comment with a response.

Stewart stepped back and nodded in farewell. "Sheriff...children." Bryce was certain that the man would have tipped his hat had he been wearing one. Even with his preppy clothes, his ancestral heritage was obvious. Despite the man's breeding, or maybe because of it, Stewart took his leave without once acknowledging his ex-wife.

IT WAS A SILENT FOURSOME that made the short drive back to Bessie Thompson's. Bryce's instincts were telling him that something about the scene he had just witnessed was definitely odd. Though he didn't believe that Stewart would ever harm the twins, Bryce had the disturbing suspicion that his fight had very little to do with wanting custody. The man had no idea how to relate to children, that was obvious.

There had been something odd about Clinton's companion, as well. The older man had not been introduced, had never even turned around once Bryce's identity had been made known. Yet, as Bryce watched his side mirror on the way out of town, the dark-skinned stranger had looked back not once, but twice, as if checking to see that Bryce had gone before following Clinton into the bank. Or had the man been watching the Stewart twins instead? Did he have some interest in them that their father did not share? Bryce made a note to ask Williams who the man was.

It wasn't until the kids were kissing Shannon goodbye that Mike brought up the subject on everybody's mind. "Do you think we might lose, Mom?" he asked, searching her face.

Shannon did not hesitate, even for a moment. "No, Michael, I don't," she said.

Mike considered her words, nodded once, and hugged her goodbye.

Mindi needed a little bit more. "You really don't?" she asked. Her voice was thick with unshed tears.

"No, baby, I really don't. It's not going to happen—I promise."

Bryce remembered once before when Shannon had made a promise to her children, the night she had sent them back into the Wannamakers' with the assurance that she would not give up. She had told him then that she never broke her promises, that they were the one thing in life on which the twins could depend. He wondered if maybe she had not been a bit premature this time.

But when he saw the instant smile that transformed Mindi's little face, he couldn't blame Shannon for doing what she had to do. He only hoped she didn't have to explain later why she'd made a promise she couldn't keep.

"Hey, kids, get back here, I have a surprise for you," Bryce called just as the twins started up the walk to the front door.

Both children were back beside the car instantly. Bryce savored the eager anticipation on their faces for a moment, and then looked at Shannon. He almost laughed out loud when he saw that the expression on her lovely face matched those of her children. He'd been keeping his news for just the right moment.

"Who knows what tomorrow is?" he asked, drawing out the moment.

"The Fourth of July," three voices chorused.

"That's right, and seeing that the Fourth of July is a holiday, I just happen to have obtained permission for one Minda Marie Stewart, along with her brother, Michael Scott Stewart, to accompany me on a picnic. Their mother is invited, too, of course, if she cares to come along." Bryce barely got the words out of his mouth before both children screamed and hurled themselves at him, embracing him with four gangly arms. Nothing had ever felt better to Bryce in his entire life.

That is, until Shannon leaned forward to throw her long, slender arms around his neck. He inhaled the fresh apple smell of her hair, filling himself with the sweet essence of her, and then she was gone.

"I guess we have some plans to make," she said. Bryce heard the breathlessness in her voice, he saw the flush in her cheeks, and he knew she had been as affected as he by the brief, heady feel of that contact. It mattered not a whit that her two ten-year-olds were still attached to his midsection, a very effective barrier against a more intimate touching of adult bodies. He could just imagine how wonderful love-making would be between Shannon and him if they ever gave in to the force that was drawing them inexorably closer.

SHANNON WOKE UP the next day bubbling with the same excited anticipation she had felt each Christmas morning since the twins were born. It had done some talking, but she had finally convinced Bryce to let her bring all the food for their picnic, and she had some cooking to do before he came for her later in the morning. She had gone straight to the grocery store when he'd brought her home the day before, but that was all she'd been able to accomplish before she'd had to leave for the Tub.

She showered, towel drying her hair before combing it straight down her back and leaving it to air dry, then accented her eyes with a little liner. She debated over what to wear, which was unlike her, and finally decided on a pair of black biker's shorts that the kids had bought for her the previous Christmas because they were "in." They hugged her hips too closely for her taste, but she solved that problem by donning an oversize white shirt that fell almost to the hem of the shorts.

Looking in the mirror, she decided that she now looked too shapeless, and went back to rummage in her closet until she found a wide black belt. The belt cinched loosely around her, falling just above her hipbones. Shannon turned in front of the mirror twice, looking at herself from all angles, and finally decided she would do. For what, she was not sure, or at least she was not yet ready to admit to herself that she *was* sure. It had been a long time since Shannon had had any desire to dress to please a man.

She had packed two boxes with sliced roast beef and fried chicken, potato salad and coleslaw, sliced vegetables and fresh fruit, brownies, two kinds of soft drinks and a thermos full of lemonade by the time Bryce knocked on her door a couple of hours later.

He did not step inside right away, though she laughingly informed him that there were things to carry. He remained motionless outside the door, looking at her as if he were a thirsty man staring at a fountain. His glance moved slowly down her body, remaining on her legs a little longer than the rest, and then moved back up again. But the look in his eyes as they met hers made her feel like fine china rather than soiled linen.

"You look beautiful," he said. It was the first compliment he had ever paid her and Shannon cherished it. To her it was more valuable than gold. She could count on one hand the number of no-strings-attached compliments she had received in her life. He followed her inside.

Bryce took one look at all the stuff she had lined up in the living room waiting to go and burst out laughing. "I guess I should have expected it, after seeing the way you bake," he told her, stacking the boxes on top of each other before reaching down to lift them both at once.

"Bryce! Your shoulder—"

"—is just fine," Bryce interrupted, grinning at her over his load. "The only way to get it back to one hundred percent capacity is to use it." And so saying, he headed out to his car.

Shannon watched him go, ogling the tight muscles of his bottom as they moved back and forth within cutoffs that fit as if he had been sewn into them. He was wearing that T-shirt again, too—the one that talked about boaters doing it. It was a darn good thing the twins were going to be chaperoning all day.

Mindi and Mike were all wound up when they arrived at the Thompson home. Waving to Bessie, who was watching from the window, they raced down the walk to the car, both of them talking at once.

"What'd you bring to eat, Mom?" Mike asked, climbing into the car first.

"Where're we going, Mommy?" Mindi asked, right behind him.

Shannon laughed, loving their excitement. "All of your favorites, Mike, and your sister's, too, and I don't know where we're going. You'll have to ask Bryce."

Both heads swiveled toward their driver.

"Where're we going, Bryce?" the twins asked in unison, then looked at each other and laughed.

Bryce sent them a stern look in the rearview mirror, but his grin broke through as soon as he opened his mouth to speak. "Don't I even get a hello?" he demanded, but any disciplinary effect was lost behind the grin.

"Hi, Bryce, where're we going?" the two in the back chorused again. It had become a game to them now.

Bryce pulled away from the curb, turned around in Mrs. Thompson's driveway and headed back the way he and Shannon had just come. "We're going to a secret place not far from here," he said, drawing out the suspense.

"What secret place?" Mindi asked, enthralled by the mystery. Bryce could almost see the fairy tales running through her mind.

"My secret place," Bryce admitted, wondering if he was making a mistake sharing this part of himself with Shannon and her family. How did he know when they were getting too close? When did empathy change to something more? Where did he draw the line?

"But I thought you just moved here," Shannon said, obviously as curious as her children.

"I did. But my aunt and uncle have lived here longer than I've been alive. I used to come up here every summer and spend a few weeks out on their farm. It's not far from town, but it always seemed to be a world all its own. I found this little field of grass one summer when I was wandering in the evergreen forest behind their place, and I've loved it ever since. Of course, it helps that there's great fishing nearby."

"A meadow growing in the middle of a dark pine forest?" Shannon asked, sounding as enchanted as her daughter had.

"It's the craziest thing I've ever seen," Bryce confirmed. "Right in the middle of the forest, there's a patch of land that has no trees. The closest I could figure was that since there were no branches to block the sun, grass was able to sprout and grow. Where the seeds came from, I leave up to a higher authority," he said.

"Do we have to walk in the forest to get there?"

"Can I fish?"

The questions were fired at him simultaneously, but for once Bryce heard them both separately. Maybe he was getting the hang of— He pulled his thoughts back abruptly. He had no business complimenting himself on his parenting abilities, especially not where the twins were concerned.

"Yes, we have to walk in the forest, but don't worry, honey, you and your mom will have two strong men to protect you from goblins every step of the way. And yes, we'll be able to fish if you want to, Mike. I brought a couple of rods along just in case."

"Are there wolves in the forest?"

"What about bait?"

Bryce smiled as he pulled onto his uncle's property. Aunt Martha and Uncle Oliver were downtown participating in Southlakes's annual parade and festivities, but they knew Bryce was bringing Shannon and her children out to the forest. Under the circumstances, the children were sure to benefit more from a day spent alone with Shannon, than one spent in town where they ran the high probability of running into their father again.

"There are no wolves in this forest, or anything else that you need to be afraid of. Mostly there are deer and rabbits, squirrels and birds, and maybe one or two other little critters that would be more afraid of you than you are of them. We dig for worms to use as bait."

Bryce could not resist a glance over at Shannon to see if she had noticed how adept he was becoming at fielding the questions. She had. She sent him a quick grin, sharing with him the silent communication of understanding, of satisfaction, that he had oftentimes seen pass between parents on the sitcom reruns he used to watch. Bryce pulled himself up abruptly. With thoughts like those, he was setting a trap for himself that would be all too easy to fall into, and pure hell to get out of.

A month ago, he had never even considered what it would be like to have children in his life. He had been too young during his brief marriage to give any thought to fatherhood, and since then, the possibility of children had always loomed somewhere out in the distant future, waiting until "someday," after he had found someone to mother them.

He had no need to consider impending fatherhood now, either, he decided as he drove into a clearing and stopped the car. It was a holiday, and he was not going to spoil the day with thoughts of tomorrow. He was going to enjoy the next few hours spent in the company of a woman he did not mind being with, and the two children who belonged to her. He would just have to keep in mind, in the far reaches of his mind at least, that they were with him only because they were in his custody.

CHAPTER ELEVEN

"GEE, MOM, YOU SURE did bring a lot of stuff," Mike said as he stood by the trunk of the car and surveyed the pile of things he was responsible for carrying into the woods.

"Yeah, she wanted to make sure she had enough food for everyone, ants and flies included," Bryce teased as he hefted the two boxes of food onto his shoulder.

Mike and Mindi were carrying bags of napkins and plates, paper towels, plastic utensils, cups, and Bryce had no idea what else. Those were just the things he had seen poking through the tops of the bags. Shannon had a small cooler in one hand, and a gallon thermos in the other.

They set off, walking single file through the pine forest with Bryce in the lead, and Mike bringing up the rear at his own insistence, so he could keep an eye on his mother and sister.

"How do you know how to find this place?" Mike asked about five minutes into the forest.

"Landmarks," Bryce said over his shoulder. "If you pay close attention, each tree looks different."

"You memorize what every one of these trees looks like?" Mindi asked, looking around her with awe.

"No, honey, just a few," Bryce answered, keeping his grin facing forward. "See that tree over there?" He motioned off to the left with his head.

"The one that looks like a slingshot?" Mike asked.

"That's the one," Bryce agreed. "That's one of my landmarks. I pick the most distinctive trees so I don't get confused," he explained.

They trooped along in silence for a while, and Bryce felt the peace of the forest settle over him. It never failed to find him. He inhaled the strong pine scent, feeling its freshness seep into his lungs. Golden brown pine needles crackled underfoot, while long, fresh, green boughs hung high overhead in such thick abundance that they blocked the sun, leaving the forest basking in a dim, dusky glow. The stillness was incredible.

"Are there snakes in here?" Mike called up to Bryce.

Mindi's step faltered behind Bryce. "Snakes?" Her voice sounded a couple of octaves higher than normal.

"I've never seen a single snake in the almost twenty years I've been coming here," Bryce answered quickly. "Michigan has a few, of course, but they're mostly garters or blue racers."

"Do they hurt you?" Mindi asked. Her voice sounded even smaller than usual in the middle of the vast forest.

Bryce sent her a reassuring smile over his shoulder. "Neither are poisonous, honey. A blue racer might chase someone if he's provoked, but that's it, he chases. He isn't poisonous."

Wondering at Shannon's silence, Bryce glanced back to see her trekking along between her children, looking around her as if she had just discovered heaven. Serene is the only word he could think of to describe the look on her face—serene and beautiful. *Custody.* She was in his custody for a reason, he reminded himself.

It took them half an hour to reach the small clearing in the middle of the forest, and by the time they arrived, Bryce was carrying Mindi's bag of supplies on top of the two boxes of food.

"It's beautiful!" Shannon said as she broke through the trees and got her first glimpse of the soft green grass growing lush and wild.

"Look! There's even a couple of apple trees," she added, pointing to one edge of the clearing. Her voice, her face, her outspread arms spoke of her amazement at nature's unexpected, unexplainable gifts.

Bryce could not help but smile, taking pride in the place even though all he'd done was find it years ago. It was his place just as much as his apartment was, and he was suddenly glad he had decided to share it with her.

"I'm going to dig for worms," Mike announced, setting down his bag of supplies.

"Take the tin can beside the tackle box," Bryce instructed.

"Do we have to eat it if he catches something, Mommy?" Mindi protested, her nose scrunched up at the thought.

"Yeah, Mom, will you cook whatever I catch?" Mike asked with the enthusiasm of a ten-year-old.

Shannon looked toward Bryce as if to say, *this is your doing, do something.*

He looked at Mindi first. "Your mom brought enough food so that you don't have to eat anything you don't want, just for today," he said, hoping he wasn't getting himself into trouble with Shannon. And then he looked at Mike. "We'll clean whatever you catch, sport, and then we can build a fire, but a true fisherman must cook his own catch. I can show you how to use a stick as a roasting bit. What d'ya say?"

Mike nodded, looking very satisfied. "You got it," he said with a grin.

And so their party, such as it was, began. Bryce and Mike went to dig for worms and Shannon and Mindi laid out blankets, side by side, end to end, making one big table, and unpacked their picnic. As soon as everything was done, Mindi ran off to chase butterflies. Shannon removed her tennis shoes, wiggling her toes in the fresh air and then leaned back on the blanket with her hands behind her hips and let the purity in the atmosphere wash over her. Inhaling the smell of fresh pine that scented the meadow, she lifted her face to the sky, closing her eyes as the sun warmed her features. A slight breeze blew over, caressing her skin, bathing her, washing away the impurities in her life. It was hard to believe that the day was not as completely perfect as it seemed, until she let her fantasies travel just a little too far, until she tried to pretend that the meadow she was lying in belonged to a man with whom she was lovingly involved, not a cop who did not trust her. . . .

"Here, Mommy, these are for you." Mindi's excited voice brought Shannon back to the beauty that did exist in the day. She opened her eyes to see Mindi holding out a bouquet of flowering weeds with bright golden petals surrounding brown button centers.

"They're beautiful, sweetheart," she said, wrapping an arm around her daughter's legs and giving them a squeeze. She had much to be thankful for and she was not going to spoil things by wanting more than she could have. "We'll use them for a centerpiece."

She had Mindi fill a foam cup with enough dirt to support the "flowers" and then helped her make an arrangement out of them that would have been the envy of any florist. They substituted wild clover for baby's breath, and pine boughs for greenery, and they thought the end result was breathtaking.

BRYCE WAS HAVING the time of his life. There was something elemental about teaching a boy how to be a man, especially when the teacher had a pupil as eager and willing as Mike. Bryce showed him how to overturn soft earth and then sift through the exposed clods of dirt to find the night crawlers living there, explaining how much easier the job is right after a rain because the worms are all up closer to the surface. Mike dug in with enthusiasm and in less than twenty minutes they had collected enough worms to last them all day.

"Have you ever been fishing?" Bryce asked as he and Mike walked side by side down to the stream that ran along the back edge of the forest.

"Nope. My father's always been too busy to take me," Mike admitted, but he sounded more excited about the prospect of finally going fishing now than he did disappointed that he had not already done so.

Bryce smiled, giving Shannon credit for the boy's attitude. She had that same ability to look for what good was there, and not dwell on the bad. If only he could be sure that all of Shannon's influences were as positive.

"You need to be quiet now as we approach the stream. This is all natural out here. Nobody stocks the stream with fish that were raised in a hatchery. These guys are not used to human sounds, they're sly, and they'll swim right by the biggest, most tempting worm if they sense anything unfamiliar at all," Bryce whispered as he led Mike to a spot in the stream that was deep and usually produced good-size trout.

He showed Mike how to bait the hook and then had him find a comfortable rock on which to sit while he waited to feel a tug on his line. Bryce baited a line for himself, dropped it into the water a short distance downstream from Mike, and then settled back to daydream.

Before he knew what was happening, he found himself wondering how it would be to have a son, to have a family, to know that his wife and daughter were close by, that the soft blankets spread in his meadow, the pounds of good food that lay prepared and waiting, were the result of loving preparations for him, as well as the children. He wondered what it would be like to be a part of the feeling of unconditional acceptance, of the willingness among each one of them to get along, to enjoy each other and the day, to look out for one another.

"Bryce! Bryce! Come quick! I got one! I got one! He's huge! Bryce, come quick!" Mike's earsplitting squeals filled the air, drumming up a beat in Bryce's heart that probably equaled the boy's.

Bryce yanked his line out of the water and ran over to stand behind Mike.

"Here, you take it," Mike said, passing the rod back.

"It's your fish, you bring him in." Bryce refused, knowing even if Mike did not, that he would be robbing the boy of the best part of catching a fish if he took over now.

He stayed just behind the boy, close enough that he could grab the pole if it became necessary, but far enough away to give Mike room to work. "You need to jerk your line tight, to make sure you have him hooked, and then keep it tight. If you leave too much slack you give him room to get loose and swim away," he advised, keeping his voice calm and even.

His heart continued to thud. He wanted this to be as big a moment for Mike as it had been for Bryce all those years ago when he had reeled in his first fish. It was a moment that a man never forgot, no matter how young he was when it happened, or how old he got afterward.

"I got it! Look, Bryce, there he is. Isn't he a beauty?" Mike enthused as Bryce helped him net the fish.

Bryce looked at the thirteen-inch brown trout and had to agree. The little guy was just barely a keeper, but he was the biggest catch Bryce had ever seen.

"What would you do if you didn't have a net?" Mike asked as Bryce showed the boy how to take the hook out of the fish's mouth.

"Swing him far enough back on land that if he squirms off the hook, he can't plop back into the water," Bryce said, sliding the threader through the fish's gill to string him up.

"Guess I kinda scared the rest away, huh?" Mike asked when he turned back toward the stream.

Bryce walked back to collect his rod, and started packing up the tackle box.

"That's okay, sport. We can come back later this afternoon. I would've been disappointed if you didn't whoop and holler a little on your first catch."

Mike looked up at Bryce, uncertainty marring his brow. "Did you?"

Looking down into earnest eyes that were the exact color of Shannon's, Bryce would probably have been tempted to lie in order to reassure the boy. Thankfully he did not have to. "I sure did," he admitted. "My dad and uncle thought I should learn to fish nature's way before they spoiled me with a fishing pole and so my first time out I had nothing but a stick I had to break off a tree myself, a safety pin and a couple of pieces of string."

"No hooks?" Mike asked, falling in beside Bryce as they headed back to the meadow.

"Nope, a safety pin," Bryce replied. "I had to tie a piece of string to one end of the stick, bend the pin, tie it onto the other end of the string, and bait it."

"Did it work? Did you catch anything?" Mike asked. His avid interest intrigued Bryce. A man could become addicted to having a boy hang onto his every word. But not this boy, he reminded himself. This boy was strictly off-limits. Maybe he needed to find a Big Brothers program somewhere, or coach Little League. He would have to remember to ask Oliver about such opportunities the first chance he had.

"It worked. But I only caught one," Bryce admitted. "I hollered so loud I scared the rest of the fish clear into the next county."

Mike giggled and Bryce noticed that the boy moved in a little closer to him as they walked through the trees. Even as his heart swelled, his conscience was reminding him that it was not fair to encourage the boy's affection when there was no future in it for either of them.

SHANNON AND MINDI were collecting pine cones when the fishermen returned with their catch. Shannon was almost as excited over her son's success as Mike was. She pulled a little Instamatic camera out of one of the bags and took more pictures of that single fish than Bryce would have believed possible. Everybody had to take a turn posing with Mike, and then Mike posed by himself. Bryce manned the camera while Shannon posed with her son, and then Shannon and Mindi posed one on each side of the boy. Bryce could not remain immune to the holiday feeling in the air, nor could he put a damper on it with thoughts of tomorrow. Whatever else happened, Shannon and her family deserved some carefree hours.

"If we don't stop soon, I'm going to pass out from malnutrition," he complained laughingly when it looked like Shannon was going to be content to take pictures for the rest of the afternoon. She was moving Mike over to get the apple trees in the background.

She laughed with Bryce, meeting his eyes with shared merriment, and then put the camera away. "Yes, sir, Sheriff, we can't have you falling down on your job," she replied with a curtsy. It was the first time she had ever called him Sheriff without an undertone of dislike. And yet her words, playful though they were, reminded both of them for a moment of the real circumstances behind the day. They were not a couple spending the day together out of a decision to be together; they were two adults caught in the system, trying their best to make a couple of kids happy.

But that did not mean they were not allowed to enjoy themselves, Bryce argued with himself as he watched Shannon move around the blanket laying out containers and foil-wrapped packages, bags of chips and plastic bags full of sliced vegetables. Her perfectly rounded bottom was in the air as she moved around the four corners of their makeshift table, allowing Bryce a view he was not likely to forget. The black spandex covering her hips outlined more than it concealed. He pulled his eyes away.

"Mmm. That's how I like my women. Barefoot and in the kitchen," he teased just before he turned away.

"Oh yeah?" The playful challenge in Shannon's voice lured him. He turned back in time to be struck by a marshmallow in the hollow of his left cheek.

Had the children not been there, Bryce knew just how he would have retaliated, but they were there, and Bryce decided it was a good thing, even though they were laughing as hard as their mother was. He determined that it was prudent to quit while he was ahead, or at least before he got any further behind.

"Come on, sport, let's get that fish cleaned."

LUNCH WAS LONG AND LAZY, and Shannon found herself wishing the day could last forever, uncaring at the moment how dangerous such a sentiment would be to her emotional health. She was almost getting used to the way her nerves jumped in response any time she got too close to Bryce, and even sometimes when she didn't. Regardless of what her head told her, her body had apparently determined that Bryce was the man it had been made for.

"Mom, can I take Mindi down to show her the stream?" Mike asked as the four of them gathered up the leftovers from lunch. They had decided to save the marshmallows for roasting later when they built the fire to cook Mike's fish.

"Yeah, Mommy, can he?" Mindi begged.

Shannon did not like the idea. She had immediate visions of one or both of her children falling into a swift current and being swept away. And yet she knew she could not coddle them forever. They were not babies anymore, and if she wanted them to be self-confident, she had to show confidence in them.

"What do you think?" she asked, looking to Bryce for guidance. After all, it was his river.

He was quiet for a moment, as if giving the situation proper consideration. "I've been going down there alone since I was eight years old," he said with a shrug. "There's much more danger on a playground than there is out here." He leaned over to put the mustard back in the cooler.

Shannon sat on the blanket, her legs pulled up beneath her. "But what about the current?" she asked. She couldn't help it—she was a mother, and mothers worried.

Bryce rolled the top down on a bag of chips. "A puppy could beat that current, Shannon," he said with a smile. "It's a lazy stream."

Shannon looked up at Mike with serious, piercing eyes. "Okay, you can go, but you watch out for your sister, young man."

Mike's hastily given "I will" was lost as he and Mindi raced away across the field.

The children were not gone ten seconds before Shannon realized the real danger of their going. She and Bryce were sitting in the middle of a warm blanket, out in the center of God's green earth, all alone.

"Don't look so scared, I won't pounce," Bryce said, putting away the last of the leftovers.

Shannon didn't smile. "Maybe not, but I might," she whispered, her fear forcing her to be honest.

Bryce stretched out his legs, leaning back against his left hand where it lay on the blanket behind him, trying for a sense of calm when in reality Shannon's words had had the same effect on him as a horse kick in the gut. She had finally openly acknowledged that the mind-destroying attraction he had been battling for weeks was not completely one-sided. He knew in the back of his mind that he was treading in some dangerous waters, that he was straddling a very thin line between professional ethics and personal involvement.

He reminded himself that Shannon's words could merely be a practiced ploy to sucker him into influencing her case against the Stewarts, but even as the thought was born, he dismissed it as ridiculous. He knew her better than that. And while yes, he was a cop, he was also a man, one who was feeling something special, something different, something worth a risk or two. And that was why he had to believe he could wear his two hats without jeopardizing either one of them.

"Would that be so bad?" he finally replied to her bald confession, picking a weed to chew on the stem.

Shannon's gaze devoured him for several seconds while she remembered all of the reasons why it would be wrong for her to surrender herself to this man. He was the cop who was waiting for her police record—the one thing which was sure to destroy her life—and she couldn't tell him about it, because until it showed up, there was still a chance that it would not. She had to consider the risk to Bryce, as well. She knew, even if he did not, that if he were to become involved with her while he was in a position to influence the nasty court battle looming in her near future, his career could be all but ruined. The county would laugh him back to Detroit if he stood up for her and then she was run out of town.

And selfishly Shannon could not risk involvement with Bryce, either. She had trusted her own husband to stand up for her once, to see beyond her parentage to the person she was, and look where it had gotten her—divorced and fighting for the right to raise her own children. What it all boiled down to was trust, and that was one thing she and Bryce did not share. Still, her heart hammered for him.

"You're a cop," she said, picking at a piece of lint on the blanket. She could not talk about this and look at him at the same time.

"I'm not going to forget that, Shannon. But I'm also a man and it's up to me to keep the two straight. It's not as if you were a wanted criminal or anything."

No, but she had a prostitution conviction he knew nothing about.

She looked across at him, absorbing the heat in his determined brown gaze. "I still think it would be bad." She forced the words with a voice thick with a passion she could not hide.

"Why?"

"You don't completely trust me, for one."

"Maybe not completely, but I do care about you, and I'm trying," Bryce said. Shannon was gratified that he did not attempt to deny her accusation, but even more, thrilled by the closest thing to a declaration of love she had ever had.

"I care about you, too," she whispered, and then looked down again. She had to think straight and when she looked at Bryce she couldn't seem to think at all.

"I'm giving you the benefit of the doubt." His words caressed her.

He was. She knew he was. But still . . .

"There are things about me you don't know," she said, daring to give him that much.

"*Are* you a wanted criminal?" he asked, half in jest. His warm brown eyes did things to her stomach that should be illegal.

"No! Of course not," Shannon said with a nervous laugh. She had served her sentence, twice over.

Bryce shrugged. "Then what's the harm in two willing adults expressing their appreciation for one another?" He made it sound so mature, so casual, such a simple solution for the awareness that had been steadily eating away at her composure.

Shannon did not have an answer to that except that, whether he believed it or not, she just could not see how lovemaking between them could ever be casual, or how she could give him her body and still keep her heart intact.

Bryce leaned over, bracing his weight on his elbow, and lifted his free hand to brush her hair back from her face. "You worry too much," he murmured, sending shivers through every nerve ending in her body.

She did. She always had. It probably came from never having had anyone to worry about her.

"Maybe," she conceded, not wanting to tarnish her memories of this special place with the uglier facts of life.

She knew she should pull away from Bryce's touch on her face. If she allowed him any further entry into her life, she stood a good chance of being burned, and so did he. Yet, as if her body had a will all its own, she did not pull away. She leaned forward instead, burying her cheek in his tender caress.

"I'm going to kiss you, Shannon. Just kiss you," he said.

Shannon was fascinated by the movement of his lips as he spoke. She could not pull her gaze away from them.

His hand slid underneath her hair to her neck, guiding her forward. She inhaled his fresh male scent, afraid that she wasn't going to feel complete again until she had taken the rest of him into her in every way possible. The sun was shining down upon them, but its heat was tempered by the light breeze blowing across their private meadow. The heat she was feeling had nothing at all to do with the weather.

Her gaze pleaded with him to stop, begged him to continue. She closed her eyes just before his lips touched hers.

Shannon had fantasized about his kiss so many times, in so many different ways, especially after his mouth had grazed hers last Saturday night, but nothing had prepared her for the sensation that shot through her as his warm, firm lips caressed hers. He took his time, lingering on her upper lip, before moving on to pay homage to her lower one.

He was touching no other part of her body except her lips and her neck. Shannon was still seated beside him, facing him, leaning over just enough for their mouths to meet, and yet every pore in her body responded to the veneration she felt in his kiss.

"Lie down with me," he whispered against her mouth.

Shannon gave no thought to denying him. She was suddenly discovering what could be so all encompassing about the physical acts between a man and a woman, and she could not have stopped at that point to save her life. Kissing Bryce was just as she used to dream kissing could be, dreams she had relegated to the world of make-believe long before her sixteenth birthday. She was not doing this because she felt it was her duty; he was not taking it because it was his right. They were communicating, honestly, beautifully, each giving, each taking.

He slid his arms around her waist, supporting her weight as she stretched out beside him, breast to chest, belly to stomach, thigh to thigh. She felt him everywhere, and everywhere she felt him he was warm, hard muscle.

"You feel so good," Bryce murmured in her ear. His tongue dipped gently, tasting her lobe.

"You feel...incredible," Shannon told him, running her hands up and down his back, exploring, discovering, wondering if she would ever get enough to calm the unfamiliar fires raging through her blood.

His lips captured hers again, pushing her back to lie flat against the blanket while he half lay on top of her. His leg slid in between hers and, supporting his weight with his left side, he placed his arms on either side of her. She could feel his heart pounding into her breast.

His breathing ragged, he lowered his lips to hers once more. "Kiss me back," he demanded. She felt the words as much as she heard them, and she complied. Her tongue moved hesitantly at first, exploring his lips tentatively, but when she had crossed over the barriers to touch her tongue to his, all uncertainty was gone.

He slid his right hand down to touch her hip, as he had touched it once before, and then moved his fingers slowly upward, leaving a trail of fire in their wake. He stopped at her ribs, and the heat of his palm seeped into her.

When his hand was finally covering her breast, Shannon moaned, hardly able to comprehend how right his touch felt, how proper that he was taking these intimacies from her, how good she felt allowing them. His thumb brushed her nipple through the thin material covering her, teasing her sensitized nerves.

His lips continued to take from hers everything she had to give, and Shannon was beyond thought, beyond doubts, aware only of the need she felt in him—a need that was equal to the intensity of her own. He slid his hand back down her body, reaching for the buckle of her belt....

Sanity returned with a thud.

Shannon pulled her mouth away from his with an effort that was almost superhuman, so desperately did she want it to stay right where it was. "Stop," she panted. "We have to stop."

Bryce's hand stilled instantly, as did his lips, but he continued to lie against her. He looked down at her, with a question written clearly in his eyes.

"The children. I can't go any farther knowing that the twins might be back at any moment," she said, offering the only excuse she could think of. The excuse was legitimate, but it was not the only reason she had stopped him. No matter how good or right he felt, Shannon Stewart making love with the county sheriff was not a good idea at all.

Bryce rolled off her, cursing himself beneath his breath. "I'm sorry, Shannon," he said, after drawing a couple of deep breaths. "It's no excuse, but I just plain forgot about the kids for a minute," he admitted.

Shannon sat up with a regretful smile, reaching over to run her fingers through the hair that fell to just below his collar. He was such a proper man in so many ways, and yet he kept his hair such a rakish length. She loved that about him. He had principles, but he also had the ability to see that all was not black and white. "Don't feel bad," she told him. "I almost forgot, too, and they're my kids."

Bryce stood up, adjusted the fly of his shorts slightly, and then slid his hands into his pockets, as if he did not trust them on the loose. "I'm sure that by tomorrow we'll both feel that it's for the best that it worked out this way."

Shannon understood what he was saying. His actions had been controlled by his body, not his head. She only wished things were as simple for her. "I'm sure you're right." It was what pride demanded she say, not what was in her heart.

He turned around for a minute, as if he was going to walk away, and then turned to face her again. "This isn't going to be easy."

Shannon was not sure what "this" he was referring to, exactly. Did he mean fighting their attraction was not going to be easy, or embarking on a relationship wasn't going to be easy?

"No," she agreed, figuring her reply was safe either way. Was he worried that she would not have stopped him if it had not been for the children? Was he afraid of what might have happened then? Was he going to say he could no longer chaperon her and the kids?

"I can't make any promises for the future, Shannon," he warned.

She knew that already; she knew it even better than he did. But she respected the fact that he was willing to admit it to her. He was a cop with a conscience, but he was still a cop.

"I know," she said. Until the custody hearing was over, there was no future.

He stood above her, looking down at her broodingly for several long seconds. "Lord, I want you," he swore. The words sounded as if they had been torn from him. Before Shannon could respond, he turned away, striding off in the direction the children had gone.

CHAPTER TWELVE

BRYCE BROUGHT HER flowers on Sunday—not red roses, or even white ones, not an arrangement of assorted hothouse blooms, but a handpicked bouquet of lilies of the valley.

He was dressed in full uniform, with a bulging holster at his hip and his shiny, engraved name badge on his chest. His bubble-topped cruiser was parked, though still running, on the shoulder of the apartment driveway.

"These are for you." He handed her the bouquet in lieu of a greeting. She noticed a small white envelope sticking out from in between two stems. "I can't stay, I'm on duty," he continued. With a smile and a wave, he was gone.

Shannon stood in the open doorway, a slow smile replacing the surprise on her face, as she watched him walk to his car, loving the way a lock of his hair had crept behind his collar. She had waited and watched for him to show up at the Tub through her whole shift the night before. When he hadn't, she had cursed herself for being a fool. And then, during the long, dark hours of the night, she had begun to believe that her response to him in the meadow had convinced him that she was everything Clinton accused her of being. Now she didn't know what to think.

She buried her nose in the fragrant wild flowers, taking them straight to the kitchen and a ceramic vase. She waited until they were arranged to her satisfaction before she allowed herself to open the card.

"Lily-white, beautiful, and resilient—they reminded me of you. I'm trying." The card was signed simply, "Bryce."

She gazed at the tiny bell-like petals that grew along the stalks of the lily plants, happy tears in her eyes. Was it possible that things could work for them somehow, some day, if she held on long enough?

HER HOPE LASTED RIGHT UP until Darla called late that night. She was surprised to hear her mother's voice when she picked up the phone, but then, she had been the one to initiate contact when she had called asking Darla for help.

"I had a visitor yesterday, Shannon," she said as soon as she assured herself that Shannon had received the money. Shannon's heart dropped with a thud, because Darla sounded troubled, and there was not much that troubled Darla.

"Who?" Shannon asked, not really wanting to hear about Darla's "visitor." The kind of entertaining her mother did made Shannon physically ill.

"A legal representative, a Stewart legal representative." Shannon felt the blood drain from her face.

"What for?" she asked, as soon as she could force the words past the constriction in her throat.

"Your ex-husband wants me to come up to testify against you. He wants to use me to prove that the environment you provide your children is neither 'suitable nor morally chaste.'" Darla mimicked what was obviously a stuffy Stewart lawyer. "They offered to buy a big house in the swankiest section of Havenville and pay me quite a handsome salary to be its caretaker."

Shannon slid down to the kitchen floor, running her hand along her scalp. This was worse than her worst nightmare. She covered her free ear with her palm, as if she could shut out her mother's last words. If she refused to hear them, they could not touch her. Had Darla lied to her about her financial situation? Had her mother sent her all the money she had? Was Darla now in a financial bind, needy?

"What did you tell them?" she asked. She had to know what she was up against. She wished she had not already sent Brad a sizable advance.

"What do you think I told them?" Darla asked, taking offense. "How could I testify against my own daughter?"

Yeah, how? Shannon wondered, agonizing as she imagined the Stewart clan picking every piece of nasty garbage they could find out about Darla Howard, then asking the courts if this was the kind of familial influence that two impressionable ten-year-olds should be exposed to.

She rubbed her eyes, suddenly more tired than she could bear, wondering how much pond scum one person from the wrong side of the tracks had to wade through before she was allowed to swim in the pool. She was frightened at Darla's continued power to hurt her, and the steady knowledge that she could never be sure that Darla would not. Darla would always care more about Shannon than any other individual on earth, except herself. Darla always cared about Darla first.

"Do you need the money?" she asked, determining somehow to come up with something to help her mother out—at least enough to help her overcome the temptation of Stewart cash. Maybe, if she fired Brad Channing she could get the advance back.

"No, dear, I don't need the money. I told you I'm doing okay. I just wanted you to know what you're up against. Maybe you should consider the tidy settlement you could probably get if you gave up this battle. Lord knows, the Stewarts can afford it. And if they want those children so badly, they can't be all bad. Think of how much more they have to offer two kids, and how much further you can go if you aren't tied down to them, being a single woman and all...."

Shannon stared at the tile on her kitchen floor, picking out patterns among the multi-colored squares. She knew Darla meant well, she *knew* it. Which is why she held her tongue and choked back her tears. Because no matter what happened from now until the end of her life, Shannon finally saw clearly that Darla would always be Darla. And to Darla, having things was more important than anything else on earth. She could not understand that to Shannon, things had never been important at all.

She had still hoped, even after her mother had betrayed her in the deepest sense, that someday Darla would learn that love was more important than anything else on earth. But as Shannon listened to her mother's words, she finally acknowledged that love was probably not even a word in Darla Howard's vocabulary. How could it be? She had only been offered it once in her life, and by then, by the time Darla had had a little girl who had openly adored her pretty mother, Darla had already been too firmly molded into the woman she was to recognize the preciousness of the gift she had been offered.

Shannon hung up the phone as soon as she possibly could without offending Darla, her mother's last words still echoing in her ears. Darla had assured Shannon that if she insisted on going ahead with the court battle, Darla would stay out of it, but Shannon wasn't sure she believed it. Her mother honestly felt that Shannon and the twins would be better off if Clinton won the custody suit. But the fact that her mother stood to gain from the victory as well worried Shannon most of all.

SHE SPENT THE NEXT DAY engrossed in her accounting textbook. Not only was she trying to complete her degree by the first of the year, she was also hoping to find something that would occupy her mind long enough to give her emotions some peace and quiet for a while.

She was interrupted midafternoon by a phone call from her lawyer. Brad Channing reported that both the twins' schoolteachers from the previous year were willing to testify on Shannon's behalf. But he had not yet received any information from the bank regarding Clinton's accounts and the custody hearing was only twelve days away. She told Brad about the Stewarts' attempt to have Darla testify, and Brad told her not to worry about it. But then, Brad did not know Darla.

It rained during her visiting time with the twins on Thursday, preventing the trip to the park they had planned, but the bad weather turned out to be good news. Since the rain was forcing them indoors, Shannon had a logical excuse to bring the children home for a couple of hours. She set off with Bryce to get her children, determined to enjoy every minute of the day.

The twins were delighted to be home, and Shannon and Bryce spent a lazy afternoon playing board games with them in the middle of Shannon's living-room floor. There was one difficult moment when Shannon stretched to get a kink out of her back and caught Bryce staring at her breasts, but the moment passed and Shannon knew she had to let it go.

BRYCE DROVE TO WORK Friday morning feeling good about the way things were shaping up with Shannon and her children. It had been tough the day before to be with her all afternoon without touching her, to watch her sprawled out so deliciously on the floor without climbing on top of her, but all in all he had had a wonderful time. He was a little uneasy with quite how wonderful it had been. He could not allow himself to be swept away by the budding feelings be-

ween him and Shannon; he couldn't lose sight of his po-
ition as sheriff in this tight-knit little town.

Out of habit, he slowed as he drove down Main Street,
eying Stewart's department store, the library and other
usinesses, ensuring that all was well. He noticed Clinton
Stewart's vintage Jaguar parked in front of the bank again
and glanced toward the door of the establishment, finding
t curious that he had seen Stewart twice in the past week
and both times had been at Southlakes's only bank. His
eyes narrowed as he saw Stewart coming out, accompanied by off-duty Deputy Williams.

Bryce had been trying to reach Williams all week to ask
him about the older man he had seen with Clinton, but his
attempts had all been fruitless. Williams was on vaca-
ion—supposedly out of town. Bryce was definitely going
o have to corner his deputy, and soon.

He arrived at work with time enough to stop in the mini-
kitchen for a drink of chocolate milk, and then headed for
his desk. An envelope from records was waiting for him
here—a copy of someone's police record. Apprehension
ightened his stomach; the only record Bryce had requested since he had arrived in Southlakes was Shannon's.
Not having received it, he'd been hoping it meant that she
didn't have a record.

He pulled back his desk chair and sat down hard, reach-
ng for the envelope. This was not a statewide computer
printout. It had been mailed directly from the county sher-
ff's office in Valdine County, Michigan's southernmost
county.

Cloaked with a numbness born of fatalism, he slit open
the envelope. He told himself he felt no anxiety, no dread,
nothing. He was just a cop doing his job.

He took in her basic biographical information, noting
that her maiden name was Howard, that she came from a

little town called Havenville and that her father was unknown. *Unknown?*

He read as if every fact meant the difference between life
and death, as if it mattered that at the time of her arrest she
had been employed by the Burger Barn. His eyes studied,
his brain computed, but the rest of him was completely
numb. He was not even surprised, realizing that, deep
down, he must have been expecting something like this all
along.

The numbness continued right up until he read the details of the arrest, the charge, the conviction, the word
"prostitution." And then he was consumed by a dread so
frightening he felt as if his heart was going to explode in his
chest. Had he been taken in by a pair of lying eyes? He had
known women in the past who had done some pretty des-
picable things in an effort to fulfill whatever emotional
need was driving them. But was Shannon really capable of
the same calculated, self-serving deceit Bryce's ex-wife had
practiced on him all those years ago? The same deceit The
King's woman had used to fool Bryce's father?

Even as his head asked the question, his heart cried out
in denial. He could not deny that Shannon had lied in the
past; it was public record that she had lied when she had
first come to Southlakes. But surely she had not set out to
hurt anyone. Bryce wanted to believe that more than anything at that moment. Despite the past betrayals he did not
want to believe that he had been fooled again.

He read the report for a second time, and then a third,
and a fourth, like a curious passerby irresistibly drawn to
the horror of a car accident. He implanted every detail in
his mind. But by the time he had read the damning words
for the fifth time, another emotion was threatening to
strangle him—red-hot jealousy. How could she do it? How
many had there been? How many were there still? How
many more would there be?

None. There had been none, not in that way. He had to believe that. He had to believe that someone had made a terrible mistake.

After his ninth time through the report, agony started to creep in. He massaged the muscles tightening in his right shoulder as he thought of Mindi and Mike. He thought of what a wonderful mother Shannon was to them, how obvious it was that she loved them, how much they adored her, and he hurt for all three of them. He thought of Shannon's optimism, her strength, her willingness to understand when Bryce could not give her any assurances that he was with her for the long haul. And he thought of the times she had escaped within herself, expecting no help, no understanding.

It finally hit him that she had known what he was going to find, that she had known it on the Fourth of July when they had lain together in his meadow. Whatever truth there might or might not be in her police report suddenly paled in comparison to what Bryce now saw as a deliberate act against him personally. She had known about the record's existence, and yet she had not told him. She had not trusted or cared for him enough to have prepared him for this, or even had the decency to give him an explanation. An explanation he suddenly needed more than the air he breathed.

SHANNON STEPPED UNDER the cool spray, flinching as the water stung her heated flesh. How many cold showers would she have to take before she got used to the barbs of the icy needles against her skin? She forced herself to take the pain, while sensuous images of Bryce still floated through her mind. If only she knew how long it was going to be until he could trust her, really trust her, or what path her life was going to take after the custody hearing....

She waited until she had goose bumps on every inch of her body before she relented and reached down to turn on the hot water, but there was a muted banging on her front door and she paused, listening. Alarm clutched her stomach as the disruptive pounding came again. Galvanized into action, she turned off the shower and threw back the curtain. And then she heard the pealing of her doorbell.

There was only one person she knew who had ever rung her bell and pounded on her front door at the same time. He had only done it once, and he had been impatient to reach her then. Judging by his persistence, he was impatient to reach her now, as well. Had something happened to the twins? *Dear God, dear, dear God, please let them be all right.*

She did not waste time drying off, but ran dripping wet into her bedroom to grab her robe off her closet door.

She had the front door unlocked and swung wide open by the time the doorbell rang a third time. Bryce almost fell inside, as if he'd been leaning against the door.

"What's wrong? Has something happened to the twins?" she asked, moving back as he stepped the rest of the way inside.

His face looked strange, as if he was in shock. He was pale, haggard, his eyes expressionless. He was looking at her, but it was as if he didn't even see her. He didn't say a word.

"Tell me!" she demanded, panic raising her voice to a shrill pitch. "Has something happened? Are the twins hurt?"

Bryce continued to stare at her, saying nothing, while Shannon's chest slowly constricted, suffocating her. She finally looked down, in a desperate attempt to escape from the frightening emotions she was reading in his eyes, and she saw the official-looking papers he clutched within his fist.

Suddenly, she knew. It all made sense—the doubt in his eyes, the uniform. He had finally received the record on Shannon Howard, and just as she had expected, he had believed every damning word without even giving her the benefit of the doubt. He was The Law again, and The Law had never once been willing to hear her side of anything.

"Oh," she said, gathering the familiar cloak of detachment around her shivering body, waiting for him to say whatever he had come to say and then leave.

"Go put some clothes on," he said, his disappointment ricocheting off the walls of the hallway. The only thing familiar about him then was his faint, woodsy scent.

Shannon went, not because he told her to, but because she would be more comfortable facing the accusations that he was obviously ready to spew if she were not standing before him half-naked, and because she was cold.

She hurried into a pair of comfortably baggy shorts and an oversize blouse, more grateful than usual for the concealment they offered. She would have liked to have kept him waiting, to have forced him to cool his heels alone in the room that had been filled with love and laughter just the day before, but she could not tolerate having him in her apartment any longer than she must. He was standing at the living-room window, his back to the room, when she returned.

He stiffened when she entered. His silence stretched out. Shannon had no concept of time as she stood there waiting for him to say something. She was numb to the situation, escaping far within herself to a place she had discovered when most girls her age were still playing with Barbie dolls.

She did not sit; she was not going to give him the opportunity to tower over her. And she came no farther into the room than the archway that led into it, refusing to feel trapped in her own home, especially not by an officer of the law.

"Why?" The word, when it finally came from him, sounded like a curse.

Shannon did not dignify it with an answer. There was no point.

He spun around then, pinning her with his stare. She withstood the visual attack, seemingly unaffected. *Here it comes.* The realization was more an awareness than a conscious thought.

He advanced farther into the room, closing in on her, his bulging holster moving back and forth against his hip with every step he took. Shannon stood her ground, refusing to allow him to intimidate her.

"You've grown amazingly quiet all of a sudden, just like the woman I first met several weeks ago. Is she the real Shannon Stewart? Or should I say Shannon *Howard?*"

Bryce was not proud of himself, of the venom he heard hissing from his own mouth, but he was too disappointed, too hurt, to stop the angry flow. He had seen Shannon glance at the damning papers, still clutched in his fist, while they'd been standing in the hallway; he had seen realization dawn on her finely carved features, evidence that she had known, that she had deliberately kept the knowledge from him. He had waited, then, for her explanation, but he had waited in vain.

By the time she had returned from her bedroom, he had finally faced the fact that there probably was no explanation. In the face of her silence, he could no longer keep his doubts at bay. At least at some point in her life, a very young point according to the damaging papers he still held, Shannon Stewart had been a prostitute.

He still didn't want to believe the evidence, but he just could not get by the fact that Shannon had deliberately withheld information from him.

He threw the mangled police report on the coffee table. "Is this some kind of game to you?" he asked.

Shannon held herself stoically before Bryce, unwilling to credit his challenge with a response, clutching her wounded heart so tightly that it could not feel the pain he was inflicting.

"I need to hear your explanation, Shannon."

Shannon was a child again, playing freeze tag at recess with the children at school. She loved the game because she was always the best. Someone would tag her and she would have to stand perfectly still in whatever position they found her—become a statue of ice. Sometimes she was still standing motionless when the bell rang for class to resume. It was the one time she could ever remember any of the other kids admiring her for anything.

"Why didn't you tell me? I thought I made it perfectly obvious that I was trying to help you. The least you could have done was let me know who I was dealing with. What was the point in waiting for me to find out on my own?"

Shannon thought she saw his features soften with a hint of disappointment, but the coldness returned so rapidly she could not be sure. She squeezed a little harder on her heart, refusing to feel.

Bryce came closer, stopping just inches away from her, until she was inhaling his fresh outdoor smell with every breath she took. She concentrated on the lines that bracketed his mouth, refusing to see his lips, or to allow him to pierce her again with the cold barbs she had seen in his eyes earlier.

"What is it with you, Shannon?" he asked, but something had changed. His growing frustration was evident, but the horrible anger, suddenly, was not. "Why don't you even try to explain, to defend yourself?" he asked. This question was hesitant, searching, coming from the man, not the sheriff.

Shannon's gaze flew to Bryce's. She had to know that she was not just imagining the change in him, that she was not just conjuring up images of the man she wanted him to be. His liquid brown eyes were warm again—warm and confused. The damaging police report had done more than anger him, it had hurt him.

"It's what you want to believe," she said, unable to deny the man the reply she had to deny the cop.

He pulled back as if she had hit him, but she did not know whether his reaction was due to a possible truth he heard in her words, or to the fact that she had spoken them at all. He studied her for several long seconds, and she let him, despite the feeling that he was looking deep into her soul, seeing everything she protected there.

"How can I believe anything else?" His words were barely audible, muffled by deeply conflicting emotions, yet she felt their blow more potently than any others.

She could not answer his question. She had no answers. She did not know herself how she could have hoped, even briefly, that if that old record ever showed up, he would take one look at it and know that something did not fit. She was twenty-nine years old, not ten; she had ceased to be starry-eyed long, long ago. And yet, no matter how much pressure she put on the wound, it still hurt that he did not see her for what she was, that he did not *know* that she could never have committed the crime for which she had been convicted.

It was that pain that imprisoned an explanation still. If she told him what really happened twelve years ago, and he, like those other officers before him, could not believe her, then the wound that had been inflicted on a seventeen-year-old girl would be ripped wide open, hurting like never before, because this time she cared about the man whose faith she sought. She needed him to trust her, to believe that she could never sell her body to anyone, before she could tell him about the night she lost her innocence, if not her virginity.

"That's just it. You honestly don't see how you can believe anything else. What about faith, or trust? Can you give me those? Can you promise me that if I confide in you, I'd be talking to someone who believes in me rather than someone who's ready to believe the worst of me?"

She did not have to watch the struggle going on in his eyes. His silence was her answer. "I understand," she said, tightening her hold on herself. She could not allow the hurt, the anger to get control of her. Those sinister emotions led to bitterness. They could destroy her in minutes. "But then there's no point in putting myself through this another time, for another cop. The case was closed years ago."

It was Shannon's unnatural acceptance of his defamation that finally got through to Bryce. He saw the mask slip back over her face, taking the life out of her beautifully sculpted features, and knew that he could not leave things this way. He remembered back to that time in court when she had accepted the charges of kidnapping without defending her reasons for having done so. But she had had a reason—a good reason. It dawned on Bryce suddenly, sickeningly, that there could also be an explanation for what she had done, some desperate situation that had left her believing she had no other choice.

Only Shannon knew what had really prompted her arrest twelve years ago; only Shannon could tell him what had driven her to commit such an ugly crime against herself. Yet, Bryce knew that she was going to give him nothing—not now. How could he expect her to? How could he expect her to trust him, when he had just proven that he still didn't completely trust her?

Bryce walked over to sit on one end of the worn beige couch, knowing that he owed it to her to try to explain. "As much as I want to trust you, Shannon, it doesn't come easily. Especially under the circumstances." His gaze locked with hers as she stood in the doorway, willing her to come closer, to allow herself to listen to him. His eyes remained locked with hers as she finally crossed the room to sit on the opposite end of the couch.

There was no warmth in her eyes, no hint of emotion on her expressionless face, not even a clenching of hands or a stiffness of shoulders to give any indication of tension. She watched him, waiting. Bryce looked away.

He took a deep breath, wondering where one began when pouring one's deepest agony out to a body made of stone. If he had ever, in the darkest hours of the night, considered telling Shannon about his past, it had never been like this. Her arms should be around him, offering him the powerful peace he had begun to crave from her, giving him the comfort he had never felt from feminine arms.

"I never knew my mother," he started, talking to the faint, blurred image of himself and Shannon reflected back at him from the silent television set across the room. He was surprised at the words coming out of his mouth. He had made no conscious decision to go back quite that far. But once he had started, he found that he could not stop the flow that poured from him. "She left right after I was born. All the years of my growing up, it was just my dad and me. My old man was a cop, the best there ever was. I was riding in a squad car before I was out of diapers. As I grew up, there was never any doubt in my mind that I wanted to be just like him. I wanted to be a cop, too. Together we were going to be the best team ever, and bring down every bad guy in the city." Bryce leaned forward with his elbows on his knees, smiling sadly at the images of innocence his memory was dredging up.

He rubbed his hands together, following their motion with his eyes, needing some sort of contact, even if it was with himself. "Funny thing is, that's just what happened...." He stopped speaking when he heard Shannon's sharply drawn breath.

He reached down between his knees to brush a speck of lint from his shiny black shoes. "I graduated from the academy top of my class, worked my way up, made detective, and was assigned to work with Pop. It wasn't all easy," he admitted, remembering. "I got married my second year out of the academy and that slowed things up for a while."

"Married?" Shannon echoed.

Muscles Bryce had not even been aware of holding tense suddenly relaxed a little. She was letting him in. He continued to study his hands as he nodded.

"Briefly," he conceded, holding that old bitterness at bay. "It was the only time Pop and I had a serious confrontation. We didn't talk for six months. He tried to warn me about her, but I was too young, too hot-headed to listen. She was older than I was by almost ten years, but she was a looker. We'd only been married a few months when I found out she was seeing someone else. Another cop. She had a thing for cops. Made her feel safe, or something."

"What happened?" Shannon asked. Her voice was soft again, carrying a wealth of empathy.

Bryce shrugged. "I was ruled by my pride for a while, refusing to admit to anyone what a fool I'd been. It wasn't until I caught her down at the station one day that I realized there were some things more important than misplaced pride, like my self-respect."

"And because of one mistake you lost faith in humanity?" Shannon asked, obviously having trouble buying that fact.

Bryce left his memories behind, along with the young man whose head had been turned by the experience of an older woman, as he turned to look at Shannon. Her hands were clasped together in her lap, and her long black hair, still slightly wet from her shower, fell around her shoulders. In her face he saw her need to understand, accompanied by her inability to do so.

"That's only part of it," he admitted, knowing he was going to have to give her the rest, the worst, the part he could not seem to escape.

Her beautiful brow puckered with confusion. "Then what?" she asked, searching his eyes for the truth.

Bryce did not look away as he told her the rest, bluntly, sparing neither her nor himself.

"Last year, when we were following The King, the ringleader I told you about, Pop met a woman whose sister had supposedly fallen into The King's debt, been forced into service and eventually died on the streets. Darcy had some information that could help us bring The King down. I guess Pop was taken in by her big blue eyes, her sad story, the unfairness of it all. Something didn't seem right to me, but I couldn't put my finger on what it was, so I never told Pop about my doubts. Anyway, Darcy led us straight to our man all right, when he was fully armed and expecting us. Pop went in first. I followed, catching one of the bullets in my right shoulder. By the time I got to Pop his uniform was soaked with blood. I was sitting there, holding him, begging him to hang on, when I saw Darcy hurry past on the arm of The King. By that time I'd lost too much blood to go after them. Pop died in my arms a few minutes later."

Suddenly, Bryce was there again, sitting on the cold concrete floor of an abandoned warehouse beneath the weight of his dead father. He felt the desperation welling up inside him as it had done that night, as it did every time he relived those horrible minutes in his nightmares. His skin felt cold, clammy, as the sweat poured out of him.

"Darcy's sister had been arrested for drug trafficking years ago. She'd killed herself rather than go to jail. Pop was the arresting officer." He forced the final words past the lump blocking his throat.

Bryce had never again spoken of that night, and wouldn't have done so today if he'd been aware of how difficult the telling was going to be. He wasn't even aware of the lone tear sliding down his cheek, until Shannon wiped it away.

He jumped up from the couch, resuming his place at the window. He hated his doubts, hated the fact that he was hurting her when just being with her made him feel good.

Shannon joined him at the window. She didn't touch him, but he felt her presence reaching out to him. "And now you can't be sure it isn't happening again, can you?" she whispered.

"I want to believe." He thumped his chest hard, once, with his fist. "What I feel in here tells me to believe, but my head keeps telling me different. I wish I could tell you that it's going to change, but I'm just not sure it ever will."

He turned to look at her, to see the understanding in her eyes. He reached for her then, crushing her against him, burying his face in the damp strands of her hair. He was a cop who had to do his job, but he was also a man, a human being with faults and wants and needs. And he needed Shannon. He needed the sanctuary he found in her arms. Somehow, he vowed, he was going to prove to himself, and to the rest of this town, that she was just who she claimed to be—a human being with faults and wants and needs—but a good, loving woman, just the same.

CHAPTER THIRTEEN

SHANNON WRAPPED HER ARMS around Bryce's waist, driven by a need for reassurance as much as by her need to comfort him. They were two soldiers carrying battle scars, but as long as they had the ability to console each other, they had the means to recover. Perhaps this was why they had met; why they continued to draw inexorably closer despite their differences. Perhaps this was meant to be.

"I didn't do it." The words were muffled against his chest. She hated to dispel the closeness that they shared, to tarnish the moment with her sordid past, but she knew that Bryce needed to hear the words almost as badly as she needed not to speak them.

His grip on her loosened slightly, but he continued to hold her. At least he hadn't pulled away as Shannon had feared. "Then why the report?" he asked.

Shannon concentrated on his warmth. She continued to rest her cheek against the solid muscles of his chest. "After being caught in a compromising situation, I was accused. The trial was fixed and I was convicted. But I didn't do it."

"The trial was fixed?"

His doubts were still too obvious, but as the pain sliced through Shannon, she reminded herself that he had been hurt, that he was entitled to his doubts, that he believed in the system he upheld.

"A couple of witnesses lied. They stood to lose a whole lot more than I did. One of them was also a whole lot more respectable than I was. It was his word against mine."

Bryce digested her words in silence, giving her no clues to his thoughts, to whether or not he even believed her. But when his arms tightened around her, pulling her more fully into his body, she knew that, for now, he was allowing his doubts to rest. And she was needy enough to accept what she could get.

She felt heady under the tentative support he was offering her, and even more lighthearted to realize that he was taking some form of support from her, as well. No one, other than her children, had ever found her worthy enough to accept from her the abundance of caring she had to give. In spite of the prostitution conviction, Bryce was still trying.

Just when the need in his embrace turned from emotional to physical, Shannon was not sure, but as she gradually became aware of the hardness pressing against her stomach, she gave in to the special passion he evoked.

She lifted her face to him with an eagerness she had never felt before, trying to believe that, given time, she and Bryce might find their way together. She parted her lips at his coaxing, opening beneath him, a willing participant.

Shannon gloried in the response Bryce was able to rouse in her, the wonders he was teaching her about herself, her womanhood. Her skin tingled wherever he touched. Her nerves vibrated and the feeling in her stomach was excitement, not fortitude.

Even while she recognized that she wanted more of him, that she wanted to feel him crazy with desire for her, she suddenly knew that she did not want it like this. She was afraid that it would cheapen the beautiful feeling flowering within her, that the excitement would be replaced by shame, if she went to him before he was hers for keeps. And she knew that as things stood, the chances of him being hers for anything more than an hour or two were slim. Darla might have settled for an hour or two; Shannon could not.

As Shannon's thoughts cooled her ardor, sanity and rational thought returned. She had no business becoming personally involved with Bryce. Now, more than ever, their relationship had to be platonic. His reputation would be shattered in an instant if it ever got out that the sheriff was bedding a convicted prostitute. And even if her police record was not made public, there was every chance that she could still lose the custody case. Darla might testify. Shannon might be unable to prove that she had not received money from Clinton. She might be publicly branded a tarnished woman—a woman unfit to raise her own children—certainly not wife material for the local sheriff.

Bryce felt the change in her kiss immediately. She wasn't pulling away from him, but the passion was gone from her response. He loosened his hold on her, lifting his head to search her burning violet eyes. His lips parted in a smile of commiseration when he read the resolve, mixed with a healthy dose of frustration, that was shining up at him. She wasn't ready, but she wanted him. That was enough for now.

Shannon shifted slightly to the right, removing herself from within the circle of his thighs. "You're on duty, Sheriff," she reminded him. As excuses went, it was pretty poor, but Bryce understood.

He rubbed his hand along her hip. "I took an early lunch."

"Then you should eat or you'll be hungry later, right when you have to chase down a gang of thieves."

He knew that she was trying to tease him, to get things back on an even footing, but as she spoke, he was watching her lips, pink and swollen from his kisses.

He pulled her fully up against him again, wrapping his arms around her until his fingers brushed the sides of her breasts. He realigned her hips with his. "I'm already hungry," he growled into her ear, taking a gentle nip before he finally released her. If this was going to go no further, then he needed to get out of there and cool off.

"I'll be back," he warned, heading toward the door.

Shannon followed him into the hall. "I have to work tonight."

He turned, caressing her with a look. "So I'll wait."

Shannon slowly shook her head. "Not yet, Bryce," she said. She just didn't have the heart to say "not ever."

He searched her face and the desire in his eyes was slowly replaced by resignation. "We have time," he said.

Shannon tried to believe him, but time was becoming a precious commodity to her these days. She only had one week until the custody hearing, and nothing solid to stand on. One way or another, Shannon figured her time was running out.

MIKE HATED TEA. How could anyone expect a kid to like tea? And even if a kid did like tea, he sure wouldn't want hot tea on a summer afternoon. He wondered if his grandparents had ever tasted lemonade.

"That's enough sugar in your tea, Minda. Too much sugar will rot your teeth." Grandmother Stewart always reminded Mike of the spinster schoolteacher they always had on the Old-West movies his mother rented. He exchanged looks with Mindi.

"Yes, ma'am," she said, taking a small sip from her cup. She didn't like tea, either.

Mike could think of a lot better ways to spend a Friday afternoon than sitting around in a stuffy room drinking hot tea. He'd even choose reading a book over this. He had never liked living in this huge house. A guy always had to be so careful not to get things dirty. Even in their own wing their father had always insisted that Mom keep the place looking like a museum—except he called it "proper."

"We have some good news for you, children. Your father told us he hinted at it last week...." Mike listened to Grandmother Stewart build up to whatever she was going to say, wondering how much longer he was going to have to sit still in his grandparents' formal living room with his shirt collar itching his neck to high heaven. He didn't think he could take it much longer, especially if he had to swallow much more of that horrible tea. He already had to use the bathroom, but he figured Grandmother and Grandfather would harrumph and frown if he interrupted right now. Besides, he didn't really want to leave Mindi here, having to keep up the conversation all alone.

"...couldn't do anything while your mother still had custody of you. She refused to hear of it. She didn't realize what a wonderful opportunity this is for both of you. But it's not too late..." Mike perked up, realizing all of a sudden that this time his grandparents just might have something really important to say. He looked at Mindi again, to see if she had picked up on it, too. She had.

"...you've both received acceptances into the best boarding schools in the country. You, Mike, to your father's alma mater, and Mindi, to mine."

"Boarding school?" Mindi's question was asked in a frightened little voice.

"Separate boarding schools?" Mike knew he sounded horrified, but he just couldn't help it. First they talked about taking him and Mindi away from Mom, then they wanted to send them away to school, and now they wanted to split them up? Didn't these people care about him and Mindi at all? Why would anyone's grandparents want to make their grandkids so unhappy?

Grandfather Stewart put down his pipe and sat forward in his chair. Grandfather usually only spoke to him and Mindi when he figured they needed to be set straight about something. This was serious.

"You children clearly don't understand what a coup this is. Neither of you are straight-A students, your mother is not of a name that would impress anybody, you don't excel in sports, and we still managed to get you accepted into schools that usually have waiting lists years long."

Mike didn't know what a "coup" was for sure, but whatever it was, he didn't think this was good news at all. He wished he was so far down on the waiting list that he would be done with school before his turn came. He looked across at Mindi, saw the telltale quiver of her chin, and for once felt as hopeless, as helpless as she did. Mike just plain did not know what to do about this one.

BRYCE OCCUPIED his usual table at the Tub the next two nights, but the only passionate things he shared with Shannon were the intimate glances he sent her every time she sped past. He did not touch her again, though he saw her safely to her door each night. He wanted her as badly as ever, probably worse, but he was a cop first and a man second. He was no longer sure he could wear both hats at once.

For the time being, he was keeping her damaging police report to himself, not only because he was under no obligation to publicize it unless the record was subpoenaed, but also because he needed to hear the whole story before he could decide whether or not it was in the children's best interest to let the Stewarts know about the report. He spent hours wondering what compromising situation she had been in to appear as though she were selling herself. He dreaded the answer.

He cared about her a lot. He was no longer trying to fool himself on that point. And he was going to do everything in his power to show this town that she was a decent, law-abiding citizen. But until he had some more answers, it was hands off Shannon Stewart.

HE CORNERED WILLIAMS at his locker Monday afternoon, three days after receiving Shannon's police report.

"Oh, you mean B.J.," Williams answered when Bryce questioned him about the third man who had been in the Jaguar that night. Bryce was surprised at Williams's willingness to chat. He had expected the deputy to be uncomfortable, evasive.

"B.J.?" he asked, needing more than a couple of initials to run a check on the man.

"Yeah, B. J. Roberts. He's from Detroit, but he gets up this way to pit his skills against Clinton Stewart every now and then. He and Clinton have been hunting buddies for years," Williams explained.

"But hunting season isn't for another couple of months," Bryce pointed out.

Williams shrugged, seemingly at ease, as if he was doing nothing more than passing small talk with his superior. And maybe he was.

"Clinton talked B.J. into trying his hand at some serious fishing. We all went up to the Upper Peninsula last week to try for some coho."

Bryce nodded, satisfied with the explanation. There was nothing sinister about male friends socializing. There were also no stammering, no shifting eyes, no body language to indicate that Williams was lying or hiding something.

"Catch anything?" Bryce asked, not because he cared, but because if he were merely chitchatting he would have asked.

"Not this year," Williams admitted with a shrug. "It rained all week. We ended up coming back early."

Bryce commiserated with his deputy over his ruined vacation, and then continued searching.

"You've known Stewart a long time, then, huh?" he asked.

Williams grinned and nodded. "All my life."

"What do you think of him?" Bryce asked, trying for nonchalance.

"Oh, he's a great guy, one of the best, always looking out for his own," Williams assured him.

"His children included?"

"Absolutely. Don't let anything their mother says convince you differently, sir. Clinton's real bothered by this thing. Mostly he can't even talk about it. He just keeps saying he'll be real relieved to have those kids home where they belong."

Bryce chatted with Deputy Williams for a few minutes longer before heading back to his desk. Bryce's instincts told him that Williams had been straight with him. His deputy believed that Clinton Stewart was all he seemed to be, all the whole town believed him to be. So was Williams right, or had he been snowed right along with the rest of the town? Or was Bryce, perhaps, the one who was deluding himself?

Before he left for the day he placed a quick call to the Detroit Police Department, Inner-City District. He had enough friends in high places to insure a rapid, but confidential rundown on one B. J. Roberts. If the man had ever had a traffic ticket, Bryce would soon know about it.

He stopped at Aunt Hattie's for some take-out burgers and then drove slowly home. He was not going to go to the Tub that night. He needed to get things into perspective and the only way he could think of to do that, was to put some distance between himself and Shannon.

It was fact that the woman had grown up in an unsavory atmosphere, that her early formative years had been spent with a prostitute. It was fact that she had been convicted of prostitution herself before her eighteenth birthday. It was fact that she worked as a scantily dressed cocktail waitress in the roughest bar in town, in spite of the handsome support payments she was supposed to be receiving. It was also fact that in spite of all the evidence, Bryce's instincts told him she was everything he, personally, had perceived her to be—warm, loving, moral. The few times she had defended herself to him, her explanations had been logical and viable. And he did not share the town's affection for Clinton Stewart.

Every time he was close to believing in Shannon, though, something else came up. The way she looked so at home in the clothes she wore to work, her lack of money, her police record. How much more was there? How could he trust someone who kept him so completely in the dark? Yet, how could he *not* trust the woman who had wrapped herself around his lonely heart and healed some of the hurts he thought he would carry with him to his grave? How could he *not* care about a woman who baked dozens of cookies to convince her son that he was a special little boy?

SHANNON MISSED BRYCE. It was only Tuesday, just two days since he had been to see her at the Tub, and yet she was mooning over him like some kind of lovesick teenager. She had driven to St. Joe the day before, to the privacy of an out-of-town doctor to prepare herself for the possibility that she and Bryce would become lovers. She felt a little silly, and a lot embarrassed, as she stood in her bathroom, preparing to swallow the little pill, but she did it anyway. Where there was hope, there was possibility.

With that thought, she put away the pastel-colored packet with its one little foil circle ripped out, collected a gallon water jug from her kitchen and went to check on her plants. They were little green nubbins now, and as she attended to them her mind returned to the worries that had become her constant companions. The custody hearing was only three days away, and so far she had nothing conclusive on which to base her case. She had had several conversations with Brad during the past week and though he had repeatedly told her not to worry, he had not given her any substantial reason not to. The bank was stalling with Clinton's records, and without them she had no way to prove that she had not been receiving child support. She watched the dirt greedily suck up the life-sustaining moisture she was giving it and reminded herself that it was not necessarily the mightiest that survived, but the most resilient. And while she did not have any solid proof on which to base her case, neither did Clinton.

Then there was Darla to consider. Would Darla testify? Could they make Shannon's mother testify against her even if Darla did continue to refuse to do so? Would the courts accept Darla as evidence of an unsavory environment for the twins?

Shannon reached the only little pot that, so far, was not showing any visible signs of growth, and frowned. She had planted all of her seeds exactly the same way, with the same bag of dirt, had cared for them all equally, given them the same amounts of water and plant food, so why was one little guy not growing? She ran her finger lightly over the dirt, searching by touch, just in case her eye had missed something....

The doorbell rang. Shannon grabbed a paper towel to wipe her hands as she hurried to see who was there, her heart beating in anticipation, hoping it was Bryce and not some boy wanting her to subscribe to the *Southlakes Gazette*.

The man standing outside her door was not a boy, but he definitely was not Bryce, either. Shannon's heart continued to thud, now with dread. Why was he here? He had not sought out her company in ten years. Why would he do so now?

"Clinton," she said, wrapping herself immediately in a cloak of numbness. She did not invite him inside.

He came in, anyway. "We need to talk," he said, walking around her into the living room. Shannon didn't miss his obvious maneuver not to touch her. In the ten years since Darla had shown up in Southlakes, Clinton had only touched Shannon when he was too drunk to stop himself. From the first time he had found out about Shannon's unsavory background, he had always sought his physical satisfaction elsewhere, and as time passed, Shannon had been more relieved than anything else. Being a Stewart, Clinton had always been extremely discreet; Shannon had learned to be satisfied with that.

She followed him into the living room, knowing how much it was costing him to be there. She was living proof, at least in his mind, that Clinton Stewart had been made to look like a fool. Besides, he was a result of generations of social conditioning. How would it look if a Stewart *chose* to associate with a prostitute's daughter?

"Say what you've come to say," she said, frightened by his uncharacteristic visit. She remained in the entryway to the living room. Clinton crossed over to the far side of the room—as far away from her as he could get—as if he thought being from the wrong side of the tracks was a contagious disease. She would have thought she would be numb to the pain after all these years, but Clinton's obvious distaste for her still hurt. Not because she loved him, but because he had once thought her worthy enough to be his wife, because she had once wanted nothing more than to please him enough to remain his wife.

"I want you to give up this craziness and sign the children over to my care. It would be best for everyone, including yourself, Shannon, if we can keep this among ourselves. You stand to lose more from a dirty court battle than we do."

Shannon's stomach cramped with apprehension. She had seen it as a good sign that Clinton had not already done something to try to avoid public scandal. She had thought that meant that maybe, just maybe, he was not sure of himself, that he would be the one to give up when she did not. Was he only now believing, with the court date looming so close, that she was actually going to go through with things? And did he honestly think he could come in here and talk her out of it? He did not know her at all if he thought anything short of death would keep her from fighting for her children.

She lifted her chin to meet him eye to eye, praying for strength. "That remains to be seen, Clinton. I will never willingly give up my children."

He thrust his hands into his pockets. Shannon wondered if he ever got hot in his proper suits and ties, and if Stewarts were allowed to sweat. When she had first known him he had still been little more than a boy, but even the athletic clothes he had worn then had looked starchy on him. She had teased him when he'd insisted on changing sometimes two and three times a day. But as she looked back on it, she could never remember him sharing the joke.

"Be reasonable, Shannon. Not only will you lose the hearing, you will never be able to hold your head up in this town again." His tone was carefully modulated, but Shannon knew him well enough to recognize the telltale sign of ire, as he rocked back and forth on his heels. The Stewarts had succeeded in suffocating most of Clinton's emotions in the cradle, but they had failed to completely suppress his temper. They had managed, however, to teach him to cover it well.

She braced herself against his words, afraid of them, afraid for her children. She didn't reply. She couldn't. There might be complete truth in what he said.

Clinton obviously took her silence as a sign of capitulation. His eyes lost their feral gleam. "I will see that you get a settlement big enough to start over in a new town, Shannon," he offered.

Anger rose within her, suffocating her fear, cloaking her worries with strength. It wasn't so much the fact that he thought he could buy her off that infuriated her; she expected that. In Clinton's frame of reference, anyone with her meager background could be bought. But the fact that he wanted her in a new town struck her like lightning. Did he expect her *never* to see her kids again? Even if she lost?

"I don't want your money any more now than I did two years ago," she said, gritting her teeth to keep from shrieking at him. "And even if I did, we both know I would never see it. You didn't even send me the support for *your* children that the court ordered you to send. I'm not the fool you take me for, Clinton."

She expected to see him start rocking back and forth again in his expensive leather shoes and was alarmed when he stood still and smiled instead.

"But that's where you're wrong, Shannon. There has been a bank account in your name since the day the divorce was final. And on the fifth of every month, a deposit was made in the exact amount you were due to receive."

"Then the money is still there, proof that I haven't touched it," Shannon said as her stomach muscles tightened another notch. Clinton was many things, but stupid was not one of them. He would not be telling her this unless he were sure she could not benefit from the information.

Clinton slid his hands into his pockets, riffling his change, something he always did when he was feeling particularly confident.

"I was in talking with Barry Collins down at the bank, you remember him, don't you?" Clinton asked.

Of course she remembered him. Clinton had spent more time with his select, "respectable" friends during their marriage than he had at home. Collins, Williams and Stewart—the three musketeers.

"Get on with it," she said through clenched teeth, wrapping her arms around her middle, attempting to soothe the pressure that was threatening to double her over with pain.

"It's just that Barry happened to mention that the money was withdrawn like clockwork."

"But that's impossible. I never even knew about the account. How could I possibly have taken money out of it?"

Clinton shrugged, no longer smiling. "It's not for me to determine how, only to show that it was done. You see, Shannon, it's like I've been telling you for years. You picked the wrong man to be your patsy. You may have managed to make a fool out of me when I was younger, but I will never allow you to do so again." His eyes were sharp again. "Now, I *need* those kids. And I intend to have them." If Shannon had not been reeling from the information he had just given her, she might have heard the desperation that slipped in and out of his tone.

"My patience is running out, Shannon. Remember, it was you who walked out on me in front of this whole town, forcing me to admit not only to my parents, but to Judge Donovan, that I'd been duped by a seventeen-year-old tart. I've had to endure pitying looks when I walk downtown, or into one of my stores, for more than two years now. No one's going to fault me if my next offer to you is not nearly as generous.''

Shannon was frightened, more frightened than she had ever been in her life. She felt as though her chest were shrinking, squeezing the air out of her lungs, forcing her heart to beat much too hard. But still, she would not back down.

He left without another word, walking around her in the entryway, ever careful not to so much as brush against her.

Shannon held herself together until she heard the click of her front door and then she stumbled through the living room on trembling limbs and sank down to the edge of the couch. Her back was straight, her muscles held firmly in check, as if by controlling her body, she could control the pain. She could not allow the tears to fall. She might not ever be able to make them stop.

He had her. She was going to lose the twins. It was her word against his, always, and she knew who would be believed. Clinton and his family owned more than half the town and employed the other half. She had no idea how he had managed to deposit money in her name and then have it disappear, but she did not doubt for a minute that if he said he had proof, he did.

Moving like an automaton she picked up the phone, dialed, and waited for the ring to be answered.

"Tub of Suds!"

"Ory? It's me. Clinton just left. I don't know if I'm going to make it in tonight. You think Sheila can cover for me?"

"'Course, no problem. She owes you. You gonna be okay?"

"I'm not sure just now, Ory, can I get back to you?" Part of her registered the absurdity of her reply, but it was the best she could do.

"You need some help?"

She waited while he coughed. "No, but thanks. I think I just need some time," she told him. And it was true. She did need time, about ten years of it. Then the twins would be too old to be hurt by Clinton Stewart.

"You got it. You'll get that ex of yours, too. You just wait and see," he said.

Shannon was not so sure, but she wasn't going to take up any more of Ory's time debating with him about it. It wouldn't solve anything. Ory had no way of knowing what the judge's decision was going to be. With a weary "thanks" she hung up the phone.

She remained perched on the edge of the couch, stiffly upright, warding off the world and agonizing for her children. What was going to happen to them? Would their spirits shrivel up and die in the Stewart mansion? Was she really going to lose them? And when she did, would they ever trust her again? Would she ever see them again?

Shannon suddenly jumped up from the couch, grabbed her keys, and ran from the apartment. The walls of her life were closing in on her and she had to get away... to find some fresh air... to breathe.

"SHERIFF? LINE TWO," Deputy Adams called from the dispatch desk Tuesday afternoon. Bryce's shift had been over an hour ago, but a cop was always on duty.

Bryce punched the second blinking button on his phone as soon as he unburied it from the mound of paperwork he was sorting through. "Sheriff Donovan here."

"Bryce? It's Aunt Martha." The unusually hesitant tones of his aunt came over the line.

Bryce stiffened. "Aunt Martha? What's wrong? Are you all right?"

"Yes, Bryce, I'm fine. Everything's fine, it's just that something a little strange is going on. I told Oliver about it when he phoned from the office a few minutes ago, and he thought I ought to give you a call.''

Bryce leaned back in his chair, propping one ankle against his knee. If Oliver wasn't rushing home, Aunt Martha was not in danger. "What is it?" he asked, curiosity replacing concern.

"Well, there's this strange car parked on our property, close to the pine forest. I wouldn't even have noticed except Babsy got out and I had to chase her down...."

Bryce smiled as he pictured his plump aunt chasing the little dog through a field of weeds. His smile turned back to a frown as he realized what else she had said.

"What kind of strange car?" he asked, all business now.

"I don't know the make, but it's a four-door, it's blue and it's empty."

"You didn't go near it, did you?" he demanded.

There was a brief silence on the other end of the line and Bryce stifled a groan. "Well, yes, I did, actually. I wanted to be sure no one needed a doctor or anything."

"It's not smart to approach an unfamiliar, illegally parked car, even in Southlakes." Bryce felt obligated to scold. His aunt was entirely too trusting, and though that was one of the things he loved about her, it also worried him sometimes. Not even small towns were as safe as they used to be.

"I know, dear, but I did get the license number," she said as if that made up for her foolishness.

"Let me have it, then, and I'll find out what we've got. In the meantime, it might not be a bad idea to stay inside," Bryce instructed, knowing that Aunt Martha would never stand for staying inside if Babsy needed to go out.

He typed the digits into the computer himself as soon as he hung up the phone, and then tapped his thumbs impatiently against his desk while he waited for the corresponding registration information to appear on his screen. It was probably nothing. Kids, most likely, out in the woods necking, but with his aunt out at the farm all alone, he would feel better knowing for sure.

The machine in front of him beeped, and then lines of fluorescent green letters began to scroll across the screen. He paused the information as soon as it reached owner identification.

Bryce's heart began to hammer in earnest then. Aunt Martha was not in danger. Kids were not necking in the woods. But something was definitely wrong. The computer had just flashed out Shannon Stewart's car registration.

Bryce straightened his desk, checked out with Adams, changed into the jeans and T-shirt he kept in his locker and was in his car heading out of town ten minutes after Aunt Martha's call. He had no idea why Shannon was trespassing on his aunt's property, but he knew he was not going to rest until he found out.

CHAPTER FOURTEEN

SHE WAS UNDERNEATH the apple tree, her back resting against the trunk, her knees pulled up tightly against her chest, her head lowered. Her soft, slender arms were wrapped around her knees, as if she was giving herself the comfort she wouldn't allow herself to seek from anyone else. Sunlight passed through small gaps in the leaves and blossoms above her, glinting off her long dark hair like tears.

Bryce slowed as he reached the clearing, wondering, all of a sudden, what he was going to say to her, how his being there was going to make her feel when she so clearly believed she was all alone. She obviously had not heard his approach and he was uncomfortably aware that he was invading her privacy, despite the fact that she was trespassing in *his* meadow.

He heard what could have been a sniffle and stiffened. If Shannon was crying, something definitely was not right. The only time he had ever seen her shed a tear had been the day he had taken her bruised daughter out of her arms. Yet he knew nothing was wrong with the twins this time; he would have been notified.

Wrenching sobs rose, disrupting the natural peacefulness of the meadow, sending Bryce into action. Pine cones crunched beneath his feet as he approached the apple tree, warning her that she was no longer alone, but she never lifted her head from her knees, so lost in her pain that she did not know or, perhaps, was beyond caring that he was there.

He slid down beside her, pulling her against him without hesitation, cradling her shuddering body against his chest. She was like a rag doll in his arms, neither resisting his hold nor moving into it, as her sobs continued. Her lack of reaction worried him. "Shannon? I'm here, hon," he said, uncaring how inane the words sounded. "Sssh. It's all right. Everything's going to be okay," he continued, kissing the top of her head. The words meant nothing. He had no way of knowing if things would be okay or not without knowing first what was wrong, but he didn't know how else to comfort her. Her slim, feminine form, racked by hiccupping sobs, continued to tremble against him.

He braced himself against the tree and pulled her more fully into his arms against his side. He stroked her hair, continuing to whisper words of reassurance, dropping an occasional kiss near her ear, trying desperately to reach her, all too aware that he was out of his depth.

Moans of pain erupted from within her and Bryce swallowed thickly. He slid his hands along her back, caressing her thighs, her arms, her neck, his nonsexual strokes touching her everywhere, spurred instinctively by an urgency to reach her, to give her an awareness of the reality around her, to make her feel something besides the despair that was obviously controlling her. "Sssh. It's okay, Shannon. I'm here. You're not alone anymore," he promised her, speaking gently but firmly. He did not even question his compulsion to stay with her, to make sure that if she was traveling to hell and back, she did not go alone. A murder on Main Street could not have taken him away from Shannon right then.

"Let it out, honey, just let it all out. I'm here with you. I'm right here...."

He's here. Bryce is here. As soon as the thought gradually registered, Shannon held on to it, using it to fight her way out of the tunnel of grief that had consumed her. She had no idea how Bryce had come to be there, to be holding on to her so fervently, but the whys and hows didn't matter. All that mattered were his arms around her, his voice in her ear and the fact that having him there made the world so much less threatening.

As she came slowly back to awareness, she moved her hands over the firm muscles of his chest where she had been lying so listlessly. He was warm and solid. She felt him still beneath her touch, as if he was afraid that moving might send her off again. Filled with a rush of wonder at his caring, she slid her hands around his waist, clutching him desperately, then buried her nose in the security of his damp shirt. She inhaled his familiar woodsy scent.

"Oh, Bryce," she said, drawing out his name with a wealth of meaning she could not put into words. "Thank you" could in no way express what it meant to her that he had pulled her out of a void so deep, so dark, so terrifying, that she had lost all sense of time and place.

"Shh. It's okay," he said against the top of her head. Her scalp tingled where his breath brushed against it.

For a moment, Shannon willed his words to be the truth. For just a second or two, she allowed herself to float along on the tide of security he had wrapped around her. She lay in his embrace like a child seeking reassurance that a frightening nightmare was only a dream. He continued to stroke her slowly, offering that reassurance. The soft breeze in the meadow dried the tears upon her cheeks.

"What happened?" His words shattered the illusion Shannon had created to provide the calm after her storm, but somehow Bryce's arms around her, his body beneath her, cushioned her return to reality.

She lessened her hold on him, but did not sit up. With her head still snuggled into the warmth of his chest, she moved one hand from his back to pick at a piece of lint on his shirt. "Clinton...came...by," she admitted, hesitant to say too much. Bryce was there for her, but there was no guarantee he would stay, no promises that he was not going to go away and leave her stranded. Yet she needed someone to talk to, someone to confide in. She needed *him*.

His hand stilled in her hair. "And?" he prompted.

"How much time do you have?" she asked dryly, playing with a little string hanging from the seam of his pocket.

He tilted up her chin until she was looking straight into his deep brown eyes. "As much time as it takes." He voiced the words, while his eyes made the promise.

Shannon held his gaze for several seconds and then closed her eyes, searching for a way to begin. She remembered how hard it had been for him to tell her about the circumstances that had led to his father's death, and the memory gave her the push she needed. Maybe this sharing of one's deepest self was what falling in love was really about, not the hungry groping for bodies that she had always assumed it to be.

"He came by to remind me that he's more powerful than I am," she finally confessed, returning her attention to the string on his shirt.

"How so?" She felt the rumble of Bryce's voice beneath her ear on his chest.

Shannon took a deep breath. "I guess for you to understand I need to explain a few things." She committed herself more fully to the telling. With each breath that he took, she took comfort from the movement like a baby being rocked into a semblance of security.

Bryce moved his hands to clasp them together behind her waist. "Okay." He was assuring her of his willingness to listen, but he wasn't pulling anything from her. Once again, Shannon was grateful to him.

"I'm sure you've been told how I grew up," she began, twisting the loose string around her index finger.

Bryce unwrapped her finger and then threaded his right hand with her left, bringing them to rest, clasped together, on his chest. "I'd like to hear it from you," he said, offering her the opportunity to explain herself, an opportunity she had always been denied in the past. She left her hand in his possession.

"My mother was raised in a shack with eight little brothers and sisters in the slums of Havenville. She hated it, of course, and was determined to provide herself with the luxuries she had missed out on, come hell or high water. With no formal schooling, the only thing she had going for her was her looks, and she felt no shame whatsoever in using them to her advantage. I was the one mistake she ever made. She never told me who my father was—if she even knew—but I always suspected that she kept me because she thought I might give her some hold over him someday." Shannon paused, not sure how to continue, how much to say, what to leave unsaid.

Bryce remained silent, as if leaving the choice entirely up to her. His thumb caressed the back of her hand, but otherwise their bodies were still, her hip nestled against the side of his, one of her breasts pressing against his chest.

"Needless to say, there were enough men in and out of our house to fill the United States Army." She forced the words out, past the memories that they conjured up.

Everywhere her body touched his, Bryce could feel her tension and knew how hard it was for her to talk to him. He hurt for her, but he forced himself to remain silent, to ask no questions. He had to know, but it had to come from her voluntarily, or it might as well not come at all.

"As I grew old enough to understand what was going on, Darla started scheduling her appointments during the times I was away at school, and later, at work." Shannon fell silent, pulling her hand from his to start in again on the string hanging from his pocket.

Bryce allowed her to fiddle, understanding her need for the diversion, wishing he had one of his own. As much as he was compelled to know her secrets, Bryce wanted to stop her, to put a halt to her words before they could escape, before they could hurt them anymore. He felt physically ill at the picture she was drawing. He closed his eyes and saw her, a pretty, impressionable, dark-haired little girl with her big, violet eyes, watching her mother parading yet another strange man through the house. Opening his eyes, he tried to banish the image, but it wouldn't go away. He didn't even want to think about that pretty little girl developing into a desirable young woman....

"Then one night, when I was seventeen, I got sick at work." Her words were coming in a rush now, as if she had to get them out quickly or have them remain stuck inside her forever. He braced himself, knowing instinctively that he was not going to like what he was about to hear.

"My boss drove me home. There was a strange car in the driveway, but I was too sick to notice. I barely made it to the bathroom before I lost everything I had eaten that day. By the time I was finished, I was almost too weak to stand up, but somehow I made it to my bedroom before I passed out. I never gave a thought to Darla, or heard the noises that were coming from her bedroom. I only heard about them later, when she berated me for being so careless."

She paused again as her voice grew weak with suppressed emotion and Bryce swallowed thickly past the lump in his own throat. He couldn't move. He could only sit and wait, and listen.

"The next thing I remember is...hands...big hands...pulling at the waistband of my pants." Her speech was sporadic, wooden. She was pulling back into the shell that saw her through life's worst moments.

Bryce had had enough. He knew what was coming now, knew he was hearing about her "compromising situation" and he was no longer sure he could stomach the details. "Stop, honey. It's all right. You don't have to say any more," he said, pulling her farther up against him, settling her in the crook of his left shoulder.

"I fought him." Her words continued to come as if they were being driven out of her. All inflection was gone from her voice. Bryce forced himself to listen to her, to live through it with her, to be there for her this time.

"He ripped my shirt...he grabbed at me." Tears trickled slowly down her cheeks, seeping into his shirt.

His hand froze against her. He was afraid to move, to make any new contact with her body, afraid that she would associate his touch with the memories she was reliving. He was not sure he was going to make it through the next minutes without becoming physically ill or slamming his fist through the tree behind him, or both. His heart was pounding so hard he could hear it behind his ears.

"But before he could get what he was after, he was gone. Someone had pulled him off me, a cop."

The relief that flooded through Bryce made him almost giddy, more proud than ever that he was a policeman. He felt an instant, brotherly love for his fellow officer who had been there to take care of Shannon long before Bryce had met her.

He was not sure which came first, the realization that, though she had been saved the humiliating degradation that had almost befallen her, she had still been convicted of prostitution, or her next words.

"I had never been lucky before, not once, but I was never so glad in my life. I lay there on my bed and figured out that my share of luck had just been storing up, waiting for a time when I really needed it."

Bryce's stomach knotted as he heard the bitterness in her voice. That should have been a happy statement.

"But the joke was on me, see, 'cause the policeman wasn't there to save me, but to arrest me. He didn't stop the jerk because he was trying to help me, but because he did not want me to have the opportunity to satisfy my *customer*."

Bryce sat stunned, digesting her words, afraid of what he knew had to follow. Had that been it? Had a near rape to an innocent teenager been the grounds that constituted a conviction for prostitution?

Shannon pulled away from him, as if suddenly remembering who Bryce was, what he was, and he let her go. The regard for his fellow officer turned sour, the pride in his profession into nausea.

She stood up and walked into the sunshine, lifting her face to its brilliance. If he never saw her again, Bryce would always remember how she looked at that moment. Even dressed as she was in worn gray sweatpants and an old blue T-shirt, she was a picture of untouched femininity. He wondered how he had ever dared touch her, kiss her. Her breasts heaved as she took in a long, slow breath, and then settled as she released it again.

"They had been trying to nail my mother for months, and she let me take the rap. She testified against me," Shannon said, meeting his eyes for the first time since she had begun her confession. "I was underage. They'd go much easier on me than they would've on her."

Bryce could not turn away from her, but neither could he keep the piercing anger from his expression. "What about the guy?'' he asked, hoping without hope that somehow the tragic situation had been remedied.

He hated. the bitter laugh that came from deep within Shannon. ''Of course he corroborated my mother's story. Why wouldn't he? His other choice was to face a charge for attempted rape. He also happened to own the dry-goods store in town, and guess who folks believed? Not the seventeen-year-old daughter of the local tramp, I can promise you that.''

''Wasn't there any evidence?''

''By the time someone got around to thinking about that, I'd scrubbed myself raw trying to get rid of the feel of that filthy man's touch. Not that it would have mattered, anyway. That a sexual act had almost occurred was obvious. The question was whether or not I had invited it with the intent to make money.''

Bryce hated to ask the next question. But he was a cop. He knew procedure. If he ever had to defend Shannon against these charges, he needed to have all of the angles covered. Besides, if he didn't ask, he would always wonder, and he never wanted Shannon to have to speak about those events again after today, not unless she chose to. ''What about a medical exam?'' he asked, hoping she would understand what he was asking without him having to embarrass her further by spelling it out.

''No one asked for one,'' Shannon said. She looked toward the sky again, as if looking for the freshness she had not found in her life on earth. ''Like I said, the sexual act itself wasn't even an issue. Everyone knew that the cop pulled the guy off me before he could finish what he was doing, so there was no point in exploring any further. Even if an exam proved my virginity, it didn't mean I wasn't selling sex that night.''

Bryce remained seated, one knee pulled up to his chest. He picked a blade of grass, tore it into pieces and picked another. "So you ran away, made a new identity for yourself and started over," he summed up, hating the fact that she had been taught such a bitter lesson, but at the same time admiring the grit that she had shown, her refusal to give up, to give in, to be the kind of woman the world was trying to make her be.

He looked up, meeting her gaze, giving her the understanding she so desperately needed, but for which she would never ask. "I couldn't stay in that town, Bryce. People were scandalized after the trial. Mothers wouldn't let their daughters near me, or their sons, either, for that matter. One girl who had tried to befriend me in school actually crossed the street rather than walk by me. But the worst part was the men. Oh, they stood beside their wives in public and scorned me, but that didn't stop them from trying to get me alone. It got to the point where innuendos rang in my ears from morning to night. I was afraid I was going to go crazy, or accept myself for what they saw me to be, so I ran."

Bryce threw away the blade of grass he had been destroying. "Come here," he said, patting the ground beside him.

Shannon moved slowly forward, but she didn't sit next to him as he had requested. She sat down in front of him instead, far enough away that he couldn't reach her.

"I lied, Bryce. I lied to everyone here, but I never meant to hurt anyone. Never. All I ever wanted was to be a good person, and to be treated like one. I used to devour books from the library on etiquette and manners. I figured that if I could portray myself as different from my mother, then people would see me differently. I hitchhiked a ride one day after I'd left Havenville and heard on the news about a fire in a textile mill in the U.P. and the family who died in it. I ended up in Southlakes a few days later and fell in love with it. People were actually friendly to me, and when Clinton asked me where I was from, I just kind of took that textile family for my own. I hadn't planned to do it, it just sort of happened.''

Bryce leaned forward, reaching for her hands, but she resisted. And then he remembered that there was more. All of this had been leading up to something. Something that had to do with Stewart's power. Something that had upset her today.

''When Clinton Stewart asked me to marry him, I was so happy I went back to the room I was renting and cried for hours. I was finally being accepted as the kind of woman I wanted to be, I was finally being given the respect most girls take for granted, and I promised myself that I'd be the best wife he could ever find.''

''Did you love him?'' He didn't want to know, but he had to know. He didn't understand how Shannon could ever have been in love with someone as lacking in compassion as Clinton Stewart.

She shrugged. ''What did I know about love? I knew enough about men to know that Clinton was physically aroused every time he came near me. Yet, when I demurred, he never got angry with me. He offered to marry me instead. I loved him for that. I tried to tell him I wasn't sure if I was *in* love yet, but he said people put way too much stock in love. He said that we had all the right ingredients to make a successful marriage, and that a stronger affection would grow in time. I believed him.'' She turned her head to the side, looking out over the meadow, no longer meeting Bryce's eyes. ''In the beginning, Clinton was very attentive to me. I may have been little more than a possession, but I was a highly valued one. And I was a member of the most reputable family in town. I could walk down Main Street and everyone would smile at me and say hello, they would invite me to lunch, or to sit on a board for a charity dance, instead of sneering and looking the other way. I did my best to please my husband, I was treated with appreciation, and I was happier than I had ever been. All of that was worth way more to me than the passion I had only read about in books. I wasn't even sure it existed, anyway.''

''So what happened?''

''Darla showed up shortly after I found out I was pregnant with Mindi and Mike. She'd been looking for me for months. Having discovered she had a conscience, she wanted to make reparation for what she had done to me. But instead, she destroyed the life I had made for myself. She didn't know about the lies I had told, and when Clinton found out he was actually married to the daughter of a tramp, he saw red. He figured that being my mother's daughter, I had to be like her and that I'd married him for financial gain. I tried to explain, of course, but he dismissed my pleas as attempts to hold on to his money. He believes I deliberately set out to play him for a fool, and as if that wasn't bad enough, I had tricked him into fathering tarnished children. He was horrified when he realized his heirs would have Darla's blood mingled with his. I had done the unforgivable. I had tainted the Stewart name. It's something he's never gotten over, or forgiven me for.''

''So why did the marriage last another eight years?'' Bryce asked.

''Because of the twins. I knew I could never provide for them as well as Clinton could, but I couldn't leave them to be raised without love.''

''Why do you think he let you stay, if he despised you so much?''

Shannon pulled on the elastic at the leg of her sweats. ''I know why. How would it look if his marriage failed? You have to remember that to a Stewart, appearances are just about everything. As Clinton saw it, I'd stained Stewart blood, but as long as we stayed married, as long as we were cordial to each other in public, no one would know. We had our own wing in the Stewart mansion, and Clinton slept in another room and never spoke to me in private unless he had to, but he insisted that we keep up appearances whenever anyone else was around—including his parents. They didn't find out about any of it until the divorce.''

Bryce mulled over all that she had told him, hearing what she wouldn't say—how difficult it must have been for her to live with Clinton's disdain, how difficult to keep up appearances of an affection that no longer existed—and all because she wouldn't rob her children of the security they deserved.

''So why did you leave him two years ago?'' he asked, bringing up the part of the story that still didn't fit.

She looked away, out over the meadow, toward the forest beyond. The sun was getting lower in the sky, shining on the back of her head, giving the impression that she was wearing a halo. Bryce didn't know if that was an omen or a warning.

''Shortly after the twins were born, Clinton started to drink more than he should have. Some evenings he would just sit in the den with a decanter of whiskey and stare out the window. Then he stopped staying home, but he didn't stop drinking. Twice, he was stopped for drunk driving. His buddy, your Deputy Williams, took care of a couple of charges that had come up against him, which put Clinton in his debt. One night, shortly after the second charge, Drew came over and he and Clinton started drinking. After they cracked the second bottle, Drew confessed to Clinton that he'd always been attracted to me. Clinton was drunk enough to think he could pay the debt to his friend by serving me up. He knew Drew would keep things quiet.'' Her voice was a monotone once again.

Bryce stiffened, remembering Oliver's statement that Clinton had caught Shannon with one of his friends, but that the accusation had never been proven. He had dismissed it long ago as hearsay, but had it been more than that? Had Shannon been forced to give away favors after all? He felt sick at heart, angry at a world that could ask such things of a woman who only wanted to provide for her children.

"So you left," he said, not wanting to hear the details of Clinton's sickening offer. He was afraid that with two drunk men, Shannon would have had no way of escaping. He was afraid he was going to beat Deputy Williams into a pulp the next time he saw him.

Shannon looked up, her velvety eyes burning into him. "So, as soon as I realized what was happening, I grabbed Mindi, locked the three of us in Mike's room until Clinton and Drew passed out, and then we left," she stated, leaving no doubt about what she did *not* do. Bryce wanted to take her in his arms and cherish her as she deserved to be cherished. He wanted her to know that he was proud of her, of her ability to take care of herself. He contented himself with breathing normally again.

"Why didn't you leave town after the divorce?" he asked. If nothing else, at least he was getting many of the answers that had been eluding him for weeks.

"I couldn't take my children," she said, as if the possibility of leaving without them didn't even exist. "Clinton had joint custody," she explained as he raised his brow in question.

"And you didn't fight him when he neglected to pay child support, as long as he agreed to leave you alone," he summed up, remembering her words in his car that day.

Shannon nodded, gratified by his understanding, but still aware that there was more to come. Was he still going to believe her when she told him the particulars of Clinton's visit? Bryce was her friend, there was no doubting that now, but he was still a cop. Could she tell him about Clinton's proof of bank transactions that had never taken place and expect him to believe her?

CHAPTER FIFTEEN

THE HARD GROUND beneath the apple tree was beginning to take its toll on Bryce's tailbone and he leaned sideways, bracing his weight on the elbow of his good arm, getting more comfortable. He had been waiting much too long for some answers and for the ability to see a way clear to helping her, to stop now.

"So what happened today?" he asked, drawing her out, needing to know what they were dealing with, so he could determine how best to proceed.

Shannon leaned back, too, placing both hands behind her, supporting her weight. "Clinton's going to insist he's been paying support all along," she said.

Bryce frowned, leaning forward while he pulled up a weed. Shannon liked the way his hair rose from beneath his collar with the movement. She didn't know what it was about him that made him so attractive to her. Lord knew, she had seen enough men in her life to have become immune to the pull of rugged masculinity, but somehow everything about Bryce's looks pleased her.

He looked across at her, chewing the stem of his weed. "So what makes that any different from a week ago?" he finally asked.

Shannon shrugged one shoulder. "He's pretty convincing," she admitted. "Don't you see, whatever he says will be believed? He says he paid me and I believe he'll even lie about it in court if it comes to that. It's his word against mine." She was scaring herself anew with her words. She could claim she knew nothing about that bank account, but if Clinton had some sort of proof, who would believe her?

"As long as he doesn't have any canceled checks with your signature, as long as he has no receipts, or any other proof that you received that money, his words will mean nothing," Bryce assured her.

Shannon turned onto her side, mirroring his pose, facing him, meeting his gaze directly. "What if he does have proof?" she asked, taking one of the biggest gambles of her life.

She felt as though she had just jumped from a plane without a parachute as she saw his expression cloud with doubt. She held her breath and watched as the doubt was chased away by anger and then finally replaced with confusion. His words when they came were quiet, controlled.

"Would you mind explaining that?"

If she was not so worried, Shannon would have smiled with relief at his carefully phrased question. He was not demanding. He was not shutting her out. She had not lost him, yet.

"I wish I could. I have never received, taken, or otherwise touched a cent of Stewart money since I left Clinton, but he says he opened a special account for me two years ago, that he's been depositing my child support there on the fifth of each month, and that Barry Collins, son of the president of Southlakes Bank, has proof that the money is being withdrawn like clockwork. Logically, my head tells me there's no way they can prove I took money from an account that I didn't even know existed, but Barry and Clinton have been buddies since they were in diapers. With Barry's knowledge of, and access to, bank procedures, who knows what they could have done?"

"Clinton's probably just bluffing, Shannon. I assume he had a purpose for telling you about this supposed account?"

Shannon did smile then, briefly. Bryce's first instinct had been to make sense out of the nonexistent account, not to suspect that the account existed. He might change his mind when he had more time to think about it, but she would always know that, at least for a brief time, he had believed in her.

"Yeah, he had a purpose. He wants me to give up the custody battle before it goes to court. But I don't think he was bluffing. I know him too well. He wouldn't have told me about that account unless he was feeling pretty confident about his evidence. That's what scares me."

"But don't you see, Shan, he knows you, too, and he's just trying to scare you into doing what he wants. He obviously knew just how to do it. If you're really worried, you can call Brad Channing in the morning and have him check it out. Since he can narrow it down to one account now, as opposed to all of Clinton's various financial dealings, Channing shouldn't have much trouble locating it—especially if it has your name on it. I think you'll find that no such account exists. With modern day banking security systems, it'd be virtually impossible to prove that you've been taking money when you haven't."

"I hope you're right," Shannon said, not at all convinced. Bryce had not spent years witnessing all of the "impossible" things Clinton could do. All you had to do was have the right people in your debt....

"He's just trying to get at you, Shannon. Since he's so positive he's going to win one way or the other, what other purpose could he have had for today's visit?" Bryce asked, more as if he was proving his point than expecting an answer.

Shannon picked a weed similar to the one Bryce was chewing, stuck the stem just past her lips, and bit down gently. Its fresh, minty taste surprised her. She continued to chew as she considered his question, thinking back over

Clinton's visit that afternoon. Now that she was calm, and able to look at the conversation logically, Shannon suddenly began to wonder if maybe Bryce had not just unknowingly hit on something.

She had wondered all along why Clinton had started this custody fight. Why now, after years of shafting her and the twins had he suddenly taken his parents' point of view and decided the twins should be raised as Stewarts? As she replayed their conversation in her mind more calmly, something clicked for the first time. Clinton had said that he *needed* the twins, not that he wanted them. There had been almost a note of desperation in his tone. In anyone else, herself included, that might not have been so unusual. But Clinton was a Stewart, and the only thing Stewarts valued were their reputations and their money. So which was at stake, she wondered. Which did he need Mike and Mindi to help him secure? Nothing more had happened to change his reputation, so that only left . . .

"Maybe Clinton's parents are behind this whole thing," she ventured tentatively, piecing a few things together for the first time. She tried not to let herself get too excited as, suddenly, it all began making sense. Clinton had never wanted custody of his children in the past, but the elder Stewarts had made no secret of the fact that they believed their grandchildren should be raised by Stewarts.

Bryce pulled his stem out of his mouth, obviously surprised. "I was under the impression that they wanted the twins all along, so why should Clinton all of a sudden start listening to them?"

Shannon thought about the bank account. Was it possible that Clinton had needed it to appear that he was paying her, because he was actually using the money himself? Maybe, instead of paying her out of his own funds, he had set up monthly withdrawals from the Stewart fortune, the fortune his father still controlled, to be deposited into an account for her. An account that, if he had access to it, would increase his monthly allowance considerably. Did he *need* that money, while at the same time needing proof that he did not use it?

It had never even occurred to her that Clinton Stewart, one of *the* Stewarts, would ever be short of cash. But why else would Clinton risk concocting a fake bank account unless he had to have the money she was supposed to be getting? Tampering with bank records was committing a federal offense, not something one did lightly.

"Because they control the money," she said, speaking to herself as much as to Bryce. Excited chills spread up into her scalp. She wasn't sure what, if anything, this hunch could do for her, but she was eager to explore the possibilities, hopeful that maybe, just maybe, she was coming up with a way to win after all.

"The money?"

"Mmm-hmm," Shannon answered, thinking it all through. "I've suspected for years that Clinton likes to gamble. He seemed to go through money in large amounts, and he could never pass up the challenge of a wager. He even took bets on whether I was carrying a boy or a girl. That one was a bust," she related with a sad little smile.

"Anyway, maybe his hobby has turned into something more," she continued. "Maybe he lost more than he bargained for. Where would he go? His parents, of course. They'd help him, if only to keep things quiet. But what if the Stewarts took a gamble themselves, and only agreed to let him dip into the family pot if they got something in return?"

Bryce nodded, a gleam in his eye. "The twins," he said, as if it all made sense.

"The twins," Shannon confirmed.

Bryce looked across at her, approval shining from his warm dark eyes. "You'd make quite a detective, ma'am, with this sudden burst of deductive reasoning."

Shannon was insecure all of a sudden, popping her own bubble, afraid to trust that it would hold air long enough to save her. "You think it's possible?" she asked.

"Sure I think it's possible. What's more, I think it's probable. I'll do some checking around to see what I can sniff out right away, but we should probably request an extension on your hearing to give us enough time to move on this. If we can prove something like this, we stand a much better chance of convincing the town that Clinton Stewart has been lying to them all along."

"We?" Shannon asked, as thrilled by his choice of pronouns as by his message.

He reached over to rest his right hand behind her neck. "We," he repeated, pulling her forehead forward to rest against his. Shannon gazed into his eyes, so close to him that she could see the darker ring of brown that circled the iris. She saw the promises there, and allowed herself to hope.

Her worries were not over by far. Bryce's faith in her had not yet been tested. She would not know until they found what "proof" Clinton had whether or not Bryce would really remain true to her, whether or not the proof would be enough to sway his faith in her. And there was still the hearing to get through, but at that moment Shannon almost believed in the possibility that all four of them—Mindi, Mike, Bryce and herself—would come out unscathed.

Bryce saw hope enflame Shannon's beautiful eyes and knew he had to kiss her. She had finally opened up to him, making him greedy for more. It had only been a few days since he had tasted her, but those days seemed like decades to a man as hungry as he.

He captured her lips, opening his mouth over hers, caressing her, coaxing her to let him inside, to mesh with him, body, spirit and soul. He tasted the mint from the plant she had been chewing mixed with the salt from the tears she had shed. The fresh scent from her hair mingled with the smell of the pines, reminding him of the last time he had lain with her, whetting his appetite for more.

He explored her softness thoroughly, driven to be as much a part of her as he could possibly be. He rolled her over, onto her back, then lay half on top of her, burying his fingers in the lushness of her long, dark hair. He had had fantasies of that hair splayed across his pillow, surrounding her, surrounding him.

Her fingers crept around his neck, pressing him more firmly against her, deepening the kiss. She met his tongue boldly, and then shied away, teasing him in the way that women have been teasing men since the beginning of time. His body throbbed with desire such as he had never known before, but even as his body urged him to mount her, his heart urged that he wait. Merely possessing her body was not enough.

"I want you, Shannon, but I want you to want me, too," he said against her lips. As hot as he was for her, it had to be all or nothing, and the decision was hers.

Shannon heard the longing in his voice, the barely suppressed force that was driving him, and felt its impact in a place deep inside her where she had never before been touched. She knew what he was asking of her, and for the first time in her life, she was eager to give it, eager to take what he had to give. She had only been intimate with one other man in her life, but she did not question Bryce's right to have her as intimately as her husband had. It was necessary—necessary that Clinton not know her better than did the man she loved.

Her eyes flew open as she faced the truth she had just discovered, the truth that had allowed her to need him, to confide in him, to find comfort in his meadow, in him. She loved him. It was as simple and as complicated as that. Never in her adulthood had she loved another man, but it was the void that now provided her with the certainty that she was in love with Bryce Donovan.

She nodded, committing herself, surrendering to him without a single doubt. She needed Bryce to touch her, to erase the tawdry misconceptions she had about physical love, and replace them with the natural beauty she suddenly sensed it could bring.

He brushed the hair back from both sides of her face, laying her expression open before him, studying her intently. "Are you sure, love? This is what you want?"

The love in Shannon's heart overflowed. This was as it should be—she and Bryce together, in his meadow where no one could touch them, or point fingers or pass judgment. This was between the two of them and the powers that be, and Shannon was completely confident that in this exclusive company, what they were doing was not only right, but ordained.

"I'm sure, Bryce," she said tremulously, choked up with the powerful emotions raging through her.

Still he made no move to deepen their embrace. "I'm a man, not a saint, Shannon. If you need to change your mind, it has to be now." His voice was raspy, sending delicious shivers down her body.

She moved her hips against his thigh with a suggestiveness that surprised even her. "No, thank you," she replied, wondering when he was going to kiss her again.

He held himself stiffly above her. "Are you protected?" His voice was strained, as if he was about to choke.

Shannon felt heat creep up her face, amazed that she could brazenly welcome this man to her body, and still be embarrassed to tell him about starting the Pill that morning.

In the end, she just shook her head. Bryce reached into his back pocket with a trembling hand, yanked out his wallet and searched its folds almost frantically. Shannon held her breath for the seconds it took for his fingers to come up with two flattened foil wrappers.

She watched relief smooth Bryce's features, from the unwrinkling of his brow, through the hungry glint in his eyes, down the straight line of his nose, to the smiling fullness of his lips. Through a lifetime of habit, she searched for her own doubts, but came up with nothing.

He kissed her tenderly, reverently, sipping from her as if only she could satisfy his thirst. She lay pliantly beneath him, happy to have him showing her the way, trusting completely that he would see her safely home.

"You are so beautiful," he said huskily. Shannon smiled, accepting his compliment as a tribute, not a payment for something in return. She lay still, absorbing his touch as he ran lazy fingers along her arms, up over her shoulders to her neck, wanting to remember every moment of this time for the rest of her life.

"Not just here—" his palm grazed her breast "—but here." He laid his hand beneath her left breast, covering the pounding rhythm of her heart.

Shannon felt her chin begin to tremble, felt the tears spring to her eyes, but she did not attempt to hide her reaction from him. He met her eyes with a tender look and leaned over, kissing the tears from her lashes.

He continued his leisurely exploration of her body as if now that he knew for sure where he was going, he wanted to enjoy the journey. Despite the tension singing through her veins, Shannon wanted him to take all the time he desired, wanted their moments together, their first time together, to last as long as it could. She was in no hurry for the experience to end.

She quivered wherever he touched her, her ankles, the backs of her knees, her thighs, her fingers. He showed her surprising, exciting things about the body she had been living in for twenty-nine years.

He stopped long enough to remove his shirt and then moved his hands to the waistband of her T-shirt and slowly drew the material up over her torso. The fresh, warm air of the meadow caressed her stomach as he bared it to his gaze. She held her breath as her ribs were exposed, and began to tremble when she felt the material brush past her breasts and up over her head. Her bra quickly followed.

He cupped her breasts with both hands, caressing lightly.

"Do you like me to touch you this way?" he asked, searching her eyes for reassurance.

And suddenly she knew what these moments were all about. Bryce was going to take nothing, ask for nothing, that she could not give. He was doing everything he could not to remind her of other, less considerate times. But Shannon knew now that the quality of lovemaking had little to do with the degree of gentleness, it had to do with the degree of loving.

"I'd like it even more if you weren't quite so tentative," she told him with a hesitant smile. She wanted him to love her with all of his hunger visible for her to see. She wanted to feel the power she held over him.

With no further urging he lowered his mouth to her, rasping his afternoon beard against her skin.

"Ah, Shannon, how I've wanted to do this. You taste so sweet, so fresh," he groaned against her breast, and then he moved more fully on top of her, aligning himself with her, moving his mouth up to capture hers.

Shannon wrapped her arms around him, kissing him back, excited by the feel of his broad shoulders. His woodsy scent blended with the air in the meadow, and she inhaled deeply, wanting it to become a part of her. Whether she had him for an afternoon, or a lifetime, she needed this man.

She moaned in protest when he finally pulled away from her, but the moan died in her throat when he reached to open the button on the fly of his jeans, and then pull down the zipper with an exciting rasp. Shannon's limbs trembled as he rid himself of the denim and the briefs beneath them in one swoop, kicking off his tennis shoes as he stepped out of the pants. Every inch of Bryce's firmly muscled form spoke of pure masculinity.

Wordlessly he let her study him, to become familiar with him, and then he crouched at her feet, helping to take off the rest of her clothes. He looked at her with awe, making her proud of the body she usually tried to hide.

"Come to me," she whispered, holding her arms out to him.

He hesitated only long enough to use one of his foil packets and then lowered himself so that his body was just inches above hers, and took her lips in a kiss that communicated so much more than mere physical gratification. She was being consumed by a feeling she had never known before, something that took her out of rational thought and into a world of the purest emotions. Her hips thrust against him instinctively, completing their union greedily.

"Fly with it, love, let it happen." The words reached her within the swarm of sensation, giving her the encouragement she needed to grasp at the pleasure that was hanging just beyond her reach.

His thrusts grew heavier, helping her, and then she was soaring with him, high above their meadow in a delicious realm where pleasure was everywhere, anything was allowed, and loving him was so right. She had finally found the pot of gold at the end of her rainbow.

"It was your first time, wasn't it?" Bryce asked softly a few minutes later. He was lying beside her again, cradling her head in the crook of his left shoulder.

Reddening, Shannon knew immediately what he meant. "Mmm-hmm," she murmured against his chest.

"The bast—" He started to swear, but Shannon cut him off.

"Shh. It doesn't matter, not anymore. Don't you see?" she asked.

He tilted her chin and looked at her with eyes full of concern and sorrow, but he must have seen something in her easy expression, something he had not expected, her peace maybe, because his features suddenly cleared. "I guess I do see," he murmured softly, gazing at her with wonder. "You are one helluva woman, Shannon Stewart," he said, pulling her up to kiss her again. . . .

NOT WANTING TO CRAWL into his great big bed alone, Bryce drove straight to the station after he followed Shannon home much later that night. He had wanted to stay with her, but he hadn't asked, and hadn't been surprised when she didn't offer. It wasn't wrong for a grown woman to have a lover, but if the woman was Shannon Stewart, people would *make* something wrong with it. At least until the custody hearing was behind them, their affair was going to have be kept a secret between them. In the meantime, Bryce had his work cut out for him—starting with Clinton Stewart's alleged drunk-driving charges. He had learned long ago never to enter a battle unarmed.

He chatted with the deputy on night dispatch just long enough to keep from offending him, and then strode purposely down the hall to a storage room filled with file cabinets. He believed Shannon, but they still had an entire town to convince. His good name, maybe even his career, was going to be on the line when he stood up for her, and he needed some ammunition with which to defend both of them.

It took him an hour but he finally found what he was seeking. Not a police report, he had pretty much figured those wouldn't exist, but he had been searching with the hope that Deputy Williams was either too green, or too complacent, to have remembered to tamper with the dispatch records. On three separate occasions over the past four years, a report had been called in concerning a drunk-driving charge. The vehicle in question was a vintage white Jaguar, with a license plate registered to Clinton Samuel Stewart III. The suspect in question had been identified as the same Clinton Samuel Stewart III. On each of the three occasions, there had been no follow-up to that call; it was as if the calls had never come in. As far as Southlakes's paperwork detailed, Clinton Stewart's record was squeaky-clean.

Bryce knew that this discovery alone was not enough to convince Oliver, or anyone else, that Shannon was a fit mother, or that Stewart was not a fit father. But for Bryce it was a major victory. Not only was his faith in Shannon growing by leaps and bounds, but he was also now more certain than ever that she was right about Stewart. And if she was, then he was going to find a way to prove it.

Bryce was at his desk early the next morning, setting into motion his own investigation of Clinton Stewart's affairs. He was using a personal friend, an ex-cop, to do a lot of his legwork because he didn't want to tip his hand with the local law until he knew who the Stewarts did and did not own. And then, having told Shannon he would, he called Brad Channing to fill him in and suggest that he apply for an extension on the custody hearing.

Later that morning, Bryce presented himself in Oliver's chambers ten minutes before his uncle was due in court. He wanted the meeting to be short and sweet.

"You're going to be receiving a request for an extension on the Stewart custody hearing, sir, and I would like to state, for the record, that I believe there are reasonable grounds to grant the extension." He stated his business unemotionally.

Oliver frowned, looking at Bryce over his glasses. Had he not been so sure of his convictions, Bryce would have felt like a little boy again, intimidated by that look.

"What grounds?" the older man asked.

Bryce placed the dispatch records on the desk in front of Oliver, divulging his suspicions about some of the other areas of Clinton Stewart's life. He concluded with his own observations on how the man treated his children.

Oliver removed his glasses halfway through Bryce's dissertation, rubbing his eyes wearily, as if it was closer to bedtime than breakfast.

"You do realize what the Stewarts will do to you if they catch wind of these accusations and they aren't true?" he asked when Bryce fell silent.

Bryce never budged from his position in front of Oliver's desk. "Yes, sir, I do. But unless it's true, there's no reason for the Stewarts to ever hear of it. And even if they do, I wouldn't be the cop you know me to be, the man my father raised me to be, if I didn't pursue this."

Oliver steepled his fingers in front of his face, rested his elbows on his desk, looked at Bryce, studied the reports in front of him, and glanced back up at Bryce.

"If the request comes in, I'll give her a week. It's the best I can do," he finally said, but he didn't sound happy about his decision. "Make sure you know what you're doing, son," he added just as Bryce reached the door of the office.

Bryce glanced back, saw the affection in the old man's eyes, nodded once and left. He vowed he was going to get through this one without letting *anyone* down.

"MIKIE?" THE TREMULOUS whisper stole across the small, darkened room where Michael Stewart, the room's sole occupant, lay fully dressed on top of the single bed that had been assigned to him. He had been studying the white beam of light that filtered through the cotton curtains hanging beside his bed, wondering if the powers that could make something as awesome as the moon had time left over to help his mom. But at the sound of the frightened voice calling his name, his glance shot immediately toward the door.

"Yeah, Min?" he replied, sitting up as his twin tiptoed farther into the room. For once he hoped it was another one of Mindi's nightmares that had upset her. Those he had learned how to handle pretty well. It was sure turning out to be one long summer.

"I'm scared," Mindi admitted as she came closer. She was wearing one of the silky nightgowns Mom had given her last Christmas, long before everything had gone so horribly wrong.

The knot in Mike's chest tightened as he recognized the hint of tears in Mindi's voice. Her whining used to drive him nuts, back when she had cried about dumb things like E. T. or a rip in her rag doll, but she didn't cry about stupid stuff anymore, not since their time at the Wannamakers'. Now her tears scared him.

The mattress was jostled a little as she climbed onto the bed beside him. "There's nothing to be scared of, Min. Mrs. Thompson's nice enough," Mike said, telling her what he figured his mother would have said. He tried to keep his voice calm, reassuring.

"But you heard Mrs. Thompson at dinner. She says we're lucky that we're probably going to get to go home with Daddy tomorrow. Maybe she knows something they're not telling us. Maybe it's already been decided and we're never going to go home to Mommy."

Mike felt like crying himself as Mindi verbalized his own fears, the worries that had been occupying his thoughts for most of the evening.

"Mom promised," he reminded his sister, wondering if, for once, their mother had made a promise she couldn't keep. He wished now that he hadn't convinced Mindi not tell Mom about those boarding schools. He hadn't wanted to worry Mom, but he sure wished he knew what she would have said about them.

"Then why did she and Bryce tell us this afternoon at the park that the custody hearing might be delayed another week?" Mindi said, driving the fear farther into Mike's chest. Mike knew what Mindi was thinking. He was thinking it, too. Their mom must not be ready if she was hoping for more time. But maybe she wasn't going to get it. Maybe the decision had already been made without her. Maybe their father had won after all. The Stewarts were probably already making arrangements to send them away.

Mike turned to face his sister, settling himself cross-legged on the bed, his fists resting against his face. "But Mom promised, Min." He didn't know what else to say and he needed to hear the words again as badly as Mindi did. He was kind of losing hope himself, ever since his grandparents had said that they were already accepted at those darn schools. He figured even they were pretty sure of themselves. But he had to boost Mindi, anyway. Mom was counting on him.

Mindi's skinny shoulders were slumped, her head bent. He heard her sniffle. She wasn't buying it, either. An unfamiliar anger surged through him. Anger at a world that gave his sister so many reasons to cry, anger at the laws that took their mother away from them, leaving only himself to dry her tears. It was something he was not too good at.

"We gotta keep believing, Min."

Mindi raised watery eyes to meet his gaze in the moonlight. Her chin was trembling. Mike swallowed a lump in his throat. Mindi looked so much like Mom just then that the homesickness almost did him in.

"But what if it's not enough this time?" she whispered.

Mike pulled her into his arms until her face rested against his chest. He was sure it looked as if he was being strong, comforting Mindi and all, but he knew deep inside that he needed to hold her as much as she needed to be held. "They won't split us up. I promise." Awkwardly, he rocked her back and forth, thinking he might have just made a promise like Mom's—one that was impossible to keep.

CHAPTER SIXTEEN

BRYCE WAS IN A MEETING at the county seat Friday morning, sixty miles from Southlakes, when he received an urgent call from Deputy Williams.

"Sheriff! We need you here, sir. The Stewart twins are missing again."

Apprehension slithered down Bryce's spine, his heart pounded with possessive concern, but his mind was all cop.

"When and where were they last seen?" he demanded. He had a brief flash of B. J. Roberts's face peering after him and the twins as they drove out of town the day before the Fourth. *Please, God, let them be all right.*

"About an hour ago, in Bessie Thompson's backyard. They'd built a fort out of a couple of cardboard boxes, but when Mrs. Thompson got the call that the hearing had been delayed and went out to tell them, they had gone. She checked all the obvious places and then called us," Williams reported.

"Has their mother been contacted?" Bryce asked, hating himself for asking the question, even while he knew that Shannon's apartment had to be the first place they looked. The possibility that history had repeated itself, that she had taken them again, was the most logical assumption, and while he didn't believe it for a second, he knew everyone else in town would. It angered him to realize that he had to waste time proving them wrong.

"Not directly, sir. But she'd been seen driving out of town in the direction of the Thompson home earlier. She

arrived home just a little while ago, but there was no sign
of the children. I don't know where she's hidden them, but
right now she's alone. Adams is watching the place, but I
thought we better call you before we make any moves.''

Bryce heard the words with sickening dread, but still,
after all he and Shannon had shared, after all they had been
to each other, he knew, just as surely as he knew there was
salt in the ocean, that she would not go behind his back in
such an underhanded, damaging way. He knew that in spite
of his pep talks she remained convinced that her ex-
husband was powerful enough to win his custody battle. He
knew that her fears were controlling her more and more,
but he also knew that Shannon had a conscience. She
needed to do what was right almost as desperately as she
needed to breathe. She would not have taken her children.

"Send out APBs, get everyone you can out on the road
looking and continue surveillance of Mrs. Stewart's apartment. Check with Mrs. Thompson to see if anything is
missing from the twins' rooms. There's always the possibility that they've run away. I'll be there within the hour,"
Bryce said, forcing his personal demons aside. For the
moment, the safety of the two ten-year-olds he had grown
to love were his only concern. "Oh, and Williams? Make
some calls. See if you can find the whereabouts of your
friend, B. J. Roberts," Bryce added, hoping he was not
further jeopardizing things somehow by letting Williams
know of his suspicions about the man. He would have
made the calls himself, but he had to get on the road to
town immediately.

With the bubble flashing on his car, Bryce made it back
to Southlakes in under three-quarters of an hour. By the
time he drove through the city limits, he was actually hoping that somehow Shannon did have her children. At least
then their safety was assured. His heart sank when he strode
into the station and saw the reception committee that was

waiting for him. Their grim looks told him that the twins had not miraculously been returned.

Oliver was the first to speak.

"This is Fred and Thelma Stewart, Sheriff, the children's paternal grandparents." The couple nodded at Bryce. "There's been a further development in the past hour that we must consider as we determine how best to proceed," the judge continued.

Bryce watched the couple seated rigidly in front of his desk, but it was his uncle, sitting in Bryce's own chair, whom Bryce addressed.

"What's happened?" he demanded, remaining outwardly cool, professional, firmly detached, but acutely attentive. His inner turmoil was his business alone.

Oliver glanced up at him somberly. "The Stewarts found this half an hour ago," Oliver said, handing Bryce a well-handled piece of nondescript white paper with a pair of tweezers.

Bryce glanced down at the brief message that had been cut and pasted from newsprint, debilitating fear slicing into his gut.

"It's going to cost you to see the twins again."

He read the brief missive with a feeling of helplessness. He wanted to kill whoever was putting those children through this horror.

"How'd it arrive?"

"It was in the mailbox," Fred Stewart replied. His voice was unsteady, but there were no other signs of emotional turmoil.

Bryce studied the couple through narrowed eyes, amazed at their control. This is what Shannon had been trying to tell him when she'd said that Stewarts learned to control their emotions in the cradle. Even with their grandchildren missing, the older couple kept up appearances. He hadn't seen a single tear, and Bryce couldn't help but wonder if the price they paid for their control wasn't a little too high.

He wondered, too, how he was going to get their cooperation to help him find the children. Because whether they believed it or not, Shannon did not have them. Someone else did, and Bryce had to find that someone, quickly.

"Where's the envelope?" he demanded.

"It's right here," Oliver spoke up, handing it over. "It has no postmark."

Bryce studied the envelope, looking for anything—a smudge, a fragrance, a watermark—that might lead him to its origin.

"Which tells us nothing except that whoever is behind this knows where the Stewart mansion is," Bryce stated. "Williams!" he called over his shoulder.

"Yes, sir?" Williams was beside Bryce in a flash.

"Get on the phone, find out if anybody saw anyone strange hanging around town yesterday. Check with the motels, see who stayed over last night, find out where they were this morning, and where they are now. And get this letter dusted for prints."

"Yes, sir," Williams said, nodding.

"Has anybody called in anything yet?" Bryce asked.

"Just Mrs. Thompson, sir, to say that none of the kids' things are missing that she could tell. She's done their laundry enough times to know what clothes they had with them, and everything is still there."

Bryce heard the news with a growing dread. "That, along with this note, pretty much rules out the possibility that they ran away," he announced to the small gathering. None of the others showed any surprise at his words. Strangely enough, though, no one seemed to be panicking. Even Oliver was looking more somber than worried.

"Did you find Roberts?" Bryce asked. There was something about Clinton's companion still nagging at him.

"I just spoke to him myself," Williams reported. "He's in Las Vegas with Clinton. They were due back this morning, because Clinton still thought the hearing was this afternoon, but their plane's been delayed."

Bryce had wondered why the children's father was not among the stiff gathering around his desk. If he hadn't been so concerned about the twins, he would have been more interested in the knowledge that Clinton Stewart was spending time in the gambling paradise. As it was, he didn't know whether to be relieved or worried that B. J. Roberts was obviously not responsible for the twins' disappearance, at least not directly.

Bryce dismissed his deputy with a nod. "Let me know what you find out," he instructed before turning back to the older people sitting at his desk.

"We appreciate your thoroughness, Bryce, but shouldn't you check the most likely place first?" the gray-haired, older version of Clinton Stewart asked. "Apparently it's obvious to everyone but you that that woman has taken them again."

Bryce held on to his anger through sheer force of will, ready to defend Shannon even though he needed these people to have faith in his judgment. He needed their cooperation.

"I admit it's a possibility, but how is it obvious?" he asked, posing his question to all three of them.

"It's well-known that she's been after our money since she first set foot in this town. With the hearing drawing close she obviously panicked, seeing her hold over our son slipping away. She's got the motive, and besides, she's committed the crime before," Fred Stewart said. Thelma remained silent beside him, her regal carriage just a little too stiff, her back needle straight. Bryce needed to see some of the feelings she was hiding.

"That's circumstantial at best," he replied in Shannon's defence, telling himself he would have done the same for anyone in this situation. He didn't believe for one second that Shannon had stolen her children for financial gain. He didn't believe she had stolen them at all.

"But she was seen driving out toward the Thompsons' this morning," Oliver reminded him. Bryce had to admit that, from a logical point of view, Shannon was a likely suspect.

He stood silently in front of the trio, his detective's mind rapidly calculating his best mode of attack. He was going to need the help of every able body in this town to find Mike and Mindi. Somehow he had to convince the town to go along with him on this one. But he was so new to town....

"There's something else to consider, as well," Oliver added. "It only makes sense that if someone else had taken the children, their mother would have been contacted. Not only is it fairly common knowledge that she receives a sizable settlement from their father, but a kidnapper would count on her motherly instincts and panic to assure himself of a quick payoff," Oliver finished, leaving the obvious unsaid. If Shannon had been contacted, she would be sitting here with the rest of them.

Bingo. Bryce had his plan.

He walked slowly around his office, forcing himself to take his time over the next crucial minutes so as not to waste another second.

"Let's just say for a minute that you're all right. For whatever reason, Shannon Stewart took her children from Mrs. Thompson's this morning. The best way to find them then would be to keep Shannon under constant surveillance. If she's hidden the kids, she'll have to get back to them sometime, right? Eventually she will lead us to them. And in the meantime, we have every available body out searching for clues that will lead us to those kids. We may find them sooner that way. We may find them *before* Shannon leads us to them.''

Fred Stewart's piercing eyes were directed straight at Oliver. ''I say we bring her in now, make her tell us where she's hiding my grandchildren, and be done with this.''

Oliver opened his mouth to speak, but Bryce stepped forward, half-afraid his uncle was going to agree with Fred Stewart. Bringing Shannon to the police station was not going to get them any closer to finding the twins.

''You bring her in here and she's just going to deny knowing anything about it, Fred,'' Bryce said, careful not to sound condescending. ''We can't *force* her to talk.''

''Bryce is right, Fred,'' Oliver said, leaning back in his chair. ''Besides, if the mother *has* taken those children again, if she's hiding them somewhere, we may lure her into a false sense of security if we treat this like a real kidnapping.''

Bryce nodded, coming to stand beside his uncle. ''We also have to consider that we may be dealing with a real kidnapper, one who may know enough of the twins' situation to enact the perfect crime. We may very well be dealing with someone who *wants* us to believe that Shannon took those children so that we *don't* look any further. We can't take that risk. Mike and Mindi's lives may be depending on it.''

Fred and Thelma nodded, almost in unison, as if even their physical motions had been synchronized long ago to ensure that their appearances were always the best they could be. ''You'll make certain that she's watched every second?'' Fred asked, pinning Bryce with his powerful stare.

''I'll set up base in her kitchen. She won't make a move that I don't know about.''

Informing Williams where to find him, he left behind the threesome in his office. Before he was out of earshot he heard Thelma say, "Shannon's got those children."

And Oliver replied, "She may, but Bryce is a good man and a good cop. He'll find your grandchildren."

Bryce was warmed by his uncle's faith in him, but he hated putting Oliver in a position where his uncle was forced to defend him.

SHANNON COULDN'T SEEM to shake the melancholy that had been dragging her down all morning. It was ironic, really. Before she and Bryce had become lovers they had never considered that people might get ideas about them. After all, they didn't go anywhere together except when he was chaperoning her children. But now that their relationship had developed into a personal one, they were both suddenly much more fearful. In fact, ever since they had made love, they had hardly seen each other, and never alone.

She had been relieved to hear that the extension on the custody hearing had been granted earlier that morning, but she couldn't help worrying about the fact that neither Brad nor Bryce had been able to come up with anything solid against Clinton. Maybe her theory had been little more than a wild concoction born out of a mother's desperation. Maybe a couple of drunk-driving offences were the only crimes her sterling ex-husband had ever committed. Maybe she had involved Bryce in a losing battle, after all. If she wasn't careful, she thought, she was going to fail him as well as the twins.

She forced herself to make it through one chapter of her accounting text, and then rewarded herself with a trip to the blueberry stand out by the highway. When even the plump juicy berries failed to make her feel better, she turned to her plants.

As she reached the one pot that had had her worried for weeks, Shannon finally had to admit that this particular seedling was not going to grow. The thought further depressed her, it being proof that there were always going to be those who never got a chance. She watered it anyway, stubbornly refusing to give up on it, and then felt stupid for her mulishness. This particular peace lily was obviously not meant to be, and she was being naively foolish in thinking that her perseverance was going to make a difference. She picked up the container of dirt, carried it out to the kitchen, pulled out the trash can, and was just about to tip out the contents when the doorbell rang. Hurriedly setting the pot on the windowsill until she could get back to it, she slid the trash can back under the sink, and went to see who was selling what before noon on Saturday.

Her gloom fled like water down a drain when she glanced through her peephole and saw Bryce's chest filling up the view. His badge gleamed where it was pinned beneath his sheriff's star, and Shannon felt a private thrill of pleasure to think that the man she loved, the man who had acknowledged not only his attraction to her but his belief in her, was the town Sheriff. She pulled open her door, a smile of greeting on her lips.

One look at his troubled face and her smile faltered.

"I'm sorry, honey. So sorry," he said, stepping into the apartment and taking her in his arms.

Alarm shot through her, freezing her against his chest. The only thought in her head was that they really should close the door before someone saw them embracing.

Not that they were embracing, really. Shannon's arms were pinned to her sides, and she felt no passion from Bryce. He was frighteningly tense, but not from wanting her.

She pushed against his chest, fighting to get out of his arms, not even sure why she needed to do so. He gave her one last squeeze and then let her go.

Shannon whirled back a few steps, as if by doing so she could ward off whatever news he had brought her. "What is it?" She heard her shrill voice, but didn't recognize it. "Just tell me, damn it. What is it?"

Had the hearing not been delayed after all? Was she going to lose her children to Clinton that very afternoon? Shannon's hands grew cold and clammy.

"It's the twins," he said softly, clearly the bearer of bad news. Shannon watched his hands clench and unclench. She raised her gaze up to meet his and recognized not only sympathy on his face but worry, too. Her blood froze in her veins. She sank back against the wall, terror robbing her of strength.

"They've been missing for a couple of hours, honey." Shannon heard his words, but it was as if he spoke a foreign language for all the sense they made. While a part of her noted that something terribly wrong was happening, she remained paralyzed, warding off the nausea that was threatening to choke her. She concentrated on her physical discomfort, holding it back, somehow figuring that if she could control her upset stomach, she could control the rest of what was to come.

Bryce came closer, taking a firm grip of her shoulders, as if he sensed she was about to collapse. "I'll find them, Shan. I'll bring them back to you if it's the last thing I do."

Shannon felt woozy. Her face was suddenly cold and she was short of breath. "Find them?" she asked unevenly. The high, frail voice she heard did not sound like her own. It was coming from a long way off.

"Shannon?" Bryce's voice seemed muffled as if it were coming over a long-distance telephone wire. But she knew he was standing right in front of her. Not six inches in front of her eyes his star was starting to blur, all five points of it. He shook her gently and then stopped. He rubbed her shoulders, transmitting urgency, but tenderness, too. "Honey? I need your help. Can you think of anyone who may have taken them? Anyone who holds a grudge against the Stewarts? Anyone who's shown an unusual amount of interest in the twins?" He sounded almost as scared as she was.

She shook her head, but even as she tried to concentrate only one thought pierced the numb shell her mind was holding protectively around her.

"My babies... someone has my babies...." Her frozen lips could barely move.

Bryce saw the signs of shock in Shannon's vacant stare, her rapid breathing. He had to get on the phone and get every available set of ears and eyes out looking for Mike and Mindi, but he was worried about Shannon, too. He couldn't just leave her like this.

"Shannon? Talk to me, hon," he murmured, shaking her lightly again. She looked so deathly pale. Rage coursed through him as he imagined the horrors she must be seeing in her mind.

And then she was pulling away from him, running through the house to get shoes and find her keys. "We have to find them, Bryce. We have to go find them right now."

He caught up with her in the foyer again, and grabbed her up against his body, holding her steady. She was shaking badly. "We *will* find them," he promised. There was no other alternative.

He held her close to his heart, trying to calm her frantic worries and knew that he loved this woman. He loved her and he loved her children. He would find them. It was his job to find them, both publicly and privately. The Sheriff and the man had become one.

As she continued to tremble he led her over to the couch, where she flopped down like a rag doll, so lifeless Bryce almost wished she would start tearing around the house again. He strode down the hall to the bathroom, wet a washcloth with cold water, and came back to bathe her forehead. She made no sound, didn't even acknowledge his presence. After several frightening moments the tears started to trickle slowly down her face.

Bryce breathed a small sigh of relief, encouraging her to let it out, knowing the release was healthy. He sat down beside her, pulled her into the crook of his arm, and reached for the phone. Shannon had reached the end of her endurance. She couldn't handle losing her children, not like this.

He didn't allow himself to give in to the gut-wrenching panic that was tearing at him at the thought of the twins out there somewhere, being frightened or mistreated. He would not even consider an "or worse." But he could not seem to stop his own fingers from trembling as he dialed state police headquarters.

CHAPTER SEVENTEEN

"SHE DOESN'T KNOW anything. I want every able body in the state in on this—now! Set up teams to go door to door. Someone must have seen those children." Bryce's authoritative tone reached through the red-hot haze that was consuming Shannon, calming her panic enough to allow her to listen. She reached up to wipe at the tears streaming down her cheeks.

He turned as he felt her movement beneath his arm, searching her face with worried eyes, looking much more concerned than she wished he did. If he was that anxious...

Fear clawed her stomach as she stared back at him, waiting to hear what was going to happen next. No matter what, she was thankful that he was with her. She needed his strength.

"You believe what you must, Deputy, but this is my show and I say she does not know where those children are. It's our duty to leave no stone unturned until they're found."

She felt a moment's panic as it dawned on her that others believed that she'd taken the children, and she realized quite how far out Bryce was sticking his neck for her. But for now, the only thing that mattered was finding her children.

The rest of the day passed in a blur of endless hours staring out the window, waiting for her phone to ring, and whispered prayers. Detectives had been called in, taps had been put on her phone as well as the Stewarts's, deputies had been assigned to monitor telephone extensions in both homes, Southlakes's streets were being combed, as were the state's highways, county roads and byways. Shannon had been ordered to stay by her phone in case she was contacted. Bryce set up his headquarters at her kitchen table. Someone went to the grocery store.

Bryce's efforts on behalf of her kids, his caring, his obvious worry, were the only things that kept her going. She loved him so much. Enough that, as the hours passed, she worried what he was doing to his career, his life, by standing up to the town for her. But she couldn't ask him to stop. Right now she needed him, and he was here for her. She would deal with the rest when the twins were safe at home again.

Clinton flew in from Las Vegas, still certain that Shannon was behind the children's disappearance.

Darla was investigated, but no one was particularly surprised to find her with an airtight alibi. She did offer to come to Shannon, to wait with her, but though Shannon was warmed by her mother's uncharacteristic support, she declined. She was already dealing with enough.

Shannon was alone in the living room, slumped back against the couch, staring at a blank TV screen when Bryce found her late that afternoon. As each hour passed with no real leads, she seemed to be shrinking right before his eyes.

"You need to eat something, hon," he said, taking care not to touch her. Nothing had ever been harder in his life. He wanted to shelter her within his arms and squeeze some life back into her, but she was locked so deeply within herself that he was afraid trying to hold her would do more harm than good.

She looked up at him with tired violet eyes and attempted a smile, but she looked more pathetic than cheerful. "I'm not very hungry."

"You still need nourishment. Bessie Thompson was here and she made some chili. Please try to eat." Though he didn't have the heart to tell her, Bryce knew this ordeal could go on for days. She would waste away to nothing long before it was over if she did not force herself to eat.

"Maybe later." She turned back toward the television.

Bryce could only imagine the hell she was going through with every silent minute that passed, and he respected her need to deal with things in whatever way she could. He reassured himself with the idea that she was much too practical to starve herself to death. He gave her her space.

By ten o'clock that evening, Bryce wasn't so sure he'd made the right decision. Shannon was still in the living room, looking at the phone as if she were afraid she wouldn't hear it ring if she weren't watching for vibrations. She didn't even turn her head when Bryce entered the room. His chest tightened with pain when he noticed the worn rag doll she was clutching to her chest. The waiting was killing her, and this was still only the first day. Her way of dealing with this thing was not working. There was just too much pain to keep it locked up. Bryce was afraid that if he didn't do something she would never make it through a third or a fourth day of waiting.

"Okay, Shannon. You've had enough time to feel sorry for yourself. Now how about getting up and doing something to help out here?" He hated the look of shock and hurt that passed through her eyes, even as he rejoiced for having raised some reaction out of her.

"Wh-what can I do?" she asked. Her voice cracked, hoarse from hours of crying.

"First off, you're going to eat something if I have to hold you down and feed you myself. Don't forget I'm bigger than you are," he added to strengthen his threat. He wasn't sure he would really do such a thing, but if it meant keeping her healthy he might be tempted to give it a try.

Her gaze turned vacant again; she looked back toward the phone. "Give it up, Bryce. I'm just not hungry."

Bryce knew she was stubborn, that she had perfected the art of escaping into her inner world. But she'd never come up against someone who loved her before. She was about to find herself sharing a meal with him whether she wanted to or not. He strode over to the couch, plucked the doll from her arms, laid it gently on the couch beside her and pulled her up by the elbows. He would have carried her, aching for the chance to hold her, but he thought it would do her more good to get her circulation moving.

"Bryce!" she complained, trying to pull away from him.

Bryce smiled, but retained his hold. "Your children are going to need you when they get home, Shannon. They will have been traumatized enough, don't you think, without coming home to find their mother dehydrated and in the hospital?"

Bryce wondered for whom "tough love" was toughest.

"Just who do you think you are, Bryce Donovan, coming in here and insinuating that I am not thinking of my children? I've thought of nothing but them all day. How can I just sit down and eat as if nothing has happened when my children may be hungry and crying for food? Every moment I'm tormented by thoughts of who they're with, what's happening to them, where they are, if..."

Bryce could stand it no longer. He pulled her into his arms and breathed a sigh of relief when she buried her head against his chest and began to weep. "Shh," he comforted, knowing how important it was that she express some of the pain that was eating away at her.

"I'm doing nothing, while every moment prolongs their ordeal. They're who knows where, scared, maybe hurt, maybe..." She broke off with renewed sobs, her fears, her guilt filling the room.

Bryce had expected the guilt, misplaced though it was. He had been a cop long enough to have seen guilt in more guises than he thought possible. He had lived through a load of it himself. And he knew how destructive it could be. "Don't you think for one minute that you aren't helping those kids right this very second, Shannon Stewart."

Shannon pulled back to look up at him when she heard the vehemence in his tone. Her beautiful eyes were red-rimmed and blurry with tears. "How?" She finally choked out the words.

He rubbed his hands up and down her back, offering what comfort he could as he told her what he believed with all of his heart. "Because right now they are thinking of you here, knowing that you're pulling for them. Wherever they are, you can bet that they know that all they have to do is hold on and you'll find a way to help them. You are their strength, Shannon, their hope, don't you know that?"

She clutched his arms, digging into his skin, and searched his face for signs of his sincerity.

"What d'ya say we go eat. It'd be a little difficult for you to hold up all that weight on your shoulders if you're undernourished," he urged, smiling down at her.

The heavy feeling inside his chest lifted just a little as a tremulous smile broke on her lips.

"You win, Sheriff. Let's eat," she conceded, threading her arm through his as they made their way to the kitchen.

NEITHER ONE OF THEM slept that night, though they took turns dozing on the living-room couch, soaking up what comfort they could from each other. The helplessness was eating at Shannon as much as the worry, and her mind traveled endlessly looking for something she could do besides sitting and waiting, but each avenue she traveled ended up in a dead end, and she finally had to accept that she was needed right where she was. If the twins ever found themselves with an opportunity to call home, it was imperative that she be there for them.

SHANNON WAS IN the kitchen the next morning, cleaning up after having fixed breakfast for several of the patrols heading back out for another day of searching, when word came from the Stewarts that there had been no further contact. All they could do was sit and wait for instructions from the kidnapper.

Bryce wrapped his arms around Shannon as he told her the news, and she clung to him, taking strength from his broadness, warmth from the heartbeat thudding steadily beneath her ear.

"What are their chances?" she finally whispered through her tears. She could not keep running away. Her children were in grave danger, and they might remain so for some time to come. She was going to have to find the fortitude to get through whatever lay ahead and still be waiting for them when it was all over. First, though, she had to know what she was dealing with.

"At this point, pretty good," Bryce answered immediately.

Shannon chose to believe him. "Why?" she asked, her arms holding Bryce's waist as if he were her lifeline. Her cheek remained against his chest. She knew she was going to have to let go of him, that they were taking a terrible risk of being seen, of Bryce being exposed, with a deputy in the next room, but still she held on.

"Because the kidnappers don't have any money yet. The twins are the only guarantee they've got that this whole thing will be worth their while." She felt Bryce's chin move against the top of her head as he spoke.

Shannon froze. "They?" she asked. Until then she'd been picturing the odds as two against one. Her two little people against one big one.

Bryce kissed her temple. "Just a figure of speech, hon. It's possible that one person took the kids, one who is desperate for cash but has no intention of hurting them."

AND SO BEGAN THE LONGEST few days of Bryce's life. He ached for Shannon, for the agony he saw each time he looked into her eyes, for the toll each fruitless day was taking on her, for the gradual loss of hope. It was one of the hardest things he had ever done when he had to tell her that no fingerprints had been found on the ransom note.

The phones were monitored round the clock, but there were no further messages from the kidnapper. The countryside was combed again and again, patrols continued to search, teams questioned citizens over and over. Spots were aired on the nightly news and descriptions were sent out to radio stations all over the state, but there was only so much that could be done. It was a simple, frustrating fact that if someone truly didn't want to be found, the chances were he wouldn't be, not until a mistake was made. Bryce was going crazy waiting for that mistake.

He was sleeping at Shannon's, well aware that many people still suspected her of having had a hand in the twins' disappearance. Though she never asked him to leave, she was treating him much the same as she treated all of the deputies using her home. And though there were two spare beds in the apartment, as well as the other half of her own, she made up a cot for him in the kitchen. No one was left with any doubt that Shannon and the sheriff were not sleeping together. Bryce understood the sleeping arrangements; what he didn't understand was how polite and impersonal she had become.

She spent her days trying to stay out of Bryce's way, more and more afraid that all of the people coming and going might figure out how much she loved Bryce, and hold her love against him. She knew many of the townsfolk, and probably some of the police force, too, were watching her closely. They had the notion that she was somehow behind the kidnapping. And she was even more afraid, now that he had taken his stand about the kidnapping. He had already suffered twice at the hands of the fair sex; she could not be responsible for it happening again.

She tried to keep busy with cooking and cleaning up, though most of the crews who had been in and out of her apartment those first two days were gone. Only the deputies manning the tap on her phone, or those stopping by to report progress, were left. She found herself spending hours staring vacantly into space while she plotted scenarios of her reunion with the twins. Those hours were the best thing about her days. As Bryce had said, as long as it was possible that the twins would be found, it couldn't hurt her to believe in the possibility.

Alone in the apartment with Bryce late Wednesday afternoon, Shannon escaped to Mindi's room to clean out the closet. She had just finished alphabetizing a shelf of books when the phone rang. It was a private detective asking for Bryce.

Thinking immediately of the twins, Shannon found her heart was pounding as she watched Bryce turn off the tape recorder hooked up to her phone. She sat down at the kitchen table to listen to his side of the conversation. His crisp beige uniform shirt stretched across his shoulders as he held the phone to his ear, listening. She wondered how she was ever going to be complete again without those broad shoulders to lean on.

And then she heard Bryce's first words.

"You're sure the account is valid?" he asked with a frown.

With sinking spirits, Shannon realized they were discussing Clinton's mysterious child-support account, not the children. And apparently the phony bank account wasn't

phony, after all. She was not really surprised. She had
known there had to be some kind of proof of that account
or Clinton would never have bragged about it. But that
didn't bring her any closer to explaining it. She wouldn't
blame Bryce for thinking that she'd been lying to him all
along. But surely all this could wait until after the children
were found. What did any of it matter if Mike and Mindi
were not here to fight over?

Bryce didn't look at her as he listened to what the man
had to say.

"There has to be more to it than that. Dig a little
deeper." He paced back and forth across the kitchen, his
shiny black shoes squeaking against her linoleum.

Shannon did not know why Bryce was bothering with
this now, with the twins gone, but even more confusing was
his reaction to the discovery of Clinton's tangible proof.
Where were Bryce's doubts about her? Come to think of it,
where had they been all week?

"I'm telling you, she knows nothing about that account. She has not received money from Stewart since the
divorce." He was facing her kitchen sink, looking out over
the windowsill to the late afternoon beyond.

Shannon shook her head. Was she hearing this right?
Bryce was believing in her outright, with no explanation?
The custody hearing might have been a nonissue at that
moment, but Bryce's faith in her certainly was not. She
continued to listen.

"I agree. It seems clear. Too clear. I don't care how ac-
curate the deposits and withdrawals were, there has to be
something that doesn't add up. Why not look at an actual
bank statement, find out who made the withdrawals?"

Shannon waited.

"But what if he isn't all that rich? What if his parents are
the only rich ones these days?"

There was another brief pause.

"Yes, and maybe he's counting on the rest of the town to see things like you do. What could it hurt to check?"

Shannon fiddled with the ragged hem of her cutoffs, pulling at the strings of denim.

"Those automated teller machines have cameras. We'll subpoena the film," Bryce stated.

Shannon watched as Bryce moved stealthily back toward the wall that housed the phone's cradle. He looked like a jungle animal on the prowl.

"What can it hurt?" he repeated succinctly. Shannon decided she would have been hard put to argue with that tone.

Apparently the detective had seen the wisdom of capitulation, as well. With a satisfied acknowledgment, Bryce hung up the phone.

He turned to face Shannon, concern adding lines to his ruggedly handsome features. "There might be more trouble," he said, as if trying to spare her.

Shannon shrugged, knowing that until she had her children back, trouble with Clinton was the least of her worries. But she stood up from her chair, anyway, wrapped her arms around Bryce's neck, and held on tight. For the moment, the damage her reputation could do to his life was forgotten.

Bryce looked down at her, frowning with consternation. "Did I miss something?" he asked, but Shannon noticed that he wasted no time in pulling her more securely against him.

"No. Just thanks," she said with a relieved sigh.

"You're welcome," he said, returning her hug. "But for what?"

She snuggled into his chest. "For believing in me instead of the evidence."

He pulled away just far enough to look her squarely in the eye. "I do believe in you, Shannon. From now on. Always."

Shannon lifted her lips to his in a kiss that was full of all the gratitude and love she had to give. His belief in her was a solace to her wounded soul, a renewal of her will to fight, a source for her strength. The twins were still missing, the future still a frightening blank, but for a few brief moments she found the peace of forgetfulness in his arms.

Bryce was the first to pull away, but it was not hard for her to tell that he did so reluctantly. He had to give it a couple of tries before he managed to let her go.

"The existence of a bank account with your name on it is serious business, Shannon," he said, holding her far enough away to look directly into her eyes.

"Maybe so, but until Mike and Mindi are safe at home, I don't even care."

Bryce shook her gently. "You have to care, hon, for a couple of reasons. First, your extension was only for one week. That's up two days from now. That means that in all likelihood, as soon as the children are home, the hearing will be called. We need to be prepared to win on a moment's notice."

Shannon digested his words, seeing the sense in them, but still unable to work up any enthusiasm for a battle she might never fight. "And the other reason?" she asked, more to deter him from her lack of response than anything else.

Bryce ran his fingers through her hair and down to cup her neck. "They've already been missing for several days, Shannon. We have no way of knowing how much longer they'll be gone. You're going to need to be strong. And the best way to do that is to work positively for their return. Plan for a custody hearing. Plan to win it. Count on it. As long as you can do that, you'll keep going."

Tears glistened on Shannon's lashes, but this time she did not let them fall. Bryce was right. She was never going to make it if all she did was wander around the apartment cleaning closets. Maybe planning for the twins' return was the surest way to increase her flagging hope.

Bryce watched the haunted look that had become so familiar over the past days recede and then return to Shannon's eyes and swore that, whatever the cost, he would bring her children home to her.

AS HAD BECOME HABIT, he spent the early evening hours out driving the alleys and country roads of Southlakes and its surrounding towns. It was probable that whoever had taken the twins had them hidden close by and Bryce was not going to rest until he searched every possible hiding place himself. He could not shake the feeling that he was missing something, that there was more to this than he was seeing.

Shannon was watering her plants when he returned around nine o'clock that evening. He had grown to love so many of the little things about her over the past days of sharing a home with her. Her genuine affection for a bunch of green stems was just one of them; the way she always dressed in baggy clothes to undermine the beauty that had been abused so much in her life was another. One day he hoped to throw out every pair of baggy shorts she owned.

"You had a call come in from Detroit. An Officer Mitchell," she said, glancing at him over her shoulder.

Mitch. Finally. At least here was something he could do. He was going to make sure that when those children were found, Shannon would not just turn around and lose them again.

She followed him out to the kitchen where he dismissed the deputy who had been manning the phone while Bryce was away. He dialed Mitch's home number and listened to it ring, watching as Shannon approached the single, barren pot on her kitchen windowsill, watering it as she had all the rest. He had been wondering all week why she kept that one plant off by itself. It did not seem to be doing the mound of dirt much good.

"Mitch! Bryce here, buddy, what've you got for me?" he asked as soon as his friend picked up the line.

"B. J. Roberts is a bookie, man, wanted in more states than you got fingers. You know where he can be found?"

"Maybe," Bryce said, adrenaline pumping through his veins. *Bingo.* Their first real break. Now if he could find something solid to link Stewart to the man . . .

"Yeah, well, if you need any help bringing him in, let us know," Mitch said, and Bryce understood that it was only his friendship with the other cop that forestalled any further questions.

"Thanks, buddy. I owe you one," Bryce replied.

He hung up the phone, walked over to remove the watering can from Shannon's hand, and pulled her close. "I think we might have found a way to get Clinton, hon," he said in her ear.

Shannon pulled back far enough to study Bryce's eyes for any sign that he might be trying to make her feel better. "How?" she asked.

His look was steady and sure. "Clinton's pal, the one he was just with in Vegas, is a bookie wanted in states all across the country. If we can tie the two of them together, along with some missing money, we might have enough proof to show him for what he really is."

They still had their work cut out for them, victory was not yet assured, but Bryce figured that with the right ammunition and a good plan, Shannon was finally going to get her chance in the winner's circle. He hoped with all of his heart that her prize would be waiting when she got there.

CHAPTER EIGHTEEN

BRYCE'S FRIEND CALLED back the next morning to report that though it was going to be a lengthy process to secure signed documentation, or transaction film, he had been able to obtain copies of the bank statements from the Stewart child-support account.

"As I already told you, the deposits and withdrawals were mostly made through automatic teller machines," he told Bryce.

"Is there any particular pattern to withdrawal amounts or dates?" Bryce asked, pacing Shannon's floor. He watched the tense set of Shannon's shoulders beneath her T-shirt as she paused in her rinsing of the breakfast dishes. She seemed to be concentrating rather intensely on that lone container of dirt on the sill above the sink.

"Not that I can see," the ex-cop said slowly, as if he were perusing the statements as he spoke. "Nothing out of the ordinary, anyway.... Hold it. This might be just what you're looking for. There's a withdrawal here from an ATM in Vegas...."

"Gotcha!" Bryce said, dropping into his seat at the kitchen table as adrenalin pumped through him. He picked up the pencil and paper he had been keeping there just in case. "Give me the date and amount."

Shannon could stand no more. She grabbed a dish towel, and dried her hands as she walked across to peer over Bryce's shoulder.

The date and dollar sign he was scribbling seemed insignificant to her at first, until she noticed the abbreviations next to it. Her heart fluttered with hope. If money had been withdrawn in Las Vegas, Nevada, then they had their proof. Shannon had never been out of the state of Michigan in her life.

Bryce finally hung up the phone, and Shannon knew the news was good as soon as she saw his rugged features. His chin jutted purposefully, his eyes were alight with the glow of a man going in for the kill. The rakish ends of his hair bobbed in and out of the collar of his polo shirt as he nodded his satisfaction.

"We've got him, honey." He walked toward her, holding her gaze intently, his tennis shoes silent on the floor. He looked like a predator who had just cornered his prey.

"Enough to get him to call off the suit?" Shannon asked, afraid to hope for too much, afraid to hope at all, really, for fear of being crushed again.

"I don't even intend to try," Bryce said, confusing her.

She grabbed the back of the chair she had begun to consider his, squeezing with both hands. Surely they were not going to get this close, only to lose everything after all.

"I don't understand."

"I want this town to see, once and for all, just what Clinton Stewart is. I want him publicly stripped of his power so that he never has the ammunition to lord it over you, or anyone else, ever again. We've got him, Shannon. It's just a matter of showing the proof to convince everyone else of that fact."

Bryce slid his hands into the pockets of his white shorts, obviously convinced about the scenario he had just depicted, and Shannon tried to appear satisfied, as well. But she was not. Not at all. Bryce was a cop. He believed in the system. He truly believed that exposing Clinton would be as simple as he described it. Shannon did not have his faith n the law. She could not. The law had never come through or her, not once. Even now, half the town seemed to be vaiting for her to produce the twins. She'd seen the looks, caught a couple of double-edged remarks.

Bryce hadn't been in this town long enough to know just now all-powerful the Stewarts were. And even if they continued with the hearing, even if they were able to nail Clinton, the Stewarts could still have Darla's testimony on their side, Shannon could still lose the twins to the elder Stewarts if not to their father. Whether Bryce chose to see it or not, the Stewarts were just that powerful in this town. And Bryce, by standing beside her, by testifying on her behalf, could still be hurt beyond repair. Unless she got to Clinton irst...

But Shannon knew that no matter what Bryce said about keeping her hopes up, she just didn't have it in her to take on her ex-husband until she knew her children were safe and sound. Once they were home, she would find a way to arrange a meeting with their father.

It was much later that evening before Shannon was alone with Bryce again. She was trying to keep her hopes up, to be as optimistic as Bryce wanted her to be, but try as she might she just could not rid herself of the dreadfully dark cloud that hung over her as each day passed with no word about the children. They had been missing for more than five days. Her fear for their safety overshadowed everything else.

"The hearing has been officially postponed until the kids are home, but we know now that we're going to win," Bryce was saying as he and Shannon prepared a late dinner.

Shannon whipped the eggs she was scrambling until they began to resemble a not-so-fluffy meringue. She couldn't tell him how wrong he was, couldn't tell him that if the hearing ever made it to court, she didn't want him beside her. She couldn't even find the heart to care about the hearing. Without Mike and Mindi, there wouldn't be one.

How much longer was she going to have to wait to hear anything about her children? Another week? Two? A year? Ever?

Shannon finished the eggs, what there were left of them, put the pan on a back burner, and turned to watch as Bryce buttered another slice of toast. His solid shoulders looked endearingly out of place as he bent over his task. She thought of all the weight those shoulders had carried for her over the past weeks, and knew she did not regret one minute of knowing Bryce. He had restored her faith in herself. She would always love him for that.

Bryce turned around when Shannon remained silent, searching his mind for more optimistic platitudes to help keep her spirits up. But after one look at her distraught face, he dropped the toast on the counter, wiped his hands on a towel, and wrapped her in his arms. He hadn't meant to hurt her by his talk about winning her custody battle when the children were still missing. He was only trying to ensure that once the twins were found, Shannon would know that she was not going to lose them again. But it had been a long day. He should have seen that now was not the time for a pep talk.

"I love you, Shannon Stewart. Do you know that?" Now probably wasn't the time to confess his love, either. But she looked so forlorn, so lost and alone. He wanted her to know she was never going to be alone again.

She looked ready to crumble. He gathered her into his arms. "We're going to find those kids before you know it, Shan. We'll bring them home safe and sound."

Shannon pulled back to study his face. "What'd you just say?"

"I said we're going to find..."

"Not that part, you know, before." She remained stiff in his embrace.

Bryce rubbed her back, trying to loosen some of her tension. "I love you," he said again slowly, telling her with his eyes and hands as well as his words.

She continued to study him, though her hands tightened around his waist, locking him within her grasp. "You do?" she finally asked, sounding more like her daughter than herself.

"I do," Bryce confirmed, completely serious. And then he took her lips in a kiss that left her in no doubt as to the extent of his caring.

"I love you, too, Bryce." Her words, whispered a few minutes later, sounded more sad than anything else, but Bryce knew he couldn't expect anything else from a mother worried sick about her children.

BRYCE WAS AWAKE much too early the next morning. He was so tired his bones ached, but his mind wouldn't let him rest. He was careful not to disturb Shannon as he slid off the couch where they had fallen asleep some time after midnight. Her sleep had been erratic, her relaxed features interrupted by all too frequent frowns. He headed for the shower, massaging his right shoulder. He had had many fantasies of sleeping all night with Shannon in his arms, of waking beside her, and not one of them had allowed for her worn beige couch.

Bryce's mind was spinning as he showered and dressed, planning a mental map of the area he was going to search that day. Two children just did not evaporate into thin air. Someplace there had to be a clue to their whereabouts.

He skipped shaving and went straight to the kitchen to fill a thermos full of coffee. As soon as a deputy arrived to relieve him of phone duty he was going to be on his way. He was sitting at the table fifteen minutes later, drumming his fingers impatiently against the Formica, when the phone rang.

"Donovan here," he said, grabbing up the instrument before it woke Shannon. It was awfully early for a phone call.

"It's Fred Stewart, Sheriff. I've got a second note. I'm on my way over."

Bryce held the dead receiver in a hand that was not quite steady, his heart pounding. He wouldn't know what his next move had to be until he read the note, but he experienced a heady rush of adrenaline just knowing that something was finally happening, and a heavy dose of alarm as he acknowledged that the note probably meant the children's time was running out. He replaced the receiver and walked into the living room.

He stared down at a sleeping Shannon with his stomach in knots. He had to wake her just so he could hit her with bad news. But he knew he had no choice. She was the children's mother. She deserved to hear the news as soon as he did.

SHANNON WAS DRESSED in fresh jeans and a T-shirt and waiting at the edge of the foyer when the doorbell rang five minutes later. She nodded silently when Bryce offered to answer the door.

Fred pushed past Bryce before the door was even completely open, looking for and finding Shannon.

"This is it!" he thundered at her. "This has gone on long enough, and you've gone too far. I want those children, and I want them now. You have one hour to produce them, or so help me, I'll have your behind hauled into jail so fast your head will spin." Bryce saw the blood drain from Shannon's face, leaving her a pasty white.

He moved forward, standing between the threatening an and Shannon, issuing a silent warning. "I need to see e note, Fred," he said.

"Sure, see it, Sheriff." Fred pulled the note out of his ack pocket and thrust it at Bryce, but Fred's accusing glare ever left Shannon's stricken face. "See what she's doing? he wants me to buy my own grandchildren. It's what she's anted all along."

Bryce unfolded the note, careful to get as few finger-rints on it as possible. His heart began to thud anew as he ead, but he remained outwardly calm. He passed the note Shannon, wanting to know if she saw what he did.

He watched as her lips silently formed the words on the aper. "You will never see the twins again if you do not ave a satchel with one hundred thousand dollars in the eserted barn on Blue Star Highway at County Road umber 68. Do not bother with a stakeout." And he atched as hope dawned. Her mouth formed a perfect O ut not a sound came out. She saw what he saw.

Bryce placed one hand on the back of Fred Stewart's oulder and urged him toward the door. "I've got to re-ort this, Fred, and have it dusted for prints. As for the rest f your allegations, I'm sure once you think about it, you'll alize Shannon would have nothing to gain by sending you letter like this. I'll be in touch as soon as I know any-ing."

Fred Stewart stopped in his tracks, shrugging off Bryce's and. "Even you have to realize now that we're not deal-g with any big-time kidnapper, Sheriff. No one's going to ut his hide so far on the line and only ask for a quarter of million dollars when I'm worth fifty million."

Bryce opened Shannon's front door for the older man, nxious for Stewart to go so he could follow up on the unch that had hit him as soon as he'd read that note. And don't you think Shannon's smart enough to realize that, sir? If she were behind this, if all this was about he getting your money, then why *doesn't* the note ask fo more?"

"I give her an hour." With a shake of his head, Stewar was gone.

"They faked their own kidnapping," Shannon said a soon as Bryce shut the front door. She was standing righ behind him, shaking like a body in subzero temperatures Her fingers still clutched the note.

Bryce intended to warn her not to get her hopes up, evei though he was not taking heed of the warning himself, bu she never gave him a chance to speak.

"Fred's right. The amount is way too low—and exactl the amount you quoted to Mike when you were talkin about that woman's faked kidnapping in Detroit." Her eye scanned the letter again. "Look, Bryce, it even warn against a stakeout. No one else would word it like that— except for Mike and Mindi, that is, because of that stor you told them."

She clutched the note to her chest and inhaled deeply, a if she could somehow take in its essence through touch an smell. Bryce knew what she was doing, and why. She be lieved she was holding a piece of paper that had come di rectly from the hands of her children. Bryce thought sc too.

He walked over to her, carefully took the note from he fingers, and wrapped his arms around her trembling body "Okay, hon. I'll admit it looks exactly like you say it does but we still don't have any idea where they are. I need yor to stay here in case they phone or come home, while I rur this note down for fingerprinting. Then I'm going to stoj by Bessie Thompson's again, just to see if there isn't some thing missing that she may have forgotten. We need som clue as to where those kids went. In the meantime, I neec you to make a list of every place you can think of that the might go. Anyplace where they could hide out undetected for so long."

Shannon took a deep breath, pulled back from his embrace, and nodded.

Bryce would have said more, but he heard the deputy assigned to phone duty coming up the walk. "I'll be back as soon as I find anything," he promised. With a quick kiss on her startled lips, he was gone.

BRYCE LEFT HIS CAR running as he dropped the note at the station and was in front of Bessie Thompson's home less than twenty minutes after leaving Shannon.

"Bessie, think hard. Can you remember any food missing, the kids asking for anything out of the ordinary, anything that might have been the least bit unusual about those past couple of days?" he asked, the minute the woman opened her door.

Bessie frowned and shook her head, motioning for Bryce to step inside her home. "The only things they ever really asked for were the twine and safety pins they needed to secure their fort. I was happy to give them the stuff," she said slowly just as he was stepping in the door.

Bryce's heart began to thud harder and harder. He stopped with one foot in and one foot out of her house. "Twine and safety pins? Whose idea was it?" he asked, trying not to alarm the woman with his urgency.

"Why, young Mike's, I guess, but I'm sure they worked fine. That old fort was just made out of cardboard boxes, and it's still standing out there," she assured Bryce.

Bryce had a premonition that was growing stronger by the moment. "Mind if I take a look at it?" he asked.

"Of course not, Sheriff, come on ahead. It's right out back...."

Michael was a take-charge kind of boy. Michael would protect his sister at all costs. And Bryce had told Michael another story—one about fishing with string and safety pins. He had taught the boy how to cook fish over an open fire. He had pointed out the landmarks he used to find his secret meadow....

"See, there it is." The older woman pointed to a couple of sagging cardboard boxes.

Bryce wasted no time in tearing the boxes apart, searching for any sign of twine or pins. Just as he suspected, there were none. Apologizing for his abrupt departure, he thanked Bessie and hurried back to Shannon.

He asked the deputy in her kitchen to stay put, just in case a call came through while they were gone, and then he went in to find Shannon. She was watering her plants and had a queer look on her face.

"Shannon, what is it?" he asked, despite the news that was fairly bursting from him.

"The strangest thing, Bryce," she said slowly. "You know that old container of dirt on the windowsill in the kitchen? Well, it's never sprouted like these others, even though I planted them all at the same time." She paused, as if pondering a mystery of great importance.

"Things happen that way sometimes, honey," he said, finding it difficult to respect her concern while at the same time bubbling with a possible solution to her real problem.

"That's just it, Bryce. When I went in to water it a little while ago, there was this tiny little green bud peeping up at me from that stale clod of dirt. I was kind of beginning to see that plant as my own loss of hope, and now here it is, growing up green and healthy, after all."

Bryce didn't know what to say to that. He was no atheist, but he had never been one to have a strong communion with the powers that be, either. He had never before been face-to-face with evidence of their existence.

"I think I know where the kids are, Shannon," he finally said softly, praying with all of his heart that she was not in for another disappointment. Even if his suspicions were correct, any number of things could have happened to two children out on their own for days on end.

She whirled from the window, spraying the living room with water as she dropped her half-full jug. "Where?"

"I don't have anything but instincts to support this theory, but I think I know where to find them. Wanna come?" he asked, knowing the question was superfluous; an army couldn't have kept her away.

SHANNON KNEW WHERE they were going as soon as she saw the judge's property come into view. It eased her worry just a little to think that her children had spent the last five days in the peacefulness of Bryce's meadow, until she considered the past five nights, and the wild animals that lived there. *Please God, if you never answer another prayer, answer this one. Please let them be here. Please, please let them be all right.* Shannon continued with the silent litany as Bryce parked the car, and she hurried with him into the forest of pines.

"Could two kids survive out here for five days?" she asked Bryce. Trees blurred in her peripheral vision as she followed him through the forest, apprehensive about what they might or might not find waiting for them in the meadow. The pungent pine scent enveloped her, bringing even now a sense of well-being, an awareness that a power greater than she was watching over the twins, wherever they were.

"Yours could," he stated without hesitation. "When we were here before I told Michael a story about how I learned to fish with a piece of string tied to a stick, using a safety pin for a hook. I taught him to dig for worms. And you saw him build that fire. Twine and a box of safety pins were missing from Bessie Thompson's."

Shannon pondered that information with growing hope, afraid to allow herself to believe that she was just minutes from seeing her children, and afraid not to, as well. She could not bear it if this was just a dead end.

She and Bryce broke through the trees at a run, and then stopped. Tears streamed down Shannon's face when she saw the little camp set up under the apple tree, the fire pit, the makeshift rotisserie, the little girl huddled over the bountiful catch hanging there. Two thick, oblong piles of pine needles were fashioned into beds, side by side, directly in front of the fire. The sight blurred almost beyond recognition as happy tears continued to flow.

Renewed energy surged through her body, and she was running as fast as she could, galloping across the meadow while she screamed at the top of her lungs. "Mindi!" she cried over and over, running alone through the meadow for the couple of seconds it took for Mindi to realize what was happening.

"Mommy!" Mindi cried back, dropping her pine-bough utensil into the fire as she got up and raced for her mother.

Bryce stood back, content to watch, as the child and her mother met halfway across the meadow, falling to their knees with the force of their reunion. They held each other so tightly they appeared to be one body, a single mass of long dark hair and clinging arms.

His eyes stung with emotion as he watched the woman he loved cover her child's grimy face with tender kisses, pulling back to study the small body, and then holding it to her breast once again. He could hear Mindi's sobs, her uncontrollable litany of tearful "I knew you'd come"'s. And he knew he wanted nothing more than to be a recipient of such trusting devotion.

He heard footsteps behind him then, coming from the direction of the stream, and turned in time to see Michael's apprehensive face as the boy broke into the clearing and saw who was there. Holding his makeshift pole in front of him like a weapon, Mike glanced all around the meadow, as if looking to see if anyone else was there. Apparently satisfied, Mike dropped his fishing gear and started to run, tears streaming down his face.

Bryce watched with a huge grin, wondering how long it was going to take Shannon to notice her son racing past Bryce on his way toward her, when suddenly he was entangled in a pair of surprisingly strong, skinny little arms. "Bryce." The boy spoke with his face pressed to Bryce's rib cage, fear making his voice hesitant, even as he cried in relief. "Is it over? You came alone with Mom. Does this mean we won?"

Bryce's arms moved around the boy, holding his slight body steady. "Whoa. Hold it, son. It's not over quite yet."

Bryce felt the renewed tension in the small body he held. "It's not?" Mike looked up to search Bryce's face.

"Soon, sport, soon." Bryce was anxious to reassure the boy, to let him know that his life was going to be better from now on.

As if he could no longer be satisfied with simple promises, Mike pulled back from Bryce then. "Is everything going to be all right?" His words were laced with doubt.

"I think so, Mike. Your mother still has to go to court, but her case is much stronger now. You should be home with her in just a couple of days."

The boy twisted in Bryce's arms to look over at his mother and sister, and at the sudden longing he saw on Mike's face, Bryce released him to run across the grass to join them.

Shannon planted a series of kisses over her son's face, and then took turns, alternately kissing and studying each of the twins. Her arms were full once again, and Bryce would not have wanted it any other way. It was time they stayed that way. He intended to call Oliver just as soon as

the kids were settled back at Bessie's and request that the
hearing be scheduled for first thing Monday morning.

Eventually, the little family stood more solemn now as
they considered the hours to come before they could all go
home together. They faced him as one unit not to be di-
vided, reminding Bryce of the first time he had seen them,
the time he had ripped that unit apart. In that moment he
swore that he would burn in hell before he would ever let it
happen to them again.

He waited while they approached him, needing them
more than he needed life itself, impatient to finally put these
months behind them so he could ask Shannon to marry
him.

Michael was the first to speak up. "We're sorry, Bryce.
We just got so scared and all. Mrs. Thompson kept talking
about how lucky we were to be going to live with Dad the
next day, and about how great the boarding schools were
where they'd be sending us, and we just had to stop them
from splitting us up. We were afraid they were going to take
us away and then there wouldn't be anything Mom could
do to help us anymore. We'd never get to see Mom if they
sent us away." There were tears in the boy's eyes as he finished his explanation, his eyes pleading with Bryce to understand.

Bryce did understand, more than the boy knew, but he
couldn't let Mike think that running away was acceptable.

"What you did was dangerous and wrong, you know
that. You both know that," he felt obligated to tell the
children.

The twins nodded in unison, solemnly staring up at Bryce
with wide, serious eyes.

"And you'll stay put this time until the hearing is over?"
he asked. He knew he sounded stern, but it scared him silly
to think of what could have happened to these innocent
children out in the world all alone.

They nodded again, never taking their eyes off Bryce.

"You promise?" he asked, knowing what store the twins put in promises.

"We promise," they said together.

Bryce opened his arms wide. "Then give me a hug." His heart was full to the brim when he held the two skinny bodies against him. He was sure his heart would have overflowed, drowning him in bliss, if only Shannon had included herself in his invitation.

SHANNON CALLED CLINTON the minute she was back in her apartment alone. It was all up to him now. Her children were safe, her future was within her grasp, but only if she could convince Clinton to call off his custody suit. She knew she didn't have much time to work her miracle, but she was determined to do it just the same.

Shannon's hope began to flower when Clinton agreed to be at her house later that afternoon. He had already seen the children, and seemed as eager as she to talk. Bryce was tying up the legal end of things with the children, so she expected to have a couple of hours at least.

She prepared for the meeting with great care, wanting the confidence of looking her best, while still appearing capable of carrying out any threats she had to make. She washed her hair and pulled it back into a twist, only having to try three times before she convinced it to stay, and then used half a can of hair spray as added insurance that it would not tumble down in the middle of a weighty accusation.

Her makeup was tasteful—some liner and mascara to emphasize her eyes, a little blush to cover any unhealthy whiteness in her cheeks, and some lip gloss to draw extra attention to her words. She did not have to dawdle over a choice of clothes. She knew exactly what she was going to wear. The one-piece outfit had a split skirt and was bronze, with soft beige polka dots. It was chic without being ostentatious, elegant, but not too dressy. She felt classy in it, poised, and knew that its gathered waist complimented her figure while the silk material flowed more covertly over the rest of her feminine curves. It was the outfit she had worn to court for the finalization of her divorce.

Her outfit gave her composure, but it was her protective shroud of numbness that allowed her to follow Clinton into her living room later that afternoon. She had cloaked herself with determination fueled by the knowledge that her children were safe and sound and waiting for her to bring them home. They were counting on her. Nothing else mattered.

Clinton kept his hands in his pockets, avoiding contact with her. He looked around the room at the cheap furnishings, the framed poster that was her only artwork, and finally at the plants on her windowsill. She looked at her plants, too, but where she saw resilient little miracles, she had a feeling Clinton saw only foam containers.

"Okay, Shannon, what's this all about?" Clinton asked, as if he thought she could not possibly have anything to say that was worth the inconvenience she was putting him through. But if he thought that, then why was he here?

He sat rigidly on his end of the couch, both feet planted firmly on the floor, clearly uncomfortable. Decked out as usual in the latest expensive business attire, he oozed arrogance. His leather wing tips were so new they smelled like a saddle shop. The scent did not mix well with the strong, almost sweet-smelling cologne he wore.

Shannon sat back on the other end of the couch, half-facing him, ignoring the urge to wrap her arms around her middle. She had heard somewhere about the importance of body language and she wanted Clinton to get her message in as many ways as she could deliver it. "I've stumbled upon some things that you are going to find very interesting, maybe even interesting enough to be willing to trade your interests in the children for my silence." She didn't bother attempting to exchange civilities; they both knew he did not feel civil toward her.

"So you said on the phone." His tone was more bored than worried. "But if you want to deal, you know my terms. I'm not sure what's gotten into you, Shannon, with the hair, the clothes, even makeup, but whatever it is, you aren't convincing me."

His gaze ran over her figure, taking in all of her, from her head to her feet, putting her in her place. His perusal left Shannon feeling tainted. "When are you going to figure out that you are powerless in this town?" he continued.

"Power is a relative term, Clinton, and I have reason to believe that you are about to lose yours." She was not going to let herself be sidetracked, manipulated or belittled.

Again, Clinton did not so much as blink an eye. "And we have reason to believe that you are trying to hoodwink the county sheriff," he returned, as confident as always. Shannon's hands grew clammy. Things were not going as well as she had hoped. Clinton wasn't taking her claim seriously. He didn't appear the least bit worried.

She lifted her chin, thinking of the twins, strengthening her armor. "You're wrong." Through sheer force of will, her voice remained firm.

Clinton stood, one hand on his hip, and pointed at her. "You've somehow managed to convince that sheriff *friend* of yours that you're all sweet and innocent, but you haven't begun to convince the rest of us," he said.

Shannon wanted to stand, too, but she was afraid to move, afraid to show him too much, afraid the shaking in her limbs would become obvious. Was everyone already bad-mouthing Bryce? Could it be that she had already damaged his career? Or was Clinton, as always, merely pairing her off with the closest available man?

"How much longer are you planning to fight this?" he asked, backing up a little, as if he sensed she was close to capitulation. "Until the custody hearing? Were you really planning to go through with it? Were you hoping the sheriff might be talked into testifying on your behalf? Do you think some magic fairy is going to show up and make all your wrongs suddenly right? Even I didn't have you pegged as being stupid, Shannon. I actually thought you called me here today to work a deal to drop the hearing. I thought you'd finally come to your senses."

Shannon remained stoic, frozen, both inside and out. Even if what Clinton implied was true, even if the whole town thought she had taken up with the local sheriff in order to win the hearing, she could not lose sight of what she knew about Clinton that the town did not. She drew in a deep breath, ready to take the plunge. "I—"

"Why don't you just give it up, Shannon?" he interrupted, walking over to the doorway of the living room. "I'll see that you are amply rewarded," he coaxed.

Something inside of Shannon snapped. Her children's future happiness was being threatened, Bryce's reputation was at stake, and she was apparently going to have a nasty custody battle to face after all. She could not take Clinton's arrogant, holier-than-thou attitude on top of all that. He was no better than she was and it was time she started to believe it. Did he think he was just going to walk out on her?

She stood up, facing him squarely. "I don't need any favors from you, Clinton. After the hearing, they're going to be worth even less than they are now," she said, acting on instinct—the protective, animal instinct of a mother who smells danger approaching her young. "You've put down who and what I am for the last time. If either of us is a lower life form here, it's you. I have proof, in triplicate, of your criminal activities. I have pictures, obtained through the cameras positioned above all of the automatic tellers you've been using over the past two years, showing *you* making the withdrawals you were planning to pin on me. I have pictures and bank statements that coincide with them from Vegas. Shall I go on?'' She paused only long enough to catch her breath.

She was blowing it, she knew, but she couldn't seem to stop the flood that spewed from her. She was laying all her cards on the table, stretching the truth, leaving loopholes through which Clinton might be able to disappear, but only the end of the world could have stopped her. She was desperate. The futures of her loved ones—all three of them— rested on these next minutes. She had to get Clinton to drop the suit.

''I have conclusive evidence that you have business dealings with a B. J. Roberts. The same B. J. Roberts who is wanted all over the country for running an illegal gambling ring and a couple of other unsavory rings, as well.'' She stopped ranting when she saw the very real fear that flashed in Clinton's eyes. Could it possibly be working after all?

Shock spread across his face, distorting his pretty features until they appeared almost ugly. His nostrils flared, his lips tightened, his chin stiffened. Twice in one day, she was seeing obvious emotion from a Stewart.

''I know that you've gambled with your inheritance, that your parents know about it, and that they've threatened to cut you off from family funds until you get custody of Mike and Mindi....''

''Just a minute!'' Clinton walked back into the room, throwing his hand up in the air for silence. ''Are you trying to blackmail me?'' he asked, his voice low, dangerous, frightening Shannon. Clinton had never been physically abusive, but she had never threatened a Stewart before, either.

"I prefer to compromise with you," she said, keeping her tone soft. "I don't want your money, Clinton. I never have. I also have no sick desire to humiliate you, nor do I care what you do with your life, but I *do* want my children. I love them and I don't believe you do. All I'm suggesting is that you drop the custody suit. Your reputation remains intact, and so does my family."

Clinton's jaw was rigid, his arms stiff as he thrust his hands into his pockets. "You actually thought you could get away with this, didn't you?" he asked, as if truly amazed. "You're like a chronic disease, Shannon. We get rid of you and you just keep coming back. Well, I believe we've found the cure this time. We're going to run you so far out of town that you'll never be back." His eyes were glinting like steel, his voice low, his words carefully enunciated.

Shannon kept her voice low, as well, because she knew she had to if she were going to have any hope left of winning this battle. But she wanted to scream shrilly at him, to bang her fists against his chest, anything to get through the Stewart armor that he had been wrapped in at birth. She wrapped her arms around herself instead, body language forgotten. "And how are you going to do that? Subpoena my mother's testimony? What else can you do that you haven't done already? Face it, Clinton. *I'm not going away.*"

"You got sloppy, Shannon. You didn't cover your tracks well enough this time. Does the name Ed James mean anything to you?"

Shannon felt as if she had been shot. The pain was as intense as the realization that, in spite of everything, she had lost. Ed James. Clinton knew about Ed James. He knew about the man who had almost raped her, who had testified against her in court, who was responsible for her prostitution conviction. She was cold, so cold. She wanted to hide, to cover herself so no one would ever look at her again. She wanted to run, but she stood up to her ex-husband instead. Fighting to the death.

"Should it?" she asked. He could not have gotten his information from Bryce, so it must have come from Darla, or someone in Havenville. Maybe he did not know the whole story. Maybe he had just heard the name.

The look of disgust that crossed Clinton's face killed that hope. "I don't know, maybe not. Maybe taking thousands of dollars from a man is so commonplace for you that you don't even remember his name weeks later, or maybe you never knew his name at all."

Shannon felt a second of pure relief as she listened to the nonsense Clinton was spouting. He didn't know anything. She had never received a penny from Ed James, and certainly not in the past weeks. The only person Shannon had received money from was...Darla.... *Oh, God. Darla. Please, God, please don't let what I'm thinking be true. Please tell me Darla didn't go to that man—that the money I've been using to pay Brad Channing was payment rendered for what happened twelve years ago.*

"I can see you remember now, Shannon. It all checks out, anyway. James keeps very thorough records. The money was drawn from a savings account through James's accountant, put into a money order, sent to you, and promptly cashed. I have a copy of your signature, as well as the order for payment to be made out to you from James's accountant. Even after twelve years, we found someone in Havenville who remembered your association with James. And though no details of that association were forthcoming, we didn't have to look far to find enough evidence with which to hang you. And that's before we consider the damage your mother's testimony can do. Now, are *you* willing to make a compromise? Say, we give you twenty-four hours to sign over all rights to the twins and

leave town, and we'll forget what we know and leave your
sheriff friend alone to do his job? After all, you fooled the
best when you tricked me into marrying you, Shannon. We
can hardly blame the sheriff for making the same mistake.''

Shannon sank back down to the couch. Thoughts were
swirling so fast in her head she felt dizzy with them, dizzy
and nauseous. What was she supposed to do? No one was
ever going to believe that she didn't know where that money
had come from. But even though she was going to lose
them anyway, could she walk away from her children? And
if she didn't, would Bryce ever be able to uphold the law in
this town again? She was panicking. She knew it. But she
couldn't seem to slow herself down enough to concentrate.
She finally blurted the only coherent thought in her mind.

"I can't leave my children." Her voice sounded strange
to her own ears, as if she was a little girl begging for mercy.

But Clinton had no mercy for her. He took care of his
town, his employees, his image. But for the ex-wife who
had wronged him, he had no mercy.

He turned abruptly toward the door. "That's it, then?
That's your decision? You'd better think again, Shannon.
You'd better decide to cooperate. Because even if you did
manage to expose my little hobby, my parents will still win
custody of those children. Don't you see? You can't win."
He paused, standing by the doorway to the living room, as
if waiting for a response from her. None was forthcoming.
"I'll wait to hear from you." His final words were laced
with legendary Stewart arrogance.

Shannon heard the front door click softly as he let himself out. "His little hobby?" Clinton was so arrogant, he
actually saw losing large sums of money at the gambling
tables as a hobby. He truly believed that as long as he took
care of those who were loyal to the Stewart dynasty he could
get away with anything. And the sad part was he was prob-

ably right. Stewart money could buy him whatever he needed—a shiny vintage sports car, or immunity from the law.

And what was going to happen to her children when the Stewarts, and Stewart money, got hold of them? Were they, too, going to end up believing that they were two steps above the rest of the world?

CHAPTER NINETEEN

As SOON AS SHE FINISHED changing, Shannon picked up her bedroom phone. Darla answered on the first ring.

"Shannon? Is that you?" she asked, when Shannon said hello. "You don't sound like yourself. Is it the twins? Oh, Shannon. Have you heard something bad?"

"The twins are home, safe and sound, Darla. But tell me something. That money you sent. Was it yours?"

"What does it matter where it came from, Shannon? You needed it, and I was able to get it for you. Just leave it at that."

"I can't leave it at that, Darla. Clinton has the idea it came from Ed James. He's planning to use the information to crucify me in court. I need to know if it's true."

There was a foreboding pause on the line. "Damn it." Darla uttered the curse under her breath, but it told Shannon all she needed to know. "You have to believe I meant well, Shannon. Ed's remarried. He's running for city council. He owed you. He was more than willing to give you the money. It's not like he would even notice it missing, anyway."

"You blackmailed him?" Shannon asked, aghast.

"I didn't have to. I simply explained your plight. He figured out all by himself that he didn't want your past dragged up in a big custody suit. He *offered* to pay whatever legal fees were necessary to keep things quiet...."

PACKING THE BELONGINGS Bryce had left in her apartment, Shannon fingered Bryce's white shorts lovingly. The sturdy cotton was clean, spotless, slightly rough-textured and durable, just like Bryce. She ran her fingers lightly up and down one inseam. The shorts were large, but only large enough to mold the muscular contours they were meant to fit. The seams were even, the stitching tight and reliable. She buried her face in them, liking the course feel of them against her cheeks. And then her tears began to fall. She couldn't hold them back any longer.

She cried for her children, for Bryce and for herself. Her despair was overwhelming as she relived the moment that afternoon when she had had to say goodbye to her children once again, and as she contemplated the evening to come. But she didn't cry for the future. She couldn't think that far ahead. She had to get through life one moment at a time if she were going to get through it at all.

Her tears dulled the pain somewhat, as if the release alone was a huge relief, and eventually her sobs quietened, too. She took one last look at the shorts and then carefully folded them and added them to the pile already inside the paper bag in front of her on her kitchen floor. Bryce's toothbrush was no longer hanging beside hers in the bathroom and the cabinet was bare where his shaving cream and razor had been. Everything Bryce had brought to her apartment was now in the bag at her feet, and she was going to give it to Bryce as soon as he returned from the business of settling her kids back into custodial care.

He believed in her. If she hadn't already known so in her heart, the way he had stood beside her all week long, despite the town's suspicions, had certainly proven beyond the shadow of a doubt that, if she let him, Bryce would continue to fight her battles with her. But at what risk to himself? A ruined reputation? A ruined career? What would everyone think of him if he testified on behalf of a woman who had taken a large sum of money from the man who had once admittedly come to her for sex? Shannon loved Bryce too much to find out.

She heard his knock on the front door and nervously rolled down the top of the paper bag, carrying it with her as she went to greet him, and to say goodbye. She turned the dead bolt, focusing every ounce of her energy on *why* she had to do this, knowing that her love for Bryce would give her the strength to see things through to the end. With a deep, trembling breath, she opened the door.

He swept her up into his arms as soon as he was in the apartment. "It'll only be a little while now, honey," he said in lieu of hello. "The hearing's scheduled for Monday morning, and then they'll be home for good." With her face over his shoulder, Shannon squeezed her eyes closed tightly, holding back tears. He understood her so well. He knew how hard it had been for her to say goodbye to the twins so soon after being reunited with them, and how, more than celebrations, she needed reassurance. He'd probably been instrumental in having the hearing set so soon.

No one had ever loved her as Bryce did. But would he still be so understanding when loving her meant the loss of everything he had worked so hard for, when it meant the loss of his life's work? Would her love be worth anything to him if she allowed that to happen?

Her arms were raised, curling around his neck, and she pulled tighter, squeezing him for all she was worth, telling him goodbye. She didn't have to hide all her pain from him. It would add truth to the lies she was going to tell. The paper bag clutched in her fingers crackled against his shoulder blade.

Bryce settled one arm around her waist as he reached back with his other hand to grab the bag that dangled behind him. "What's this?" he asked, taking it from her.

Shannon stepped away from him, folding her suddenly empty hands in front of her. Her gaze was glued on the brown bag. "Your things."

The words hung baldly between them.

Shannon knew Bryce was studying her; she could feel his intent gaze like physical heat against her cheeks. She started to babble.

"I've had a lot of time to think this week, way too much, actually, but I came to a couple of conclusions that I'm ashamed of. I never meant to use you, Bryce. Or I guess I did, but I never meant to confuse it with personal involvement. It's just that you were the first person to ever even try to believe in me, you had the power to help me expose Clinton, and I was so grateful I let things go much further than I should have. I didn't mean to lead you on. I should never have told you I love you when I wasn't sure, it's just that I wanted to so badly...." Shannon's words trailed off. She stood stiffly before him, knowing she was bungling things horribly. She did not want to hurt him; she did not want to destroy the little bit of faith he had in her gender. But it was better to see their love die now than later, after his life was in ruins.

He stood before her like a giant boulder, solid and still. His face was like granite. "Just what are you saying, Shannon?" His deep, knowing voice sounded impersonal and stern, as it had that day long ago when he had told Deputy Adams to book her.

Shannon met his gaze. Her stomach was churning, her body trembling, but she forced herself to continue. "I'm trying to tell you that what happened between us, the personal part, was a mistake."

"The personal part? You mean by that the hours we spent in the meadow making love, that same day we explored each other's souls as well as our bodies?" He still didn't move, but his eyes could have cut glass.

Shannon listened to his sarcasm, feeling his shock all the way down to her toes. She bowed her head, because she wanted him to believe the shame she would have been feeling if what she were saying were true, and because she could not bear the cold, pointed look in his eyes.

"I'm sorry," she whispered through a throat thick with tears, meaning those two words more than anything she had ever said before in her life. And then she continued with the explanation she had rehearsed. "After the thing with Clinton, when you believed in me outright, I realized that the joy I felt wasn't because the man I loved had faith in me, but because an officer of the law did. I'm only sorry I didn't separate the two sooner." She looked up at Bryce then, hating the pinched look around his nose, hating the fact that she was putting it there. "I never meant to hurt you, Bryce, never." She wished there was a way for him to know just how much she meant those words.

This time it was he who looked away. He stood silently, staring toward the kitchen for a few tense seconds, and then nodded, once. "I guess there's nothing more to be said then. I'll let myself out."

And, with paper bag in hand, he did. He never once glanced her way, never even saw the tears streaming silently down to her chin.

THUNDERSTORMS WERE predicted to hit Southlakes midmorning on Monday, and as Shannon took her seat in the probate court hearing room, she thought the threatening gray clouds a fitting background for the day. But just as she knew the beautiful flowers she had planted along Main Street would withstand the day's onslaught, so would she. She had decided, over the long, lonely weekend that, no matter what, she was not going to be run out of town like some scarlet woman. She would get her degree in accounting, she would get a decent job, even if she had to commute fifty miles a day to find someone to hire her and eventually, the upright citizens of Southlakes were going to see her for what she really was. In the meantime, she was going to be around, open to the possibility of running into her children downtown now and then, available to assure them any chance she got that she loved them as much as always, that she was there for them as soon as they were old enough to come to her.

The double doors in the back of the hearing room opened, and Shannon turned to see who had arrived, careful to avoid looking in the direction where all three impeccably dressed Stewarts sat looking as confident and unconcerned as usual. She would not have turned at all, but she was a little anxious for Brad Channing to appear.

The knot in her stomach rose up to her throat. It was not Brad entering the courtroom. It was Darla Howard.

Shannon had not seen the woman in more than ten years, but not one visible line had been added to change her mother's appearance. Darla looked exactly as Shannon remembered, much younger than her age and a little too much. Her raven black hair was a little too meticulously in place, her startling violet eyes outlined a little too boldly, her unlined cheeks a little too perfect, her full lips a little too moist and rosy, and her clothes just a little too tight to be completely decent. To a casual bystander, her mother probably looked drop-dead gorgeous.

Darla glanced once, briefly, at Shannon and then, seeing Clinton's lawyer already seated on the opposite side of the room, went over to join him. Shannon saw the two whisper for a couple of minutes and then she watched as Darla swayed her way to a seat just behind the lawyer. *That's it then.* Shannon turned back to the front of the room, looking toward the judge's elevated bench with a blank stare, retreating to the place she had found years ago, deep inside herself, where no one could enter and nothing could touch her. She was suddenly very thankful that the twins had not been permitted to attend the hearing....

Bryce stepped into the courtroom just minutes before the hearing was scheduled to begin. He had cut things close purposely, knowing that if he had had more time, he might not have been able to wait until after the hearing before he gave Shannon Stewart a piece of his mind. If she thought, even for a second, that he was not going to be right beside her throughout the coming ordeal, then she had underestimated one very determined man of the law.

He saw her sitting at the front of the room. Brad Channing was beside her, but they weren't speaking. Shannon's shoulders were rigidly set, her head unnaturally erect as she faced Oliver's bench. She was wearing a silky, golden-colored outfit with beige polka dots. Chic but sedate. He was not used to seeing her dressed up, but he liked what he saw.

He walked down the short aisle to the third seat at the table where she sat with Brad, taking note of the other occupants of the room on the way. The Stewarts were, all three, sitting front and center, as were their lawyers. Bryce stopped in his tracks when he saw the beautiful woman sitting directly behind them. He knew who she was at once; the resemblance was unmistakable. She was the tarnished image of the woman he loved. Darla Howard did not look old enough to be Shannon's mother, but Bryce was in no doubt as to the woman's identity.

The woman's presence in the courtroom was reprehensible. He didn't think for one minute that Darla's testimony was going to hurt Shannon's chance to take her children home, but it filled him with blind rage to think what her mother's duplicity was going to do to Shannon.

He slipped into the seat beside her, ready for the fight to begin. He didn't look directly at Shannon—his business with her was far too personal to be conducted in a courtroom—but he felt her stiffen beside him. A sideways glance at her stoic features showed him that her armor was firmly in place, but he also saw the slight trembling of her chin. For the first time he wondered if he was doing the right thing, forcing himself on her publicly this way. He wanted to make things easier on her, not harder.

He had left her apartment hurt, betrayed and incredibly angry the other day. But as soon as he calmed down, he'd been able to look at things with the detached logic his years as a cop had given him. He'd seen the holes in Shannon's story. Her mistake had been in saying that she didn't love him. He may have bought into the part about her making love to him out of gratitude, about not separating the man from the cop, if they had made love *before* she had told him the intensely personal details about her past. But his instinct told him that Shannon Stewart could *never* have confided in him so completely, given him that part of herself so freely, if she had not also given him her heart. Bryce could not look back on their day in the meadow and make himself believe that Shannon didn't love him.

Once he'd reached the conclusion that she had lied, it hadn't taken long at all to figure out why she would have done so. Shannon might trust Bryce, but she didn't trust the system he upheld, and he didn't blame her. She still feared that she was going to be run out of town, and that if she was, he would be sent with her. He loved her for caring enough to try to protect him, but he had no intention of abandoning her just to save a job. Shannon was going to win her custody hearing, but even if she didn't, she meant more to Bryce than any career in the world. If loving her tarnished him in some people's eyes, so be it. She was stuck with him.

The first part of the hearing went pretty much as he had known it would. His uncle wanted to listen to all of one side first, and then hear the other. There was no prosecution. The caseworker gave her recommendation that the children be placed with their father, but her advice was really only token in this case. Not only had the woman probably been handpicked through Stewart influence, she also made it obvious from the beginning that she viewed the hearing merely as a technicality on the way to the obvious. Bryce let the whole thing roll over him, knowing that Oliver would pass down the fair and rightful decision once he was presented with all of the facts. Bryce knew his uncle.

He only wished he could transfer some of his faith to Shannon. Her hands were clenched into one big fist in her lap and Bryce had a pretty strong suspicion that if he opened them, there would be several red half moons dug into her palms. He wanted to take her hands into his own, to rub some reassurance from his own skin to hers, but she was still holding herself stiffly away from him. And he had to respect her right, maybe even her need to do so.

"Those who wish to present just cause for Minda Marie and Michael Scott Stewart to be permanently removed from their mother's care may do so now." Oliver's voice spread over the small hearing room.

Bryce gritted his teeth as the polished Stewart lawyers moved forward, their expressions complacent. He glanced at Shannon, hoping to offer her a reassuring smile at least, but she would not turn her head. She continued to face forward, encased in ice, watching the proceedings with the detached air of someone on the outside of the entire ordeal. Her hands lay still in her silk-covered lap, her knuckles white with strain.

The Stewart lawyers presented their case well, twisting every move Shannon had ever made to paint her as an immoral, money-hungry tramp. The lies she had told were not introduced as the desperate attempt of a young girl to escape her past, but as evidence that she had tricked Clinton Stewart into marriage. The fact that Shannon had stayed with Clinton for ten years after her marriage had in essence ended was established to show what lengths Shannon would go to for monetary gain. Clinton, of course, was portrayed as the innocent victim of Shannon's scheming. Bryce found it curious that no mention was made of the child-support payments, neither that they had been made, nor that they had been ill-spent.

And while Bryce hated the fact that he had to allow the slanderous treatment of the woman he loved, hated that Shannon had to endure such unfairness, he knew that they had only to be patient and they would have their say. By the time Brad Channing was finished, the Stewarts were going to have eaten every derogatory word they had ever said about Shannon.

Bryce's patience ran out when Ory was brought forward, established as a friend of Shannon's, and forced to give a detailed account of the seedy business he ran, the same business where Shannon *chose* to work, as evidence of the kind of people with whom Shannon *chose* to associate. He moved to jump up and protest the sleazy implications being made, but Brad's steady tap on Bryce's shoulder kept Bryce in his seat. It did nothing, however, to stay the rage that was coursing through him. Someone was going to pay for hurting Shannon this way.

Bryce glanced over at her often and was growing more and more concerned by the empty expression on her face. *Hold on, honey. Hold on,* he encouraged her silently. He prayed that the morning's events were not sending her too deeply inside herself to find her way out. Bryce kept looking for signs of her chin trembling, but even that had ceased. Was it really possible for someone to die inside—to become merely the shell of a warm human being? Was it happening now to the woman he loved, while he sat helplessly beside her letting it happen?

"We'd like to call on Darla Howard next, Your Honor."

Bryce didn't even bother to watch as the painted woman swayed to the front of the room. His attention was completely on Shannon now. He refused to let the next few minutes break her. He would fake a heart attack or something if he had to.

Shannon's expression did not change at all as Darla stated her full name and address.

"Tell the judge, please, what you do for a living, Ms Howard. We would like to remind you, before you answer, that you have been given immunity from any damages your testimony may bring upon you."

That was news to Bryce. His heart jumped as he felt Shannon move beside him.

"Is that true, Judge? Whatever I say here today will not be held against me for recourse at some future date?" Darla asked Oliver.

Oliver nodded. "Yes, ma'am. Now please, for the record, will you state your occupation?"

Bryce reached over, uncurling Shannon's fingers and bringing her hands around, one at a time, to rest on his thigh. She tried to pull them inconspicuously away, but he covered them with his much larger hand, cradling her injured palms against the soothing heat of his leg. He was finished playing things her way. Whether she knew it or not, she needed him.

"I am a prostitute." Darla's bald statement hung in the air of the now-silent courtroom.

Oliver glanced at Bryce, saw the joined hands of his nephew and Shannon Stewart, removed his glasses and rubbed his eyes. Bryce felt empathy for his uncle, but not remorse. He gave Shannon's captured hands a reassuring squeeze.

"And what is your relation to Shannon Stewart?" Bryce's anger reached boiling point as he listened to the practiced style of the highly paid Stewart lawyer. The man was treating the hearing like a criminal trial, and Shannon like the criminal.

"I am her mother, her only living blood relation, other than her children." Bryce was not looking at the older woman, but he wanted to strangle the young, sophisticated voice in her throat. How dare she claim any connection to Shannon? How dare she come to this town to flaunt a relationship Shannon had had no choice in establishing?

"Would you please describe the kind of values you instilled in your daughter as she was growing up?"

Shannon's skin tone changed from white to pale green. Bryce knew he was going to have to get her out of there. But he had to do it in a way that would postpone the hearing, not end it. He was not about to take a chance on forfeiting her right to be heard.

"I did not instill any values in my daughter." Darla's words were blunt, but sure. A murmur of voices spread through the small room. "But it wasn't from lack of trying," Darla continued as if she had not even heard the disturbance. "I wanted Shannon to know that if she wanted to get anywhere in this world, she was going to have to make use of whatever assets she had, that the real world is not TV land, that no one was going to give her anything she did not take for herself. But my daughter wouldn't look at the world that way. She was such a sensitive little person, studying those books on etiquette and proper behavior, always taking offense, getting embarrassed, worrying about things she couldn't change. I finally had to realize that she and I were never going to see eye to eye. And while I thought she was being very foolish, I tried harder to conduct my business when she was not around." Her voice was as devoid of expression as Shannon's face. Darla was looking at Oliver, but she could have been speaking to the wall for all the care she gave.

The Stewarts' lawyer looked ready to pop. His freshly shaven face was shiny with perspiration. He started to speak, to object, but Darla continued before he could stop her. Bryce had a feeling Oliver would have overruled any objections, anyway.

"When Shannon was seventeen, she caught the interest of one of my clients."

Shannon flinched beside him as she heard her mother's words. The room had grown completely quiet, everyone paying avid attention to the scene unfolding before them. Shannon bowed her head. Bryce rubbed his thumb along the sides of her hands, vowing that once they got through this, he was going to do everything in his power to see that Shannon never had to bow her head in public again.

"The man stumbled upon her, assumed she was there for the taking, and proceeded to avail himself of her services, until the local police came to shut down my operation," Darla continued. "I had a lot more to lose than Shannon did, including the means of her support, and I left through the back door. Shannon was arrested, and I testified against her at her trial." The hearing room was filled with one collective gasp, including Bryce's, but not a sound left Shannon's lips. Bryce felt his heart drop to his stomach as he considered the fact that Darla was giving too little too late to help heal the wounds inside Shannon. And then he felt the smallest of tugs, little more than a bit of pressure, really, as Shannon's fingers slowly closed around the hand imprisoning them. She continued to hold on to him while Darla finished her story.

"The man in question also testified against her, preferring a fine for buying illegal sex over a jail sentence for attempted rape. Shannon did the only thing she could do. She paid her fine and she ran as far from me as she could get. She landed in Southlakes, created a new past for herself, and was finally able to live like she had been meant to live. The second time I ruined her life, I did it unknowingly. Someone had seen Shannon, recognized her, and mentioned to me that she was living in Southlakes. I came to town, not to be a part of her life, but to apologize. My daughter and I approach life too differently to get through it together, but I didn't want bad blood between us, either. I didn't know about the past she had created for herself, and I blew it for her. The third time I ruined her life will be the last. After today, I am never going to play a part in my daughter's life again unless she invites me in."

Darla glanced briefly over at Shannon. "It will be better for both of us that way," she said, her voice losing its narrative monotone as she delivered words that were clearly directed toward her daughter. Shannon met her mother's eyes and nodded.

Darla turned back to the judge. "Several weeks ago, Shannon called me for the money to pay for the out-of-town lawyer she needed to get a fair shake at this hearing. I didn't have the money she needed, but I knew where I could get it. I finally had a way to make up to her for the wrongs I had done her. It took one phone call to the man who had nearly raped her twelve years ago, and I had as much money as I needed. He's remarried now, apparently happily this time, and was more than willing to help Shannon keep the past quiet."

Darla's voice finally stopped and the room was so quiet Bryce could hear himself breathe. He watched as Shannon's mother stepped down and walked from the room. The door closed on her swaying hips and still the room was blanketed with stunned silence.

Finally, as if realizing the next move was his, Oliver coughed. He looked toward the Stewart side of the room. "If you have nothing more to present . . ." Stewart's lawyer shook his head. "Then I turn the room over to Mr. Channing." He nodded toward the seats where Shannon, Bryce and Brad sat, still speechless.

"Uh, yes, Your Honor," Brad said, jumping to his feet. "We'd like to call Ory Jones back to the stand."

Everyone turned to watch as Ory once again proceeded to the front of the room. He winked at Shannon as he strode by and she felt fresh tears start to her eyes. Ory was a good and true friend, and she was a lucky woman to have talked him into hiring her two years before.

"Mr. Jones, would you please tell the court how many times you have met Mike and Mindi Stewart? How many times you've had the chance to influence their lives?"

"Why, none, sir."

"You've never been to their home, never even seen them, maybe across the room at the Tub."

"Nope." Ory coughed.

The room was silent, all eyes facing forward.

"And how many times did you have to cover for Shannon Stewart because her kids needed her?" Brad asked.

Shannon listened closely, not sure what Brad was trying to do. Some people might find her irresponsible for calling off work at a moment's notice.

Ory hesitated, his big face slightly screwed up as he thought. "Well, let's see, there was the time Mindi had tonsillitis, no, that was young Mike. Mindi had a school play that she forgot to tell her mother to make a costume for. And then there was the time last winter when both of them come down with them colds...."

"Are you saying that *anytime* her children needed her, Shannon called off work?" Brad asked.

Shannon smiled. She knew she had been right to hire Brad Channing.

Ory sat up straight, seeming to realize that he could be making Shannon look unreliable. "Well, yes, she did. But she always worked over for it. She always made up for the time she took, and she always stayed late if I needed her and she could."

Brad smiled. "Thank you, Mr. Jones. That will be all."

Brad called a couple of the twins' teachers forward after that, and each in their turn answered Brad's carefully worded questions in such a way that left no doubt as to Shannon's love for and moral guidance to her children.

And then, gauging the judge's reaction, Brad sat down. Shannon had made it clear before the hearing began that she wanted as little mudslinging as possible.

Oliver looked from one side of the room to the other and folded his hands in front of him. "If there's no more to be said, I see no reason why Shannon and Clinton Stewart can't continue with joint—"

"Excuse me," Brad Channing interrupted the judge, and Oliver looked over at him in surprise. "I'm sorry for the interruption, sir, but I would like a moment with my client before you make a final ruling."

"This hearing will resume in five minutes." Oliver sounded resigned.

Brad knelt in front of Shannon and Bryce, placing a hand on each of their shoulders as he pulled them forward, forming a small circle of privacy among the three of them.

"I'm assuming, from everything you've told me, that you would prefer not to have joint custody, Shannon. Am I correct?"

Shannon's expression was so dazed, Bryce was not even sure she understood what her lawyer was asking her. "I want my children, Brad, any way I can get them. I just want my children." She sounded desperate, as if she had been given hope and wasn't going to take a chance on it slipping away.

Bryce let go of her hand to slide an arm around her waist. "I think what Brad's getting at, sweetheart, is that with what we have on Stewart, we can probably get you full and permanent custody of the twins." Now was the time to see Clinton Stewart get his due.

Shannon looked at Bryce fully for the first time since he had left her house days ago. Her beautiful violet eyes were wide and frightened, but at least she wasn't still hiding from him. "I don't want any more trouble, Bryce. I just want to take my kids and go home."

Bryce understood her fears. As things stood, she would have her children, but she was afraid to rock the boat. He also knew that if she was not completely, legally free of Clinton Stewart, she would never be free of that threat.

"Stewart should pay for what he's done to you over the years, Shan. Let us bring him down for you."

Shannon wanted to please him. Bryce could see it in her eyes. But he also saw her determination. "No, Bryce." She shook her head. "If they'll make a deal to leave me alone with my children, that's all I need. There's no point in hurting Clinton's parents, in humiliating them, because of

something their son has done. I know too much how tha
feels, to be made to pay for how a member of one's family
lives. By all means, tell them what Clinton has done, use the
knowledge to get me my children free and clear, but let's do
it privately.''

Bryce loved Shannon more at that moment than at any
other time. The only need that ever controlled her was and
always had been only that she be a good person, and that
she be allowed to live as one. Shannon had something that
women like Darcy and his ex-wife had lacked—an honest
sense of decency—and he admired her more than anyone
he had ever known.

He turned to Brad. ''Do you think we can work a deal
with them? Tell Stewart's lawyers, his parents, what we
know, and then agree to let it drop in return for sole custody of the twins?''

Shannon remained still, moving not at all, as she waited
for Brad's answer. Bryce almost smiled. The woman he had
fallen so desperately in love with was filled with a conscience, but she was still able to fight.

Brad nodded, looking from Bryce to Shannon. ''You're
agreeable to this?''

''As long as his parents are in on it, I agree to it one
hundred percent. Let Clinton's parents deal with his problems. I'm sure if they were brought to light, they'd only buy
him out of trouble, anyway.''

Bryce was not so sure about that, but he would let it drop
for now. He figured that, sooner or later, Clinton Stewart
was going to make one mistake too many, one big mistake,
and Bryce would be waiting to send the man down, all the
way down to hell.

Brad was across the room only a couple of minutes, but
they were the longest minutes of Shannon's life. She leaned
against Bryce, resting her head against the solid security of
his chest, while she waited, too on edge to speak. She hardly
dared hope that the past half hour was actually real, al-

most could not believe that what was happening was even possible. But she would believe it, because she had to make it happen, because she deserved it, because her children deserved it.

Brad, accompanied by the Stewart legal entourage, approached Oliver's bench. Shannon concentrated on the calming effect of Bryce's hand as he ran it slowly up and down her spine. She didn't even bother to question how he'd come to be with her after the way she'd sent him away. Again, she was just going to accept the goodness that was sprouting all over her life—accept it, but never, ever, take it for granted.

Oliver motioned for order to be called once again, and Shannon and Bryce resumed their seats, his arm still locked firmly around her.

"As agreed upon by all parties concerned, permanent and sole custody of Minda Marie and Michael Scott Stewart is to be awarded to their mother. The children may return to their mother's home upon leaving the courthouse."

Bryce felt Shannon's slim frame start to tremble beneath his hand as she heard his uncle's words, and he turned to her, watching through the blurry haze of his own eyes as the tears flowed openly down her cheeks, free at last. Right before his eyes, twenty-nine years of ice were melting, leaving her heart exposed to all the joy that life had in store for her.

Letting her cry, he helped her from her chair and led her toward the door where he knew her children were anxiously awaiting the verdict from the morning's hearing. Eyeing the Stewart clan deep in discussion across the room, Bryce continued to propel her forward, wanting the twins to hear the news from their mother's lips.

Mike and Mindi were standing together, holding hands just outside the door. Bessie Thompson stood off to one side.

Michael saw Shannon first, and Bryce could have kicked himself over the look of pure terror that crossed the boy's face when he saw his mother's tears.

"Mom? What happened? Did we lose, Mom? What's wrong?" The boy's words were a cacophony of fear. His sister burst into tears beside him.

"Mommy?" The word came out on one long wail.

Shannon broke away from Bryce, rushing forward to drop to her knees and grasp her children in her arms, holding them close to her heart as if she would never let them go. Bryce offered up a prayer of thanks that she would never have to.

"It's okay, babies. It's okay. We won. I'm taking you home, and you can stay there until you're old and gray if you want to." Shannon's words were muffled in the top of Mindi's head, but her joy was audible for all the world to hear.

Mike pulled back to see his mother's face. "We won? We really won?" he asked, his eyes lighting up like Christmas morning. At Shannon's nod, he became the little boy Bryce had never seen. "Yyyeeess!" He screamed, jumping straight up in the air, his fist raised in victory. He was completely oblivious of the quiet solemnity of the building around him.

Mindi, as usual, was a little slower to believe. Her big brown eyes were locked on her mother. "It's all over? For good? We won forever?" she asked.

Shannon laughed through her tears, hugging both children to her sides as she stood up. "We won forever," she assured them. Her grin, even wet with tears, was the happiest sight Bryce had ever seen.

Mindi was smiling then, too, but there was still a question in her eyes. She looked up at Bryce and he lost his heart all over again.

"Are we going to be a family now?" she asked hesitantly.

Bryce looked from one pair of expectant eyes to the next, finally stopping to drown in the love he saw pouring from Shannon's. They might not need him anymore, not like they had, but Bryce was left in no doubt that they wanted him—each one of them wanted him to be a part of their whole.

"If your mother will have me, honey," he replied, his eyes locked with Shannon's.

"You will, won't you, Mom? Promise that you will," Mike said, suddenly serious, taking up his sister's cause as if only by seeing things through to the end would he be able to go back to being a kid again.

Shannon remained silent for a full minute—the longest minute of Bryce's life. She looked down at her children and back at him, until finally her lips parted and her chin started to tremble.

"Yes," she said. "I promise."

The small family threw itself into Bryce's waiting arms, joining their bodies in a new union of oneness, a fusion that was four bodies strong now, instead of three.

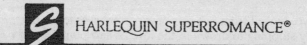

HARLEQUIN SUPERROMANCE®

HARLEQUIN SUPERROMANCE WANTS TO INTRODUCE YOU TO A DARING NEW CONCEPT IN ROMANCE...

WOMEN WHO DARE!
Bright, bold, beautiful...
Brave and caring, strong and passionate...
They're women who know their own minds
and will dare anything...for love!

One title per month in 1993, written by popular Superromance authors, will highlight our special heroines as they face unusual, challenging and sometimes dangerous situations.

The stain of a long-ago murder invigorates a ghostly presence in
#570 REUNITED by Evelyn A. Crowe

Available in November wherever Harlequin Superromance novels are sold.

If you missed any of the Women Who Dare titles and would like to order them, send your name, address, zip or postal code, along with a check or money order for $3.39 for #533, #537, #541, #545 and #549, or $3.50 for #553, #554, #558, #562 and #566, for each book ordered, plus 75¢ ($1.00 in Canada) for postage and handling, payable to Harlequin Reader Service, to:

In the U.S.	In Canada
3010 Walden Ave.	P. O. Box 613
P. O. Box 9047	Fort Erie, Ontario
Buffalo, NY 14269-9047	L2A 5X3

Please specify book title(s) with order.
Canadian residents add applicable federal and provincial taxes.

WWD-NR

1993 Keepsake

CHRISTMAS

Stories

Capture the spirit and romance of Christmas with KEEPSAKE CHRISTMAS STORIES, a collection of three stories by favorite historical authors. The perfect Christmas gift!

Don't miss these heartwarming stories, available in November wherever Harlequin books are sold:

ONCE UPON A CHRISTMAS by Curtiss Ann Matlock
A FAIRYTALE SEASON by Marianne Willman
TIDINGS OF JOY by Victoria Pade

ADD A TOUCH OF ROMANCE TO YOUR HOLIDAY SEASON WITH KEEPSAKE CHRISTMAS STORIES!

HX93

**Where do you find hot Texas nights, smooth Texas charm
and dangerously sexy cowboys?**

GUITARS, CADILLACS
Country music—Texas style!

Jessica Reynolds should be on top of the world. Fans love her music
and she is about to embark on a tour that will make her name a
household word. So why isn't her heart singing as loudly as her voice?
Could it have something to do with Crystal Creek's own sheriff?
Wayne Jackson is determined to protect Jessie from the advances of
overzealous fans...and big-time gamblers. Jessie can't help but hope
that his reason for hanging out at Zack's during her gigs is more personal than professional.

CRYSTAL CREEK reverberates with the exciting rhythm of Texas.
Each story features the rugged individuals who live and love in the
Lone Star State. And each one ends with the same invitation...

Y'ALL COME BACK...REAL SOON

Don't miss **GUITARS, CADILLACS** by Cara West.
Available in November wherever Harlequin Books are sold.

If you missed #82513 *Deep in the Heart*, #83514 *Cowboys and Cabernet*, #82515
Amarillo by Morning, #82516 *White Lightning*, #82517 *Even the Nights are Better*,
#82518 *After the Lights Go Out*, #82519 *Hearts Against the Wind* or #82520 *The
Thunder Rolls*, and would like to order them, send your name, address, zip or postal
code, along with a check or money order for $3.99 for each book ordered (do not
send cash), plus 75¢ ($1.00 in Canada) for postage and handling, payable to
Harlequin Reader Service, to:

In the U.S.	In Canada
3010 Walden Ave.	P. O. Box 609
P. O. Box 1325	Fort Erie, Ontario
Buffalo, NY 14269-1325	L2A 5X3

Please specify book title(s) with your order.
Canadian residents add applicable federal and provincial taxes.   CC-9